Julia clutched his shoulder to keep from crashing into him.

Deacon didn't flinch, his muscles and balance keeping him rock steady as she gathered herself.

"You okay?" he asked, his voice low and much too close to her ear. She nodded, the pencil forgotten as she let herself touch him for one or two seconds longer than necessary, sliding her free hand through his thick hair, relishing the contrast of soft silk and hard muscle. He rested a hand on her hip.

"I'm fine." Julia retreated, giving herself space and trying to settle her nerves. "My mom used to measure us like this on our birthdays. The marks are probably still there inside the front hall closet."

He rubbed his thumb against his lower lip and she turned her back on him, manufacturing urgency around finding the pencil. To keep herself from touching his lips.

Dear Reader,

When I write these letters, I try to choose some element of the story that resonates with me and that I hope will intrigue you. For the first time, I'm struggling with this task because so much about this book is special to me.

Deacon Fallon is exactly the kind of strong, gifted guy with deep vulnerabilities I like to write about best. He has a problem he's hidden his whole life, and it's one that he thinks makes him unlovable. Julia Bradley is not only an expert problem solver, she thinks she knows Deacon. But it will take both of them being honest and trusting with each other, in ways that feel dangerous, before they find their happy ending.

In addition to a hero and heroine I love, this book includes a thread about the relationship between Deacon and his brother, They love each other, but don't know each other. Ever since I was a little girl reading *The Outsiders* and *Tex* by S.E. Hinton, or the Sackett novels by Louis L'Amour, I've loved stories about brothers. I hope you'll fall in love with Deacon's little brother Wes, who has his own book coming in September 2012.

Extras, including behind-the-scenes facts, deleted scenes and information about my other books, are on my website, www.ellenhartman.com. I blog every month with the other Harlequin Superromance authors at www.superauthors.com. I'd love to hear from you! Send an email to ellen@ellenhartman.com.

Ellen Hartman

The Long Shot
Ellen Hartman

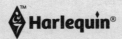
Harlequin®

TORONTO NEW YORK LONDON
AMSTERDAM PARIS SYDNEY HAMBURG
STOCKHOLM ATHENS TOKYO MILAN MADRID
PRAGUE WARSAW BUDAPEST AUCKLAND

Recycling programs
for this product may
not exist in your area.

ISBN-13: 978-0-373-71777-4

THE LONG SHOT

ABOUT THE AUTHOR

Ellen graduated from Carnegie Mellon with a degree in creative writing and then spent the next fifteen years writing technical documentation. Eventually, she worked up the courage to try fiction and has since published seven novels with the Harlequin Superromance line.

Currently, Ellen lives in a college town in New York with her husband and sons.

Books by Ellen Hartman

HARLEQUIN SUPERROMANCE
1427—WANTED MAN
1491—HIS SECRET PAST
1563—THE BOYFRIEND'S BACK
1603—PLAN B: BOYFRIEND
1665—CALLING THE SHOTS

This book is dedicated to my sister, Anne.
I don't know what I'd do without you.

CHAPTER ONE

"I'M SORRY—did you say they cut the entire athletic budget?" Julia pushed her chair back from her desk and stood to face Ty Chambers, ex-jock, current jerk, her boss and the principal of Milton High School.

"The district is in real financial trouble, Julia. You know this. The budget was voted down and we're on austerity spending. It's one of the compromises the board had to make to preserve resources for student necessities like Advanced Placement classes and guidance staff."

He gestured around her office with a look that clearly showed how little he thought of her kind of necessity.

Julia's guidance office wasn't really an office. The cubicle was carved out of a corner of the library and assembled from movable walls. It wasn't even big enough for angry pacing, which was what she needed to do right now to avoid saying something to Ty that would get her fired.

"But the whole athletic department? The board actually cut the boys' basketball program? No Milton Tigers?"

"Yes, the board cut the entire department," Ty affirmed.

Ty had been a Milton Tiger; he was wearing his state championship ring on his hand today as he did every day. He'd gained at least fifty pounds since his play-ing days, so the ring was probably stuck on his finger, but no doubt a guy like him saw that as a bonus—a perma-ring to match the Tiger tattoo he'd likely gotten during his freshman season. Most ex-Tigers took the team more seriously than they took just about anything, yet Ty was standing calmly in her office, telling her they'd cut the program. *Right.*

"The boosters put the money back for the boys, didn't they?" she asked. Not that she needed to. A first-grader would have known the answer.

The Milton Tigers basketball boosters, an indepen-dent club made up of former players, parents, commu-nity leaders and anyone who wanted to be part of the fever that gripped Milton every Friday during basket-ball season, was flush with cash and power. The boost-ers funded all kinds of perks for the boys and their fans. Why not a whole season?

"Community support through the boosters is fund-ing some programs, enabling them to continue at their current levels despite the board cuts," Ty intoned.

She moved a stack of files filled with the names of kids who needed so much more than she could offer back from the edge of her desk, praying for self-control. Ty never spouted that community-support line spontaneously. It was a rehearsed speech to cut off arguments about why her girls' team of basketball play-ers would be sitting home this winter while the boys' team went on undisturbed. "Some programs like boys' basketball."

"The Tigers are the heart of Milton High. You know that."

Ty was right. She knew all about Tigers basketball. She knew the Tigers regularly turned out state championship teams and that the booster support for one athletic team in a small community like Milton was astounding. She knew the boys' basketball team had fewer scholar-athletes and more kids who walked a thin line between exhibiting high spirits and committing juvenile offenses than any other team in the school. She also knew the sexual favors the Tiger cheerleaders allegedly handed out to the team went beyond anything their parents could conceive of. So yes, she knew what the Tigers meant to the school and she didn't like much of it.

"Boys' basketball survives and everything else gets cut?"

"Boys' basketball has the only team with an active boosters group. Other teams can start cultivating community funding."

"Basketball season begins in two weeks!"

Ty didn't smile, but she sensed how much he wanted to.

Not for the first time in her life, Julia wished she knew how to bat her eyelashes and cozy up to a guy to get what she wanted. It would get a better reception from Ty. Unfortunately, growing up with three older siblings who lived in cutthroat competition with one another, she'd learned to always follow up an elbow to the stomach with a kill shot to the groin, not bat her eyelashes. She didn't have feminine wiles and she was unlikely to find any in the drawers of her beat-up steel desk. So she stuck with what she knew how to do. When you face a problem, pummel it until it gives in.

Stepping out from behind her desk, she got right up in Ty's space. She didn't care if he was eight inches taller than her and still had the frame of a jock. She'd been at odds with him since his first year as principal when she testified at a district hearing that ended with the suspension of the team's starting forward for threatening a teacher's aide in the art room. She wasn't about to duck from Ty now. Her brothers had trained her not to show fear.

"Bullshit," she said. "You got together with your cronies and pulled a miracle for the only team you care about. But my girls get a lot out of playing. At least they're not on the streets stirring up trouble, or sleeping with one of your precious Tigers."

Ty didn't look ruffled, which pissed her off even more. He was probably loving every second of this. "The school is grateful for the help the boosters provide," he acknowledged.

"You can find some money for the girls' team and you know it," she went on.

"My hands are tied."

"What if I forgo my coaching stipend?" She used that money to provide extras for the girls on the team, like monthly pizza parties and movie nights, but she'd worry about more funding once she convinced Ty to give her team back.

"Julia…"

"You can't think this is going to fly without a protest. What about Title IX? You can't have a team for boys and not for girls. I'll file a lawsuit myself." She had no idea how to file a lawsuit, or even if she had a case, but her three older siblings were all lawyers and Ty knew it.

He turned around from the door and glared at her. "You're going to push this, aren't you?"

"Yes," she said, every molecule in her body wanting him to dare her.

"Fine. You can have girls' basketball. There won't

be much of a budget, but that's okay, because you said you'd work without a stipend. This is a bare-bones operation, Julia. You want it—you've got it. However, I guarantee you nobody cares. You'll save the girls' team and work your butt off, and nothing will change."

He'd relented so quickly it confirmed her suspicion that he'd expected her protest. He'd probably already cleared some money for the girls with the boosters, which meant she'd given up her stipend for nothing. He had no idea how much she wanted to step on his foot or spit or do something that would make an impact on his big, blond, jockish certainty that only the boys' team mattered. Her anger got the better of her.

"How about a bet?" she asked. She was gratified to see his eyebrows lift in surprise. At last she'd gotten a reaction.

"What kind of bet?"

"We make it to the state tournament."

He laughed at her.

She hated being laughed at.

"And our girls' boosters raise enough to fund the tournament trip and housing."

"Julia, you just dived right off the deep end."

"Does that mean you accept the bet?" she demanded. The logical part of her mind that had set up automatic withdrawals for her rent and her car insurance screamed at her to shut up, accept the funding and move on. But the impetuous part of her mind that had taken the bait when her brother Henry goaded her into streaking at her parents' Christmas party at the age of six told her she better not let Ty off the hook.

"What's my offer? After your team makes the tournament and your mythical boosters raise the cash, what do I owe you?"

"Full funding for next year, including a summer camp. With academic enrichment."

He snapped his fingers as if to say "chump change." "Fine. And when you lose?"

Her foot twitched toward his instep, but she controlled herself. Barely. "Name it," she said.

"You run the Boosters Bash in March. You throw the party and you plan and deliver the sincere thank-you to Coach Simon, the Milton Tigers and their fans after another championship season."

She shook his hand so fast the conversation was over before he'd finished laying out his terms. She'd rather quit her job than fete the Tigers and their supporters, but that didn't matter. What mattered was meeting Ty's smug smile with one of her own.

He left, and she felt the effects of adrenaline in her shaking hands and sweaty neck. She lifted her hair with one hand and fanned her skin with the other, musing about the bet. At least the terms were straightforward. Without boosters and a winning record her team was sunk. She'd have to get those two things. *Quick.*

School was out for the day, so she locked up her office behind her, but made sure her cell number was on the whiteboard on her door—in case any of the kids needed her.

As she cut through the library on the way to her car, she called her brother Henry, and caught him on his cell phone, at their mom's. He was taking down the awnings to prepare for winter.

"I'm stopping by," she said. "Don't leave until I get there, okay?"

Main Street in Milton was like a skeleton stripped of flesh. The storefronts were still there, but almost all the businesses were closed. A restaurant called Murphy's. A furniture and lighting store. A barbershop with a red-and-white-striped pole. The history of the town was written in the names on the open storefronts. Julia drove below the speed limit, letting the sad street sink in. She lived in a small apartment just off Main Street and walked past the tired storefronts practically every day, but she was usually so busy with her life that she never really saw her neighborhood.

Even if she was the very best guidance counselor, would anything she did alter the bleak outlook for Milton? On a good day at work, she connected a kid with a necessary resource, be it tutoring, counseling or sometimes just a website. But her reach was small and the problems in Milton were not.

It took her less than an hour to drive to Jericho, the town she'd grown up in. A mere forty miles from Milton, Jericho was thriving. The economy had a solid base in Jericho State University, one of the New York State university campuses. A pretty Adirondack setting, low crime and good jobs coupled with the culture of a college town drew young families, who built up the tax base so the Jericho public school system got better and better. Julia was, frankly, jealous of the Jericho school budget.

She pulled her Volkswagen into a space in front of the gingerbread Victorian she'd grown up in. Henry was on a stepladder, unhooking the last of the awnings from the front porch. Their two older siblings, Allison and Geoff, were partners in a Manhattan law firm, but Henry had moved back to Jericho. He'd bought the house next door to their mom a few years ago after he was hired as the vice president for legal affairs at SUNY Jericho. Julia teased him about the family compound, but her mom was happy to have one of her children so close.

"Hey, Henry," she called. "Got a basketball?"

"Garage," he said, his voice tight as he struggled to control the rolled awning.

"You want me to help with that?" she asked.

He rested the awning on the porch. "I'm pretty much done. Why do you want the basketball?"

"To see if a miracle has taken place."

She trotted down the driveway and across the grass, into Henry's yard. Inside the garage she spotted a bin of sports equipment and grabbed a basketball from the top.

Just then, her mom, Carole, opened the front door. She was wearing a red silk suit—which meant this must be one of her volunteer days. After retiring from her law practice several years ago, Carole kept herself busy with a full volunteer schedule. She and Henry walked down the steps and watched as Julia dribbled and shot the basketball at the hoop their dad had installed over the garage for Geoff's seventh birthday.

The ball missed the basket, falling far short. Julia grabbed it again and tried for a layup, but she was too far under the basket and she missed once more. The ball hit the rim and dropped fast, banging her on the head. Her mom's quiet "Oh, dear" made Julia feel foolish and compounded her irritation.

"Come on!" she said as she kicked the ball away from her feet. "You're round. The hoop is round. Why won't you just go in?"

"Maybe because you're a terrible basketball player, Coach Bradley."

"Henry, don't tease your sister," Carole said.

Julia rubbed her head as her brother dug the ball out

from under the bushes and sent it back to her with an easy bounce pass.

"The school district cut all the sports today," she said. "Austerity budget."

"I'm so sorry," her mom said.

Julia shot the ball a third time, and it hit high on the backboard before bouncing back toward her. "Not to worry. I made a little bet with the principal so he'll get the boosters to pay for the season."

Henry whistled. "Of course you did. Let me guess. He taunted you."

"Laughed at me."

"That's straight out of my playbook circa fifth grade. A little mocking laughter and you'll take any dare."

"Julia—"

"I know, Mom. It was dumb and I shouldn't lose my temper. I'm planning to work on that after I turn thirty-five." Which gave her three more years to knock heads with Ty. Maybe she'd get him trained to her will before she had to give up her temper.

Henry caught the ball when she passed it to him. He tossed it and it swished through the net.

Julia eyed him thoughtfully. He was about six foot, and for a thirty-four-year-old guy with a desk job, he was in great shape.

"Want to be my assistant coach?" she asked. "The position is up for grabs, and all you have to do is whip my girls into shape so they make the state tournament."

"That's your bet?" Even her mom's professional-grade optimism in her children's skills was shaken.

"If I can find the right assistant, we'll make it." She fist-bumped Henry's shoulder, reminding him that he was her big brother and she had total faith in him.

"Some generous, kind person who's manly and macho and good at sports."

He moved a few inches away. "That shot was a fluke," he protested.

"Maybe not. Maybe God really did send a miracle to help me win this bet. Shoot again and we'll see."

Henry picked up the ball and squinted at the basket. "This is not a bet, Julia. We haven't agreed to terms."

He shot and the ball slid easily through the hoop.

"Another fluke." He looked panicked. "Mom, you heard me say it wasn't a bet."

Carole said, "Your sister wouldn't trap you like that."

"She made me donate one hundred dollars to her uniform fund last year after she held her breath longer than me underwater at the beach." He kicked the side of Julia's shoe. "Geoff and I know she cheated."

"That accusation was never proven."

Julia settled on the bottom step of the porch, her mom two steps above her and Henry next to her.

"You don't have time to coach this semester anyway," Carole said. She turned to Julia. "Your brother is leading a seminar at the library about estate planning and charitable gifts. We're hoping to secure some new gifts to shore up our funding."

Julia sniffed. "He sucks at basketball anyway."

"No one else on the faculty wants to help?" Henry asked.

"I've reached out to people in the past, but everyone is pulled so thin."

"What about a parent from the team?" her mom inquired. "Or an aunt or uncle or something?"

"I asked last year and didn't get any interest. I can probably find someone who'd be a warm body at practice, but I need an expert—a real basketball genius. With no budget, this expert also really has to be an angel."

Henry stretched out his legs. "If you were working at a college, you'd go after the alumni. What about that famous guy from Milton who went to the pros?"

"Deacon Fallon?" Julia said. "The boosters turned the trophy case at school into a shrine to him after he graduated."

Deacon was her first, most public failure as a guidance counselor. He was a senior during her first year at Milton and had flat out refused to follow her advice to get a college education. His situation had been both painfully complicated—two dead parents, a younger brother in foster care, bad test scores and borderline grades—and desperately simple—an incredible gift for shooting the ball through the hoop and a league full of men willing to make him a millionaire if he'd put on their uniform and play.

"You sure dream big, Henry," she said. "There's no way he'd do it, and besides, I wouldn't know how to start asking him for help. What? Just call him up and invite him to coach?"

"Or maybe he'd donate money so you could hire someone. For our donors, we look at their existing relationship with the school. Does he come back? Does Fallon give money? Is he already doing stuff for the boys' team?"

"As far as I know, he turns down all their invites. He sends a check once a year but he earmarks it for the general athletic fund, so it gets split among all the sports."

A brief silence followed.

"That doesn't sound promising," her mom said.

"'Not promising' is putting it nicely. It also doesn't sound as if Deacon is your miracle." Henry stood and grabbed the rolled awnings. "I'm taking these to the garage. Be right back."

Julia scuffed the toe of her black pump in the grass. "Rubbing Deacon Fallon, or even just his check, in Ty's face would have been so satisfying."

Their mother scooted down one step so they were sitting side by side. "How much of this bet is about the team and how much is about you hating your principal?"

Julia winced. Their mom knew her too well. "The bet is personal, but the girls deserve a team. Win or lose, at least I got them one last season."

"And what have you gotten?"

"To do my job."

"You're a guidance counselor, not a coach."

"My job is helping kids. Guiding them. Connecting them with resources for them to find out what they need to succeed. I spend so much of my time tracking standardized test scores, fiddling with the district scheduling software and filing all the paperwork I generate. Every year I drown a little deeper in administrative stuff. The team is where I do real work, you know?"

"Things certainly have changed since your dad was working in the schools."

"Did he ever think about quitting? Doing something different?"

Her mom stroked her hair. "You're not your dad, Julia."

"That's for sure." Her father had died when she was ten and at the funeral so many people told stories of how he'd influenced their lives that she decided right then to be a guidance counselor. But it felt so futile most of the time. One of the students her dad had counseled recently endowed an addition to the Jericho High School library in her dad's name. She wasn't looking for that kind of acknowledgment. She just wanted to help the kids.

"I wasn't comparing your results. You approach your job differently. Frankly, you take things to heart more than he did."

"I keep feeling I should be doing more." She leaned into her mom's shoulder. "I can't lose the team. I won't."

Henry returned from the garage. "So what can we do to help?"

Julia straightened up and reached for the purse she'd set down when she'd first arrived. "My new boosters will be key to our successful year. Do you happen to have your checkbook on you?"

Henry rolled his eyes, but he went inside his house and came back with a check. Her mom wrote one as well. She dug out a pad of pink sticky notes and printed Milton Girls Basketball Supporters on the top. She drew a stick figure shooting a ball on the first one and then printed Henry's name. On the one she made for her mom, she drew two stick figures going up for a jump ball.

"So now we have two fans."

"Make two more, for Geoff and Allison. I'm going to the city this weekend, and I'll get checks from them."

"Four boosters in one day," she said. "All I need now is my coach."

SHE MEANT TO go directly home, but she stopped at her office for two student files she had to review for a special-education committee meeting the next day. She was about to duck out the rear door into the parking lot, but as she turned toward the back of the building, the lights in the trophy case in the lobby caught her eye.

Milton High School had been built in the early 1950s and it showed its age in many ways. The architecture of the lobby, with its thick marble pillars and heavy stone steps grooved deep by generations of students, was still wonderful. The solid stone reassured her. The building would be there the next day and the next, and if she persevered every day, she'd have another chance to do what she could to help the kids she had under her care.

The display case was stuffed full of awards and trophies from years of Tiger basketball dominance. Taking place of pride in the middle of the center shelf, directly under one of the spotlights, was a photo of Deacon Fallon.

He didn't look like much of a superstar. At eighteen, he had been tall and awkward off the court. Thin enough that he looked gaunt because his body mass hadn't yet caught up to his height. He'd kept his hair shaved so short his scalp showed through in places, and the combination of blond stubble and pale skin had made him appear, well, mangy. Knowing what she knew now about how some of her students' families lived, she suspected his diet hadn't provided much in the way of fruits and vegetables. He'd also suffered from serious acne and a misguided attempt to grow a mustache.

No, nothing about his appearance in the picture said superstar. But she'd seen him play way back then. She might not know how to coach the game, but she knew magic when she saw it. As hard as she'd argued for him to go to college and as much as she still regretted not being able to convince him, she acknowledged his great gift at basketball. She'd just wanted him to trade it for an education and use it as a platform for lifetime employment rather than a get-rich-quick contract.

She'd done her best to persuade him that the NBA would be around for him after college, that he shouldn't squander his chance to get an education. The entire school had watched the draft in the gym one spring afternoon, but she'd stayed holed up in her office.

She moved a step closer to the case and pulled out her phone, tilting the screen to catch the light from inside the case. She searched his name on Google and turned up a whole lot of pages about his NBA career. She changed her search terms and located him currently—or at least got a step closer to him. He was the financial backer behind a string of physical-therapy clinics, and he resided somewhere near Lake Placid. Did Ty realize he lived just a few hours from Milton, yet still snubbed the boosters?

Finding his phone number wasn't hard, and before she really thought the action through, she thumbed open her contacts and stored his number. Not that she was planning to call him. Not that he'd come back to coach, anyway. But what if she did call him? Maybe he wouldn't come himself, but what if he knew someone, or, as Henry had suggested, maybe he'd pay for a real coach? Weren't professional athletes always looking for photo opportunities for their charities?

Could that skinny, stubborn, serious kid with the sweet shot and ruthless instinct for opportunities on the court hold the key to saving her girls?

CHAPTER TWO

DEACON SLAMMED HIS hand against the glass door of the university administration building and stalked out. He made no attempt to hold the door for the idiot he called a brother. In fact, the way he felt right now, he hoped the door would hit Wes in the face. The kid desperately needed someone to knock some sense into him.

"Deacon, wait," Wes called.

He kept walking. His Porsche convertible was parked in a visitor's spot right outside the building. "Deacon!" His brother was behind him, the flip-flops he wore slapping the pavement.

"Get in the car."

"Can't you listen for one minute?"

"I was just at a meeting with your coach and a very nice woman from the dean of students office. A meeting in which I fully expected to listen to what you had to say, but— Wait a minute. You weren't there, were you? They were talking about kicking you out of school, Wes, and you couldn't be bothered to show up?"

"I got there."

"A whole hour late. The meeting was over before you managed to drop by."

"Aren't you even going to listen to my side of the story?"

"How can there possibly be 'your' side to paying

your roommate to do your work? How can there possibly be 'your' side to skipping practice? Or getting caught in a bar with a fake ID? And I'd really, really like to know how there can be 'your' side to stealing your coach's car and 'parking' it inside the weight room."

He heard Wes's barely suppressed snicker when he mentioned the car.

Deacon walked back up the sidewalk to face his brother, muscling into his space because he was angry enough that he didn't care about being nice. Deacon and Wes Fallon were both over six foot and both had spent a good part of their lives in the gym. But Deacon was ten years older and he'd shouldered responsibility for their family at an age when most boys were dreaming about learning to shave. So while he and Wes might be physically matched, he was still able to back his little brother down a step when he wanted to.

"You wouldn't be laughing if Coach Mulbrake had called the cops when he found out his car was stolen—"

"It was a joke, not auto theft."

"How is it not theft if you took his car out of his garage without his permission? The only reason he didn't file charges is that I begged him not to. I worked too damn hard to get to a place where I don't have to ask anyone for favors, and I spent the last hour doing exactly that because you think everything is a big freaking joke!"

Wes squared his shoulders and put his hands on his hips. "You're not even going to listen, are you?"

The kid might be eighteen, but he still sounded six when he thought he was being treated unfairly. Which happened more often than expected in the privileged life of Wes Fallon.

"I don't know what you could say that would convince me you haven't screwed up the sweet deal you have here to play ball and get a college degree on top of it. You're suspended, Wes, and unless we scare up three hundred hours of community service and a fistful of letters of recommendation, you can kiss your college-basketball career goodbye."

Deacon felt sick thinking about how wrong college had gone for Wes. He'd tried to give his brother everything, and he had a horrible feeling Wes didn't want any of it because he didn't know how much an education, respect, a life with value meant. How could his brother throw away his life on irresponsibility?

Wes might have been too young to know what had really happened to their parents, but Deacon had watched his dad drug his life away, day after agonizing day, until the man had died of exposure, drunk and strung out in the snow, just a few months after Wes was born. Their mom had died two short years later, killed in a fire at a club on a night when she'd called in sick to work. Deacon understood what happened to people who didn't fear consequences.

"No, Wes, I'm not in the mood to listen. Get in the car. Keep your mouth shut, and we'll talk later."

"I'm not getting in the car." Wes's cheekbones were stained with splotches of red, a sure sign he was angry. That only served to piss Deacon off more. What exactly did Wes have to be angry about?

"I'm not asking you, Wes. I'm telling you. Get in the car, because if I leave without you, I'm not coming back."

He climbed in the driver's side and slammed the

door. He took his time finding the key and fiddling with his seat belt, the whole time praying that Wes wouldn't call his bluff. Deacon felt a stab of the panic he thought he'd left behind when he signed his first pro contract—panic that he'd lose his brother because he was too stupid to figure out how to rescue him.

Wes took off, striding down the sidewalk in those stupid flip-flops, head and shoulders above most of the other college kids.

He put the car in gear and crept along, keeping behind his brother.

They'd gotten to see their mom in the hospital for a few minutes before she died. He was twelve when he promised his mom he'd look after his two-year-old brother. Not a day of his life had passed since that he hadn't worried about Wes. Which was why a big portion of his anger today was aimed squarely at himself. He'd let his brother down, and it was up to him to get him back on track.

He pulled up next to Wes. "You're acting like a child. Get in the car."

"You're treating me like a child. Screw off."

They reached a corner, and Wes crossed, while Deacon had to wait for a bunch of students to slouch past the bumper of his car, cell phones pressed to their ears, oblivious to the traffic, oblivious to the beauty of the campus or the beauty of being kids who fit in there. No wonder Wes took all this for granted. Every last one of them did. When Deacon finally had an opening, he eased the Porsche through and caught up to Wes. He hit the horn, but his brother didn't turn his head.

"You're suspended, remember?" he yelled, and three girls turned to stare. "You can't stay on campus. Where the hell are you even going?"

When Wes stopped walking abruptly, one of the girls ran into him. He grabbed her arm and helped her catch her balance. She swept her hair back off her shoulders, looking up at Wes and falling for his smile without a second thought. One of the other girls stepped closer. Moth to the flame. Deacon shook his head, watching as his brother's inexhaustible charm claimed another victim. The girls said something, and Wes shrugged. They walked off, Wes eyeing them, focusing anywhere but on him waiting in the car. Wes could follow the girls, walk right on out of Deacon's life if he wanted to. He'd turned eighteen and the legal guardianship was over. Wes was under no obligation to do what Deacon said anymore, so he did the only thing he could. He held on. Waited.

Finally, Wes opened the passenger door and slumped into the seat, his long legs, in beat-up jeans, stretching under the dashboard.

"Can you not talk to me?" Wes asked.

Yeah. He could do that.

He edged back into the campus traffic. The sooner he got them out of here, the sooner he could start making plans for how he could pull this rescue off.

They stuck to the not-talking plan while they stopped at the dorm and packed up Wes's stuff. Wes spoke once to ask if they could wait for his roommate, Oliver, whose hearing for his part in the cheating had followed the Fallons', but Deacon was mad at Oliver, too, and he said no. They didn't speak again as they loaded the car and left campus, or on their drive back north through New York toward the upstate town of Lamach Lake, where Deacon lived.

In fact, the not talking to each other lasted longer than Deacon had expected. Wes wasn't normally one for extended silences. Or brooding. If something was wrong with him, everyone in the vicinity knew all the gory details because he whined and moped and generally made a nuisance of himself until someone fixed whatever the problem was or until Wes forgot there'd been a problem in the first place.

The silence lasted so long it unnerved Deacon. He said something he'd never said to Wes: "Do you know what I had to do to give you this life you're bent on throwing away?"

Wes didn't look at him. Didn't move. Deacon should never have said that. He'd raised Wes because he loved him, and he didn't resent it. When he glanced over, Wes lifted his eyebrows as if daring him to say something else.

"You're freaking smirking at me? You have no idea how easily your life could have been utter crap. It still could if you're not careful. You can't go around not caring and blowing off opportunities forever. Someday you'll have to settle down and work."

He could hear himself yelling, hear the things he was saying, and he wanted to stop, but he was just so angry. How could Wes not know he was lucky to be where he was?

Wes's voice was clipped, controlled and utterly cold when he spoke. "I don't have to stay with you, you realize. If looking at me is going to piss you off this much, I can leave. I'm eighteen."

"Too bad you're suspended from college or you could go back there."

Wes turned his face toward the window.

"You made a commitment to your team when you took that scholarship. Fallons don't let their teams down. Doesn't that mean anything to you?"

If it did, Wes wasn't telling.

Deacon couldn't allow this situation to fester. He needed to put a game plan together quickly, before Wes decided to handle things on his own. He pulled the car off to the side of the highway and, heedless of the traffic spinning past him, got out, then slammed the door. He called Victor Odenthal, his former agent and current business partner.

"Vic, are you busy?"

"Sadly, no. I had a date tonight and she canceled on me. If a woman says she forgot about her salsa class, so she can't go out with you, are you supposed to volunteer to join the class? Was this a test?"

"Can you meet me at my house? I need to talk to you."

"Sure. Now? Where are you? Sounds like you're in a wind tunnel."

"Standing on the highway. Make it an hour," Deacon said.

"What's going on?"

"I'll tell you when I see you." He was about to hang up, but then he added, "And yes, she wants you to take dance lessons. Dance lessons are like a free pass to best-boyfriend status. Say yes to them and you could forget her *birthday* and she'd still forgive you."

"Okay. Good to know. I'll sign up while you drive home. See you in an hour."

ALMOST BEFORE THE car came to a stop in the driveway of the house, Wes practically climbed out the car window he was in that much of a hurry to get away. Vic drove in right behind them and parked his black Miata into the large turnaround at the right side of the house. Deacon reached into the backseat and grabbed the envelope he'd gotten at the meeting that morning.

He and Vic walked up the flagstone path to the side door of the house, which led directly to the indoor court. When Deacon was a kid, he'd played basketball at any neighborhood hoop he could find. Net, no net. Bent rim. Backboard with bullet holes because some hunter had used it for target practice. Cracked concrete or potholed pavement. None of that had stopped him from playing, because when he was a kid, basketball was the only thing he did that made sense.

Now he had an indoor court laid with perfectly balanced hardwood. The court was well lit and climate-controlled, and had baskets he could raise or lower using the electronic controls concealed behind a panel on the wall near the scoreboard. The same panel controlled the surround-sound system. On this court, basketball didn't just make sense—it was beautiful.

Deacon grabbed a ball and tossed it to Victor. "Let's play for fifteen before we talk." He removed his glasses and set them on the bench under the windows.

Victor dribbled the ball once and said, "You're on."

Deacon played harder than he usually did; the tension of the day had him wound so tight he needed the release. Every shot he sank centered him, chipping away some of the load of embarrassed futility that had piled up during the campus meeting. Before too long he and Vic were both sweating, cursing under their breath at missed shots or lost opportunities.

He drove for the basket, sending the ball behind Victor and taking it in. Victor gave up the chase and Deacon went up, one hand pushing the ball over the rim, before he landed lightly on the baseline.

"I had you," Vic said. Since he was standing with

his legs spread, his hands on his knees and his face dripping with sweat as he sucked in one deep breath after another, he was obviously delusional. But since he was also twenty years older than Deacon, and so lacking in natural ability that he'd never even played high school ball despite his deep desire to do so, Deacon cut him some slack.

"You did have me," he said. And then, because Vic hated condescension as much as he hated cheaters, he added, "In your dreams."

He walked to the bench and grabbed his water bottle, his glasses and the envelope with the papers about Wes. Vic sat on the ground in front of him and Deacon tossed him a water bottle before opening the envelope.

"Wes got suspended," he said. "This is the paperwork."

He looked at the papers as he handed them over one by one. As always when a page of text confronted him, his stomach clenched and the print danced and blurred. He squinted through his glasses and the squiggles on the first sheet settled down enough that he picked out his brother's name: Weston Bennett Fallon, which reflected his mom's attempt to mimic the names she heard on her favorite soap opera. He recognized a few other words, but not enough to make sense. Frustrated, he passed the rest of the set to Vic.

He propped his elbows on his knees, head bent, while Victor shuffled through the papers. The court was quiet and he wasn't sure where Wes was—the one-story modern house was big enough that they could easily avoid each other. The place was far from ostentatious, and at just over three thousand square feet, it wasn't in contention as the biggest in this Adirondack community. The court was the only true luxury. Deacon didn't waste money and he didn't spend it just to spend it. But he'd promised himself that he'd have a court of his own someday and that he did.

He didn't make many promises. But when he made one, he kept it.

Victor started to read the pages aloud. He'd been reading to Deacon for years, and his voice kept a steady pace. Deacon listened and watched him at the same time. He used to watch kids read in school. With basketball, if he saw a move—a dribble, a fake, a shot—he absorbed the lines of the action unconsciously. Once he'd seen the sequence, his muscles knew how to replicate it. Sure, when he was a kid, he wasn't perfect at everything he saw on *SportsCenter*. He had to work on technique and grow into his body. But basketball was never a struggle.

Reading was the opposite. He watched and listened to the other kids, and every time his turn came around, the page looked like a jumble of scratches. Eventually he'd learned enough simple words and patterns to fake his way through. Some of his teachers must have known he couldn't read, but once he was in fifth grade, none of them did much about it. Of course, that was the year Wes was born, and then his dad had died, so he'd missed a bunch of school. Two years later his mom died and he and Wes got sent to foster care, so maybe the teachers figured he didn't need to be hassled about his grades. He'd never been sure why no one seemed to realize how little he could read, but he guessed they looked at his parents, his address, his wardrobe and just dismissed him as another dumb kid with no future.

Victor was in the middle of the letter the teacher

had written about the assignment Wes had cheated on. Deacon interrupted his friend.

"My draft-day suit was a disaster. You never saw it, but that thing was so no-class."

"I saw a picture. Green and shiny." Vic shuddered. "If you'd been my client then, I'd have burned it."

"Right after I got drafted by the Stars, I got custody of Wes. We moved up here, and that fall, he started third grade at the Dalton Day School. I wore my draft suit to the parent-teacher conference. The teacher never blinked an eye. She treated me straight up, even though I guarantee none of the other parents in Wes's school looked the way I did. You know what she said? 'When your brother comes through the door every morning, I can count on his sunny smile.'" Deacon flattened his hands on his knees. *"His freaking sunny smile."*

Vic lowered the papers and waited.

"I felt like I was drowning. In high school, I was at the top but in the NBA, I was nothing but a scrawny teenager with acne who played a couple minutes a night off the bench and wouldn't go out to the clubs with the team. The guys didn't have any use for me. But then that teacher told me Wes was excelling in school and smiling every day, and I figured I'd pulled off the biggest upset of all time." He shrugged. "I saved that damn report card. The teacher made an actual smiley face on the bottom. I carried it with me when I went back on the road with the team and looked at it every night."

"You took care of him, D. Just like you promised your mom."

"I didn't see any stupid sunny smile today."

"Let me finish reading," Vic said as he stacked the papers back up and squared the corners.

"Can you give me a quick recap and I'll get a voice file from you later?" Deacon didn't want Wes to come in and see Victor reading to him. He clasped his hands. "Sorry for making you drive out tonight."

Vic was the only person who knew he couldn't read. Deacon hated having to ask him for help. He never would have told him, but Victor figured it out himself when they were in the midst of an intense contract negotiation about six months after they started working together. Victor invited him out for dinner, confronted him and said he didn't care if Deacon could read English, Martian or neither. They had to be honest with each other, or their partnership had no point.

Deacon thought about the meeting that morning and the additional details Victor had just given him. He couldn't make sense of the books most second-graders could read with ease, but his memory was exceptional. Without that, he'd never have been able to fake his way along so effectively.

"The community service is the key. If he does that and shows up at the next hearing at school with some letters of recommendation, he can be reinstated, right?"

Victor nodded.

"So I just need to find community service for him to do."

"Or you could let him find it."

"Right."

"Seriously, man. You've been cleaning up after Wes your whole life. How many times did he get suspended from high school? Six? Eight? And that vandalism thing when he was a sophomore?"

"That was a prank. They'd sprayed Silly String on some statue, and the town had come down on them because they were from the private school."

"Be that as it may, Deacon, he's eighteen. He's old enough to take responsibility for himself."

"What if he won't?" Deacon stood. "My parents never did. What if he's got whatever they had inside them—and this is the beginning of the end for him?"

"All the more reason you need to step back and let him stand on his own."

"You know what he'll do? He'll find someone in town to give him a cushy job and he'll live here in our cushy place. How will that change him?"

"What are you going to do? Put him into some hard-labor camp?"

"I don't know."

Victor said, "Any chance he could work for a literacy group?"

Deacon's ears went hot with shame. Victor knew he hated to talk about this. "He's not a teacher."

"You're twenty-eight years old, D. You've got years ahead of you to find a girlfriend, maybe have a kid or two, be an uncle to Wes's kids and godfather to mine if I can ever find a woman with taste impeccable enough to marry me." Vic held the eye contact. "Maybe you can do all that and keep up the lies about your reading, but it'll be hard. A part of you will always be off-limits. Is that what you want?"

"Wes doesn't have to know." And if Vic didn't shut up about it pretty quick, Deacon was going to hit him.

"I'm not trying to be a jerk, D, but you're making a mistake. When he was younger, just out of foster care, he needed you to be the adult. I respect the hell out of you for what you did, and you know it. But *he's* an adult now, or as good as. Might be nice to lean on him for some of this stuff."

"Are you telling me you don't want to help me out?"

"Don't be a jackass. I'm just saying maybe he'd like to know you've struggled with stuff."

Deacon felt sick at the thought of telling Wes. He couldn't bear to see the look on his brother's face if he found out he couldn't read. "He's so damn smart, Vic. He reads all the time. I know he's in college, but I'm still the only person he's got to steer him straight. If I tell him I was passed through school with fewer skills than an eight-year-old, he might stop listening to me altogether. How would he ever respect me again?"

"I respect you."

"That's different."

"How?"

"You don't depend on me."

"Maybe it's time for Wes to quit depending on you. You've been carrying him a long while. He might be glad to know he can do something for you."

"I don't think that would be helpful, Vic. But thank you for the suggestion."

Victor shrugged. "No need to go all Ms. Manners on me, Deacon. I knew you wouldn't want to hear it, but I had to say it. Honesty, that's why you pay me the big bucks."

Deacon nodded. "Well, honesty is annoying."

"So is stubbornness," Victor said. "I'll call you to-morrow."

They walked together to the side door.

Deacon said, "Honesty isn't annoying, Vic. I just can't tell him about this."

"You can tell him. You don't want to."

"And now we're back to annoying."

They shook hands. Deacon locked the door behind Victor, then picked up the ball. He spun it on his index finger, then gave it a bounce and spun it on his middle finger before tossing it in front of him and then in one smooth move scooping it up, passing it behind his back and tossing it into the basket. Two points. No sweat. There wasn't a thing in the world he couldn't do. Except order off a menu, pick out a birthday card or read the freaking letter when his brother got suspended from college.

WHEN THE PHONE rang an hour or so later, he was in his room, trying unsuccessfully to nap. He rolled off the bed to grab it, desperate for a distraction.

"May I speak to Deacon Fallon?"

"This is Deacon."

The pause that followed went on a little too long. "Sorry. I wasn't expecting you to answer the phone."

Must be a reporter. He didn't get as many calls as he used to, but when basketball season started, he usually received a few requests for information. Draft season never passed without a half-dozen calls from reporters looking for a quote.

He wasn't in the mood to talk about basketball and he almost hung up. But this woman's caller ID had a Milton area code and he was curious. He grabbed his glasses before he plugged in the earpiece for his phone, then tucked the phone in his pocket. He walked out of the bedroom and down the long hallway to the great room.

"Deacon, this is Julia Bradley," she said as if she thought he'd recognize her name.

"Uh, hi," he said, stalling for time and hoping she'd give him some clue about how he knew her. The remote was stuffed between two cushions on the couch and he fished it out to flick ESPN on.

"I was your guidance counselor at Milton High School. Ms. Bradley?"

Ms. Bradley. He wouldn't have put that together—he'd never called her Julia in his life. She'd been serious, he remembered. Tried like hell to get him to stay in school. She'd jabbed her finger at his coach's chest during one tense conversation. He'd been half afraid his coach would slap her. He hadn't thought about that in years, but the scene was still vivid in his memory.

She'd been new to Milton and hadn't understood how things worked there. He'd been terrified someone might listen to her and upset his plan to turn pro. Everything back then had been so touch-and-go—he sometimes thought he'd held his breath his entire senior year.

A scene from shop class came back to him. The guys had spent most of one period debating whether the new guidance counselor was wearing a thong under her dress at the student awards assembly. Just like that, the image of her at the podium, the light from the back of the stage outlining her legs and the curve of her hips under her skirt, returned as fresh as if it had happened that morning, not ten years ago.

"Ms. Bradley," he choked out. "Good to see you. I mean, hear from you." He clicked the remote again, shutting off the TV.

"Well, I hope you'll still feel that way when you find out I'm asking for a favor."

"What do you need?" Maybe a signed jersey or a ball. People phoned every once in a while asking for stuff to raffle off.

"I need a basketball coach. A reputable, skilled basketball coach who's willing to work for nothing. The athletic budget has been cut to the bone."

"A coach for the Tigers?"

"Yes."

"They let Coach Simon go? That's…unbelievable."

"Times are hard. The school board budget proposal didn't pass with the voters, so we've been forced into an austerity budget. The state sets spending levels." She rattled off the facts, but her voice had lost its warmth. He imagined she was trying to hold back her opinion of this financial state of affairs.

"Anyway, I don't want to take up any more of your time. The reason I called is that even though I realize you don't get back here very much, I'd hoped you might know someone who would be interested in helping out as coach, or maybe you wouldn't mind sending a donation to help me pay someone."

Things must have changed in Milton since he'd been there, because no way the town he remembered would have let the team go. *Man.*

His mouth went dry. Milton needed a volunteer coach.

When he'd told Victor he didn't want Wes to do easy community service, he'd meant it. He wanted Wes to see what his life could have been like and could still be if he didn't start to focus. Where better to bring that lesson home than in Milton? He and Wes would both be there still if not for basketball.

On a selfish level, if Wes worked out with the Tigers, that might give him an extra bump when it came time for the university to review his case. If he'd put the time in to stay in shape, would that show his coach he was serious about playing ball?

"You need a coach now?"

"Practice starts in two days."

"Say I can find someone. Would you be willing to write a letter of recommendation afterward?"

"For a coaching job?"

"For college."

"Guidance counselors love to write recommendations. If you know someone who'd be willing to help, I'd be more than happy to write a letter."

He didn't need to tell anyone about the suspension right away. He'd be able to keep the details quiet while Wes did his work—he could tell Ms. Bradley what she needed to know when they were done.

"Okay. I know someone."

"Thanks so much, Deacon. I mean, I'm phoning you out of the blue, and it's just so generous of you to help me out. Would it be out of line for me to ask who you have in mind?"

"Me. Well, me and my brother."

"You hate Milton." He heard what sounded like a muffled curse, and she quickly added, "Well, not hate, but you don't come home and I've heard—"

"My business is flexible, so I can work from Milton." He made the next part sound like an afterthought. "I'll bring my brother. He's the one who can use the college letter."

"So your brother is thinking about college? Good for him!"

Her tone of voice set him on edge. It was that fake-supportive thing teachers always did when they were giving an order but wanted you to believe you were making a choice. Did she think that just because he didn't go to college he wouldn't send his brother?

He'd worked hard to get where he was—no shiny green suits hanging in his closet now. He wasn't that kid with no options anymore, and high school guidance counselors certainly didn't intimidate him anymore. Not even if they were drop-dead sexy standing at the podium during assembly in a thong. He snapped out, "Of course he's going to college. Why wouldn't he?"

"No reason," she said. "I'll look forward to meeting him."

"Why are you helping out the basketball team, anyway? You weren't too supportive of the Tigers when I was playing."

"The details are different in this case," she said. "You never answered why you said yes to this, either."

Her words held a challenge, but he didn't owe her anything. He wasn't about to be baited into spilling his guts about Wes.

"Times change," he said.

"Well, even though it doesn't seem like enough, you have my gratitude."

"Go, Tigers," he said.

"Go, Tigers," she echoed.

HE FINALLY TRACKED Wes down in the gym. His brother was leaning against the wall, his eyes unfocused as he concentrated on the conversation he was having on the phone.

"Call me as soon as you hear," he said. "The minute you find out." He listened for a few more seconds and then hung up.

"Hey," he said to Deacon.

"You want to shoot around?"

Wes shrugged. "I guess."

Deacon tossed a ball onto the floor. "Want the music on?"

Wes caught the ball, but held it. "No." He jogged a few feet toward the foul line, then turned and bounced the ball back to Deacon. "We'll play to twenty. Win by two?"

Deacon didn't play against Wes. He used to when Wes was much younger. They'd played a lot. But Deacon had always held back, making sure his brother won. With ten years between them, there'd been no way to make the contest even close to fair. When Wes was about eight, he realized Deacon was letting him win. He'd pitched a fit, and when Deacon wouldn't agree to play him "like a man" in Wes's words, the boy had stormed off the court. After that, they'd shoot around, run drills, mess with tricks, but they didn't play games.

"I'm not playing you, Wes."

"Why not? I thought you'd be happy I'm trying to stay in shape so I'll be fighting fit when they decide I've learned my lesson and can be allowed back on campus."

"Who was on the phone?"

"Oliver."

He'd met Oliver during the move-in weekend. At first he'd assumed he was on the team because he was rooming with Wes, plus he was tall and well built. He looked like the other guys on the floor, but then the kid opened his mouth. Oliver was brilliant, no doubt about it, but he was pretty far off the beaten path, maybe far off the planet. At one point he'd spoken what Deacon assumed was Arabic because it sounded exactly that complicated and hard to learn, but Wes told him later it was Elvish.

There'd been a mix-up in the housing office, and somehow Oliver had been assigned to Wes's room even though he wasn't on the team and shouldn't have been on the basketball floor at the dorm.

"He has to have a second hearing. They decided there's enough evidence he was involved to suspend him, too."

"He cheated and he helped you steal a car."

"The cheating thing was a joke. Nobody would have cared about any of it if we hadn't moved that car. Coach got pissed off because we embarrassed him. He's been on me since— He's just been on me. If we hadn't touched his car, they'd have ignored everything, even the bar thing."

Deacon felt his skin go cold. Wes really didn't see why people were mad about what he'd done.

His brother went on. "Maybe I'll just drop out. I don't need college. You never went. I should skip the whole thing and get a job."

"Where? In the fast-food industry?"

"Bill Gates dropped out. Mark Zuckerberg dropped out."

"So what? You invented some new Internet technology and you've been keeping it quiet until you can drop out of school and start minting money in the stock market?"

"No, Deacon. You don't have to be a jerk," Wes said. "College is pointless. Like I said, you didn't go."

He heard Victor's voice in his mind. *Tell him. Tell Wes. He'll never know how much his education means if you don't let him see all the problems you have without it.* He told Vic to shut it.

"I *couldn't* go. There's a difference. Unless, that is, you're actually living in poverty and supporting your kid brother and have interest from NBA scouts, to boot."

His brother scowled at him.

"I lined up your community service. You're going to have an immersion course in real life for real people."

"What does that mean?"

"Look around, Wes." Deacon swept his arms out to encompass the indoor basketball court, the climate control, the sound system, the entire existence he'd built for them. "You have a sweet life. This is special and you treat it like it's nothing. Like you're owed this life. I'm done watching you screw around with this, when it's a gift."

"So you're sending me to some developing country where I can see how hard life is without indoor plumbing?"

"It's taking indoor basketball courts for granted that's the problem. We're going to Milton."

"Milton? Like our hometown Milton?"

"Exactly."

"Milton where you said you never wanted to put your foot again? Milton where you've never visited since the day we moved away? Milton where the boosters club sends you letters every year to attend the sports banquet to hand out the trophy *named for you* and you throw the letters in the garbage every time?"

"For Pete's sake, Wes. Yes. That Milton."

"Well, don't act like I'm crazy for asking. You never... Why? Why now?"

"We're going to coach basketball."

"What?"

"The Tigers need a coach—some budget crisis or something. My old guidance counselor offered us the job."

"You and I are going to coach? Together? Why?" Wes asked, sounding genuinely shocked.

This was the closest Deacon had come to getting his

brother to pay attention to him since the whole suspension issue had started. Maybe, for the first time in his life, Milton would be the solution instead of the problem.

"Because you, my brother, need three hundred hours of community service." Deacon tossed the ball through the hoop, admiring the perfect swish. "And Ms. Julia Bradley needs a coach. It's a perfect fit."

CHAPTER THREE

SHE CALLED A team meeting after school. She was expecting Deacon later that day, but wasn't going to tell the girls about him yet. For one thing, she still couldn't quite believe he'd agreed to her proposal. The way he said yes so quickly was odd because she knew he'd been asked to help before and he'd always refused. Second, there was the little matter of her allowing him to believe he was coaching the boys. When he found out about the girls, would he even stay? She felt queasy when she let herself imagine that he might leave—once again, she'd painted herself into a corner with her tendency toward brinksmanship.

The most important reason she hadn't told the team was that she didn't want to risk having Ty find out the Basketball Brothers were coming and then doing something to either sabotage their work for her team or co-opt them for the boys' team. She slipped the Fallons' district paperwork through under the catchall bucket for volunteers in the mentoring program. They weren't getting paid, so there was no requirement for her to consult with Ty about hiring them.

In the couple days since she and the brothers had spoken on the phone, the two Fallons had taken on a superhero-duo mystique in her mind. She would do her best not to refer to them out loud as the Basketball Brothers, and in return, they would rescue her program, save her sanity and help her put Ty Chambers and the boosters in their place.

Good thing Deacon Fallon was used to living up to high expectations.

Once the girls were gathered on the bleachers, she updated them about the budget cuts and then she told them about the bet. They were utterly silent for a few seconds. The only sound in the gym was the rhythmic pounding of a basketball; Max Wright was shooting alone at the other end of the court. He'd been cut from the boys' team and she'd invited him to practice with her girls, where the team philosophy didn't allow cuts. So far he hadn't joined them. He showed up in the gym every afternoon, but kept to himself.

Before she finished outlining the terms of the bet, Iris and Tali were off the bleachers and heading for the door, Tali's little brothers, Trey and Shawn, trailing after her.

"Stop," Julia said. "Where are you going?"

Tali tightened her thumbs on the cords of the gym bag she had over her shoulders. "Look, Ms. Bradley, we suck. We lost every game last year. Doing this bet? It's like we're asking everyone to laugh at us."

Iris nodded. "We appreciate what you're trying to do, but it's useless. Nobody at this school cares about anything except the boys' team."

"As I told you, I have no intention of letting them disband our team. You girls focus on having a fantastic year. I'll manage the rest."

"Fantastic? How? We don't have one thing you need for a basketball team, including a coach who knows how to coach." That was Miri. A senior, she'd been on the team since her freshman year. "Sorry, Coach."

Julia would have to consult her records to be sure,

but even without looking, she wouldn't hesitate to bet Miri hadn't scored a single point in any of her three previous years. Julia didn't mention this.

"I'm more than aware of my deficiencies as a coach."

Cora Turner snorted and Miri smiled at her knowingly.

"I believe I have found an assistant who is more than qualified to handle the basketball-specific parts of the job." *If he shows up, that is. If he stays.*

"What parts of being a basketball coach aren't basketball-specific?" Tali's posture was challenging.

If Julia hadn't been certain it would lead to more wrangling, she would have made a list, starting with letting Tali's little brothers hang around practice every day after the elementary school got out so they weren't home watching TV. Setting up movie night. Choosing the audio books they listened to on the bus. Making sure the uniforms arrived on time and fit, even if some of the girls weren't exactly built for speed. Talking to the players. Giving structure to their days. Being there in case they wanted an adult to consult with—during her time at Milton more than one basketball player had come to her about things that mattered. She was necessary. The team was necessary. The only thing that had changed this year was that winning, God help them, was also necessary.

"You understand what our team is about, Tali. Responsibility, partnership, setting goals and meeting them. We're just adding a resource with a basketball background to round things out."

"You know a basketball coach?" Cora asked.

Tali snorted. "We don't need a coach—we need a wizard."

"You think Coach knows Harry Potter?"

"Maybe if you all practiced for real and didn't spend so much time doing your nails and babysitting, you could actually get better without a wizard," Max said. "You don't entirely suck all the time."

She hadn't noticed that he'd stopped practicing and drifted over to listen. His blond hair was caught back in a ponytail and a few strands lay plastered against his neck with sweat.

"How would you know, Max?" Tali said. "Last I looked, you got cut from your tryouts."

"I know more about basketball than any of you."

"Too bad you're not on our team, then. On account of you being a boy and all," Tali retorted.

"Ms. Bradley said I can practice with you if I want to. I'm considering taking her up on it."

Tali rolled her eyes. "Between you and our new wizard coaches, we'll be all kinds of gifted this year."

Julia walked the few steps across the gym so she was next to the girl. Tali, tall and slender, with deep brown eyes, had long, thick hair she refused to put into a ponytail for games. She'd come close to flunking remedial math during her first season on the team, but because she was rostered for a sport, her record was red-flagged early in the marking period and Julia had been able to get her into tutoring to prop her up. Now, starting her junior year, she was firmly in the middle of her grade-level math class. None of that was "basketball-specific," either, but it was all important.

"You don't take anything lying down and I respect that. If you hold on to your anger, then you can put it on the court. Can we stick with each other for one more season, all in, no matter what?"

She held her breath while hoping they would respond. Instead Cora nudged Miri, who dropped her backpack and promptly turned red with embarrassment. Tali straightened up and whispered, "Please tell me that's my new basketball coach."

Julia looked toward the door and there they were, the Basketball Brothers, tall and handsome and... She did a double take. Which one was Deacon?

The younger one on the left, with his skinny neck and rail-thin body, resembled the kid she remembered. Except that young guy wasn't Deacon. She knew because his thick, inky hair was styled in an expensive, professionally messy mop that was certainly not done at home with clippers, and she knew for sure because he smiled at her and his grin was cocky and charming in a way Deacon's never had been. When Deacon had been at Milton, he'd been wound so tight and been so focused on his sport she didn't think he'd ever smiled. This kid, the younger brother, had obviously grown up in different circumstances.

So Deacon was the other one. The slightly shorter, but sweet-mother-of-grown-up-hotness-what-a-good-looking-guy one. His acne had disappeared; instead a shadow of dark beard roughened his chin. Dark blond layers of silky hair hit the back of his neck, scissoring out at the sides, and shorter layers lay in golden-brown lines across his forehead—completely erasing her memories of his clippered high school haircut. He wore glasses, which was a surprise, but the smart dark frames had a sexy edge and set off his deep blue eyes beautifully.

"Give me one minute," she said to the girls as she hurried to meet her new assistants where they stood a few feet into the gym.

Because she was a bit breathless and trying to let

her brain catch up with her eyes, she engaged the less intimidating one, Wes, first. "You don't much resemble your brother."

"Thank God for that," he said. "I can't afford plastic surgery at the moment."

Reading nonverbal clues was an essential part of navigating the tense parent-child meetings she often facilitated. The expression Deacon shot Wes was clearly a command to shut the hell up and quit screwing around. She gave him credit for saying it silently.

"Ms. Bradley," Deacon said, "this is my brother, Wes Fallon."

Wes stuck out his hand and she shook it. When she half turned, Deacon had his hand out, too. She took it, and his handshake was warm and firm. Behind his glasses, his dark blue eyes were hard to read. Did he remember her? How did she look to him after all these years?

"We're honored you asked us back to help with the team," Deacon said.

"Well." She was acutely aware of the girls waiting behind her. "We're honored to have you."

And wouldn't the boosters love to be the ones doing the honoring here? she thought. When Ty and the rest of them found out, she would be in a world of trouble.

She couldn't wait.

She'd been anticipating the Basketball Brothers, but clearly, she hadn't taken into account their being ten years older than when she'd last seen them. Their entire lives had changed in that time. The orphans from the wrong side of the tracks in a town where the right side wasn't very prosperous had grown into a pair of poised, well dressed, frankly impressive men.

Deacon had on a black dress shirt patterned in a

light gray check and a pair of dark blue jeans. The way the jeans fit, trim and taut, showed that he had filled out from his gangly high school days. But any weight he'd added was hard muscle. The sleeves of his tucked-in shirt were rolled up to his elbows, showing off more lean muscle and slightly tanned skin dusted with light brown hair. She'd dated a drummer once who'd been a total screwup and had infuriated her by spending his rent money on beer, but he'd had the nicest arms and so she'd stuck with him for a month or two longer than she should have. Deacon's arms were one hundred percent nicer than the drummer's.

She hoped he would stay and coach, because she had a sudden need to see those arms shoot a basketball.

HE DIDN'T KNOW what he'd been expecting. Maybe that Ms. Bradley would still look like a teacher, albeit a hot one, to him. He definitely hadn't anticipated the flash of attraction he'd felt as she hurried across the gym toward them, the hem of her skirt whipping around well-toned calves and then flipping up to give a glimpse of one smooth thigh.

"Dude." Wes had poked him in the ribs, and whispered behind his hand. "She's hot for an old chick."

Deacon would have smacked his head had they been alone. Manners were important even in the face of hot chicks. In the gym, he had to settle for a disgusted glare.

Now she smiled at them, appearing a bit nervous, and asked, "Are you ready to meet the team?"

And then she swept her arm toward the kids gathered on the bleachers.

"Those are girls," Deacon blurted.

"Nothing gets past him," Wes said.

Julia didn't smile. Her eyes were a light, clear gray-blue, and intense when she focused on him. She held him fixed in place when she responded, "That's right. That's my team."

Even as he spoke, he knew he was being rude, but he was shocked. This wasn't what he'd said yes to. "You told me you wanted us to coach the *Tigers.* I brought my brother here so he could work with the *Tigers.*"

Julia didn't raise her voice or even change her expression, but he had the feeling she was pissed. Which was ridiculous. He was the one who'd been duped.

"You *are* here to coach the Tigers." She pointed toward the group of girls on the other side of the gym. "Right there. Those are your Tigers."

His Tigers.

Two of them were considerably closer to five foot than six. One of them outweighed him for sure. Not a single one of the ten girls appeared remotely interested in basketball. Especially not the one perched on a ball and wearing a skirt with tights and high-heeled shoes. She had a mirror out and some tiny silver tool in her hand. "What is she doing to her face?"

"They call that tweezing," Wes said.

"Practice hasn't started yet," Julia said. "We were in a meeting. You're early."

She looked at him pointedly, but he wasn't about to apologize for throwing off her schedule when she had just pulled a whopper of a bait and switch on him. Feeling foolish because he'd misinterpreted a situation was his worst nightmare.

"She's wearing high heels. In the gym." He thought about his hardwood court at home and what heels would do to the surface. He had nothing against the girls, but he had a lot of trouble with being manipulated, especially when the manipulator was affiliated with Milton sports.

"We don't have uniforms yet." She got right up close to him, standing between him and Wes, her back to the girls and her voice pitched so no one could overhear. "Look, Deacon. I fudged the truth. You made an assumption and I should have corrected you." She edged even closer, more urgency in her voice now. "But you said you'd coach them and I couldn't believe it. I was too thrilled, and I thought if I clarified, you might not come. You're here now. Can't you see they need help? I need to know right now. Will you coach them or not?"

He was about to say *or not.* Maybe not quite that snottily, but he was ready to walk away, when Wes spoke up.

"Sure we'll coach them. We said we would. Right, Deacon? Fallons keep their word, especially to the team."

Wes looked earnest. He had this thing he could do where he somehow transformed himself from a six-foot-four-inch man into a five-year-old kid whose balloon had just blown away.

"I don't like it when you do that," he muttered. The protest was a token one and he knew it. He'd been back in Milton High School for less than twenty minutes and he was already as firmly trapped by Wes's needs and the expectations of the Milton sports program as he'd been in high school.

"What am I doing?"

"Making that face that looks like I kicked your puppy."

"I'm not."

Wes had the innocent act down so perfectly it didn't

even appear like an act. Julia probably thought he really was that innocent.

"Your brother's performance aside," Julia said, "the girls really need help."

Underneath his anger about being tricked, he was tempted because Wes wanted it, and Wes hadn't wanted anything from him since the day he got suspended. He was tempted because this time around, Julia and he were both adults and he'd gotten a tantalizing peek at her thigh and he couldn't make himself walk away without seeing more.

As he hesitated, one of the girls tossed a shot in from the baseline, and when it went in, she pumped her fist and he felt the pleasure right along with her, the satisfaction of watching a sweet shot swish free through the net.

Nothing but air.

His Tigers.

HE WAS GETTING ready to walk and she couldn't blame him. She should have come clean right from the start. He glanced at his brother and then back at the girls. Max put a beautiful shot in and Deacon's eyes lit up. He still loved the game. Would that be enough to make him say yes?

The girls were unable to control their curiosity anymore and now they were inching forward to group up behind her. She wished he'd commit so they could move on and get the season started.

Tali, putting on the tough sexy-girl act she used around cute guys, shook her hair loose around her shoulders. Cora put her hand over the pimple on her chin. Miri turned sideways, trying as always to minimize her physical presence.

The next second, the situation got even more complicated.

The double gym doors banged open behind Wes, and Ty rushed in. His golf shirt was tucked into navy blue pleated pants and his face was flushed as if he'd been running. He panted as he held out his hand to Deacon, completely ignoring Julia and Wes. "Deacon Fallon, my God. I didn't believe it when my secretary told me you signed the visitors' log, but here you are. Right here in the old gym where it all started. Welcome back."

Close behind the girls, Max hovered without actually joining the group, but she heard his awed, whispered "Deacon Fallon, no way."

Deacon hesitated and then took Ty's hand, but there was none of the old one-Tiger-to-a-fellow-Tiger heartiness she was used to seeing from Ty and the boosters. She couldn't believe this was happening. What if Ty wooed Deacon away right here with the girls watching?

"Nice to meet you," Deacon said. She gripped her left elbow with her right hand to keep from snatching Deacon from Ty.

"Oh, we've met before. Back when you were playing. Ty Chambers. I'm the principal at Milton now." He held up his right hand, flashing the championship ring. "State—1992."

She glanced down. Deacon was wearing a thick silver band on his right hand, but no championship ring. He probably had his mounted in some kind of trophy case. Maybe he thought wearing all four rings would be tacky.

"I'm sorry I wasn't around to meet you when you got in." Now Ty looked at her, but his eyes flashed with simmering anger. "I wasn't informed that you were coming."

Julia wanted to get Deacon away so they could seal their deal. If he met the girls, she just knew he wouldn't be able to say no. She edged toward him, trying to angle her shoulders between Ty and him, but the principal wasn't about to be angled any which way.

"Coach Simon is in his office." Ty put his hand on Deacon's shoulder and gestured toward the back of the gym where the coach had his office. "I'm sure he'd love to say hey. You want to walk back and see him? I can give you a tour after that and we can talk about what brought you to Milton today."

If she'd been a cat, she'd have hissed at him. How dare he swoop in and take Deacon from her? He wanted her girls to lose, he wanted her to lose, and it looked very much as though he would get his wish. Once a Tiger, always a Tiger. She knew how it worked.

Except, Deacon didn't budge. Ty must have put some pressure behind his hand, expecting forward momentum, because he stumbled, almost running into Cora, when Deacon's black boots stayed planted. Deacon's shoulders rippled, and even in that ridiculously domesticated checked dress shirt, she felt their power. Before she realized he'd moved, Ty's hand was hanging in midair and Deacon was one step closer to her than he'd been.

"You okay?" he asked Cora quietly, but with an unmistakable undertone that said he wasn't happy she'd almost been stepped on.

Behind Deacon's back, Wes lifted his chin and winked at her as if to say, *Check out my big brother.* The wink was fast, but he was clearly not worried.

Maybe the Basketball Brothers really were the good guys.

"I'd love to say hi to Coach, but I actually got here late for my appointment and I have to get a move on and meet my Tigers."

"Your Tigers?" Ty scanned the gym with a half smile—he thought Deacon was making a joke, but he wasn't sure what it was about. His gaze skipped right over the girls, dismissing them as no more likely to be Deacon's team than the bleachers were.

"My brother and I are coaching the Tigers this year."

"Coaching the Tigers?" Ty's smile faltered. He was even surer a joke was being told, but he still didn't get the punch line.

Julia did, though. She met Deacon's eyes, and knew he'd made up his mind. The girls moved, drawn in as Deacon claimed them in the face of their principal's dismissal.

Deacon nodded and took one more step so they were standing hip to hip, the gap between them and Ty more pronounced. Wes moved up to stand on her other side. In her mind, she imagined a flourish of trumpets, and it was all she could do not to pump her arms in the air. Tada! The Basketball Brothers saved the day!

An angry flush swept up Ty's neck into his face as he finally caught on. He hadn't liked her much before this—being the thorn in his professional side hadn't left room for affection—but now...she read it in his eyes. War.

Bring it!

Julia lifted her whistle to her lips, ready to get practice started.

"You're coaching the *girls?*" Ty asked.

Deacon shrugged. "The budget went haywire,

right? Ms. Bradley said she needed a coach. Wes and I weren't busy."

"The boosters have reached out to you with paid offers to run clinics, to speak at our awards dinner—hell, to show up for a game—and you never once responded."

"I sent checks."

"And now you're here for what?" Ty eyed her. She didn't blink.

"To coach the Tigers," Deacon said. He raised his arm and pointed at the girls standing behind them. "Those are my Tigers, right there. Go, Tigers."

Wes gave Ty a double thumbs-up that was both resoundingly cheerful and utterly obnoxious. Julia didn't have to say a word. Ty knew he'd lost, and she savored her triumph.

SHE BLEW HER whistle and the girls gathered in a circle a few feet away. The kids moved in real close, staring curiously from her to the Fallons, throwing an occasional nervous glance toward Ty, who stood with crossed arms, leaning against the wall near the door. Thank goodness she'd actually put the volunteer paperwork through. He would be gunning for her and Deacon. She'd have to pay strict attention to the rules so he couldn't find a vulnerability later to take them down.

"Okay, kids," she said. "I want to officially introduce you to your new coach...coaches, Deacon Fallon and Wes Fallon. Deacon played in the NBA, but before that he was a student right here at Milton." She pointed to the rafters. "That's his retired jersey up there."

Tali tossed her hair back over her shoulder, jutting out one hip to the side in a pose she probably thought was sexy, and raised her hand to ask a question. Deacon would have to figure out how to deal with this, Julia thought. They'd all have crushes on him before the season started.

"Yes?" Julia said.

"Is Coach Wes in high school?"

Cora's eyes fluttered wildly and then she asked, "Is Coach Wes going to go to Milton?"

"I can show him around," Iris volunteered. Even though her face betrayed no hint of exertion, she lifted her shirt to fan herself with the hem, purposely exposing a few inches of tanned and toned teenage stomach.

Julia was floored. The girls were preening for Wes, not Deacon. She'd registered that Wes was attractive, but he was a teenager. It made sense, of course, that they'd have a crush on him, not his brother. They were kids; Wes was a kid. Wes's looks were born of his smiling, good-natured charm, whereas Deacon had a rougher, more worn handsomeness enhanced by the laugh lines around his eyes.

The girls' reaction to Wes made her feel better about her obsession with Deacon's arms.

And shoulders.

And glasses. *Good Lord.*

That she couldn't shut out her awareness of Deacon was natural. They were both adults, and he happened to be tall and hot and standing really close to her. Her response was pure instinct. She was sure that once she got used to him, she would stop noticing every time he shifted his stance, even if his thighs in tight dark blue jeans were mesmerizing.

Wes spoke up. "I'm out of high school. I'm on a break from college to help my brother out here."

Julia caught Deacon's glance at his brother. That

answered her question about Wes and high school, but now she had to find out what was with this break from college. Maybe she wasn't the only one who'd fudged the truth on the phone the other day.

The kids posed a few more questions, and then she dismissed the team for the afternoon. Tali's hips had a distinctly forced sway as she sashayed toward the locker room. Julia made a mental note to speak to the team about appropriate interaction with their coaches.

Tali's brothers crowded up to Deacon after the girls had disappeared.

"You really played in the NBA?" Trey asked.

Deacon nodded. "You two on my team?"

Shawn giggled, but Trey scowled. "We're not girls."

Wes snapped his fingers. "I told you they were dudes, Deacon."

"Darn. I wanted them on my team."

Shawn giggled again.

Wes crouched so that he was closer to their eye level. "So what's up? Why are you hanging around the high school chicks?"

Trey rolled his eyes. "Our sister is on the team. Her name's Tali. Mom says we can't go home by ourselves after school, even though I'm in fourth grade."

"Tali says we're pests, but she has to come here after school, so we do, too."

"That's good," Deacon said. "Maybe you can give me the inside scoop on this team. You know, tell me who's really good at what."

"Man," Trey said, "Tali's team is so bad nobody's any good. You sure you want to mess around with them?"

"I'm sure," Deacon said.

"You're making a bad decision," Trey said.

"Yeah, like *really* stupid," Shawn agreed.

DEACON HOPED TALI'S brothers were wrong, but he wasn't certain.

Julia smiled at him. "I can't thank you enough for agreeing to coach," she said. "The girls were over the moon."

He glanced around, but Wes had moved off to play keep-away with the little boys, dribbling between his legs and behind their backs, while they squealed and darted after the ball.

"Look, Julia. I'm here and I'm staying to coach, but I don't appreciate being tricked, and I really don't appreciate being a pawn in whatever war you've got going with your buddy Principal Ty." He'd had enough of being played with by the boosters as a kid.

Her cheeks were pink, whether from the warmth of the gym or emotion he couldn't say.

"Ty is not my buddy. In fact, he got under my skin, and I may have made some…promises… Right before I called you, I was becoming concerned I wouldn't be able to keep those promises. I should have explained better, but you didn't exactly ask a lot of questions." Which still wasn't a real apology.

"Promises?" What the hell? She'd made promises and now he'd have to help her keep them? Wes jogged up just then. Deacon kept his eyes on Julia while he dug his keys out of his pocket. "Wes, will you go bring the car around?"

He dropped the keys to the Porsche in Wes's hand.

"Why? You never let me drive your car. Are you and Julia going to talk about me behind my back?"

"No. And she's Ms. Bradley to you."

"Then why are you trying to get rid of me?" Wes asked, even as he put his hand with the keys behind his back as if afraid Deacon would snatch them away. "And she said I could call her Julia."

"Because as of an hour ago when I accepted this job, I became the head coach and you became the assistant. The assistant does things like carry the water bottles, hold the clipboard and bring the car around. And you're a couple months out of high school. You can call her Ms."

Wes still didn't move.

"You might want to get going before I decide the assistant also does the team laundry."

Wes attempted puppy eyes on Julia. "Why does he get to be the head coach? I'm a much nicer person than he is."

"He has more experience."

"I'm taller."

She shrugged. "Not by much. Plus, he's older."

"This is age bias."

Julia grinned at him, but she shook her head. "I'm leaving personnel decisions in the hands of the guy with the most experience. But I really don't mind if you call me Julia. In fact, I'd prefer it."

"Go get the car, Wes."

"Fine." Wes spun the keys around his finger and caught them in his hand, clearly excited by the opportunity to drive the Porsche. "Don't be rude to Julia while I'm gone." He turned. "Hey, little dudes. Want to ride in my superfast car?"

The three of them ran out of the gym.

Deacon focused on the situation facing him. Coach Donny Simon, the Milton High School sports program and its boosters were the definition of *self-interested*. He knew that firsthand. He couldn't let himself forget that they never offered anything that wouldn't end with them the winners.

Where Julia stood he wasn't as sure. They might be coaching together, but that didn't mean they were on the same team.

"You have someplace private we can go so you can tell me about these promises?"

JULIA LED DEACON through the library to her office. She took him inside and then closed the door, confident anyone who needed her would knock.

She backed all the way up against her desk in an effort to put some space between her and Deacon. They'd barely spent an hour together, but she'd already realized something very dangerous about him: his eyes were lethal.

Somewhere along the way someone had told Wes he had cute eyes, and he didn't hesitate to deploy their power, but she spent her days dealing with kids trying to get out of consequences or obligations. She was immune to begging eyes, even if they were as cute as Wes's.

Deacon's, however, were a deep, dark blue and they went to navy when he ducked his head, letting his hair shadow them. They were wary, guarded and hit her in the place in her soul that wanted to save people.

Before she'd seen him, she'd worried she and Deacon wouldn't be able to work together if she couldn't stop viewing him as a former student. Now that he was in her office, taking up most of the available air, making glasses look sexy, for God's sake, she knew that fear was groundless. No one would ever mistake Deacon Fallon for a boy. His shoulders alone had enough powerful sex appeal to make her believe he'd

been born a full-grown man, because certainly someone who looked the way he did had never been anything but strong and secure.

Even when Ty with all his bulk and bluster was in
her office, the space didn't feel this small. She'd never
been so aware of the location of her thighs and chest
in relation to Ty's the way she was with Deacon.

"So you want to explain about these promises?" he
asked.

The bet with Ty painted her in a ridiculous light; she
hated to explain it. But she had to. After all, Deacon
was key to the girls winning.

"It's more of a bet than a promise. When Ty told me
the board had taken away funding for the team, I bet
him we would make it to States this year."

"You bet him you would win States?" Deacon's eyes
widened. "Seriously?"

"Not win. Just get there." Four teams went to States,
but only one could win. She much preferred the odds
for getting there.

"With this team? The one I just met?"

"Yes."

He gazed at the ceiling as if expecting to see some
other team descending from the sky to prove she'd been
teasing him all along.

He put his fingers up to his temples. "Okay. So you
bet him the girls would get to States." He was almost
talking to himself. Talking himself down, out of his
anger. "Heat of the moment. He got under your skin.
I can relate. They could be better than they look. I
haven't watched them play yet."

She wished she could let the issue go there, but she
owed Deacon full disclosure. "I also bet Ty the girls'
boosters would fundraise to pay for the trip."

"Why do I think there's something I don't know about the girls' boosters?"

She had to move. Standing there letting him pick this sorry story apart was making her itch. Yet there wasn't enough room for her to create a safe distance from Deacon. It seemed that every time she shifted, she brushed against his thigh or hip or one of those wonderfully defined arms. He was making her insane.

"The girls don't have boosters. We aren't very good, but that's not the real problem." She lifted the foam basketball she kept on her desk and aimed it at the hoop mounted on the back of the door. It missed and bounced off a stack of textbooks, right at Deacon. He caught it out of the air without even looking. He'd known where it would be and just grabbed it, because playing basketball was his magic. *Deacon Fallon was helping her coach.* That she'd pulled off a huge coup was sinking in. Maybe the season wasn't out of reach. "The problem is no one believes in them. Not even the girls themselves."

"I noticed." He returned the ball to her—a snappy little pass with just enough force to land it neatly in her hands. "You're telling me the bet had nothing to do with the fact that you'd rather set yourself on fire than be nice to your principal."

"He's wrong saying the girls' team doesn't matter."

"Just remember that Ty is your enemy, not me. I don't like mind games."

She wanted to protest that she hadn't been playing mind games, but she swallowed her defensiveness. He had a point.

"Most of the girls didn't seem too excited about basketball."

Julia pressed the ball between her hands. "We'll

change that. Now that you're here, we can make it all work."

"You hired a coach, Julia. I'll coach, but I'm not a miracle worker."

She was right up close to him again. She didn't remember moving closer.

When someone knocked on the door, she started back guiltily. He settled against the desk.

WHATEVER THE HELL spell was building between them was broken when a kid knocked on the door. Deacon bumped into a wall shelf as he ducked back, trying to give her space.

Ms. Bradley…Julia…was right next to him and he felt the silky cotton of her skirt brush against his jeans as she leaned forward to hug the girl in the doorway. The thin sweater Julia was wearing pulled tight across her back, outlining her trim waist.

He tried not to listen in on their conversation, but he couldn't help overhearing it. The girl needed help finding a person to interview for history class and Julia said she'd email her a list of possibilities.

That girl left, but a hulking boy of the no-neck football-lineman variety came in behind her. Deacon stepped around behind Julia so she could talk to the kid, and he watched as she scanned the paper No Neck handed her, then gave him a high five. No Neck had raised his science grade to passing.

So many of his teachers had let so much slide, but he remembered Ms. Bradley checking back until she was satisfied. She was apparently still working double time to connect with the students.

He'd noticed Julia's toned legs and her round hips, the warm brown hair hanging soft and loose on her shoulders and the way her big, deep blue eyes took in everything with a kind of intensity. When she interacted with the kids, her whole face was alive with interest.

As she leaned back to high-five No Neck, her backside brushed Deacon's leg and he had a vivid flashback to her silhouette at the podium and the thong. Wes was absolutely correct: Ms. Bradley was hot.

Not that he could do anything except look.

Sure, he hadn't been with anyone in a while. His last serious relationship had ended more than a year ago.

So yeah, he couldn't help appreciating Julia's looks. But he was here to help Wes. Anything else, including legs and hips and intense blue eyes, was irrelevant.

When she was finished with the kids, Deacon said, "What time tomorrow?"

He surprised himself by holding out his hand for her to shake. He pressed her palm lightly. A little innocent contact wouldn't hurt anybody. "Three o'clock, right?"

She nodded.

He'd be back for certain—even if he had no idea what to expect.

CHAPTER FOUR

HE'D RESERVED A suite for them at an extended-stay hotel while they were in Milton. It was about an hour away, back on the highway near Jericho. The GPS was programmed, but he disliked using it. The little voice telling him to turn right or left usually just confused him, especially when someone else was in the car, and he was liable to go the wrong direction. Rather than making a fool of himself in front of Wes, Deacon let him drive.

Wes, who rarely got to drive the Porsche, took full advantage of the accelerator once they hit the highway.

"You want to turn my iPod on?" Wes asked.

Deacon pushed the button and the iPod came to life. The first song on was "The Boys Are Back In Town" by Thin Lizzy.

Wes watched for Deacon's reaction out of the corner of his eye.

"Funny." He pushed the fast-forward button. The next song up was "We Are Family" by Sister Sledge.

"Two for two," Deacon said to Wes. "Funny again."

"It would have been better if we were returning to, like, our ancestral mansion, but I thought we should acknowledge the moment anyway."

Deacon let his head fall back against the seat. Wes still considered this a joke.

They checked in at the hotel, and then Deacon took

the car keys to go pick up a pizza for them. When he got back to the room, juggling the pizza, a twelve-pack of bottled water and a two-liter of Coke, Wes was nowhere to be seen. The room wasn't that big, and in less than three minutes, Deacon found the note his brother had scrawled on a piece of hotel stationery: "Gone out. Back later."

He sank onto the closest bed. Where the hell would the kid go? Wes knew Deacon was bringing food back. The only reason for his brother to skip out was to do something he didn't want Deacon to know about. There was a bar in the lobby and about a dozen chain restaurants on the highway by the hotel. Plenty of temptation for a college guy.

Deacon grabbed his cell and pressed One—the speed dial for Wes. His brother's phone went to voice mail. Deacon didn't leave a message. If Wes wasn't picking up, he wouldn't return because Deacon had left a message.

Deacon was starving, so he downed a piece of pizza and a bottle of water while he stood in front of the window, watching the parking lot. The hotel bar was having a karaoke night, and judging by the number of people he saw hurrying in through the entrance, the event was a popular one. The very last thing Deacon wanted to do was go to a karaoke night, but he could imagine that the music, the crowd, the whole scene, would have drawn Wes the same way the bounce house had at carnivals when Deacon was younger. If only the worst fear he had was that Wes would eat too much cotton candy.

TWENTY FRUSTRATING MINUTES later, Deacon had finished a tour of the bar, the lobby itself and the parking lot, but without any sign of his brother. Nothing he could do now but wait, he guessed. He made one more pass through the bar, and when he didn't see Wes, he headed for their room. It was dark and quiet with still no sign of his brother.

He'd been planning to flip a coin with Wes for who got the bedroom and who got the foldout couch, but after this rebellion, the couch was too good for Wes. Deacon took his bag in the bedroom and threw it into the closet. He turned on the TV in the room and sat down to wait.

Tension built inside him with every minute that passed. As a kid when his dad was out drinking, he and his mom would go through the same charade. They'd start out pretending everything was fine. Of course Dad would be home soon. No worries. Then, after the dinner was cold and he obviously wasn't coming, they'd stop talking about him. If they didn't talk about it, maybe it wasn't really happening. Finally, his mom would get snappy with him, sometimes mean. He'd retreat into his room and that would be the worst part, because he and his mom weren't in it together anymore. She was out in the living room, waiting for his dad, and he was alone in his room, wishing it would all end. Those hours he spent alone were when his hatred toward his dad bloomed and grew.

Now, Deacon paced from the bedroom to the door and back. He even took a shower, scrubbing himself in hot water, hoping to shed his anger toward Wes.

WHEN DEACON HAD left to get the pizza, Wes had tried to watch TV, but he couldn't sit still. Being at that school had really messed him up. His brother hadn't seemed to notice, but memorabilia from his playing days was all over the place. A big plaque in the lobby with the name of the athletes who won the Deacon Fallon Memorial Trophy every year. A trophy case practically devoted to Deacon.

After Deacon wrote his name in the guest book, the secretary did the kind of double take he'd only ever seen in cartoons, and the principal had looked as though he wanted an autograph, before Julia sent him into a rage. Deacon was a rock star in Milton, yet he avoided the place as if he were public enemy number one.

He and Deacon had a weird relationship. From his point of view, they were brothers; whereas Deacon thought of himself as the parent and Wes the child. On top of that and the ten-year gap in their ages, Deacon was so guarded he might as well have been the recipe for McDonald's secret sauce. He held everyone at arm's length, including his little brother.

Deacon's guardianship ended when Wes turned eighteen. Since he'd been home from school, his brother had been so angry, Wes had wondered if he was going to get kicked out of the house. He'd considered leaving first because he wouldn't be able to handle finding out Deacon wanted him to go.

Wes didn't blame Deacon for resenting him. Deacon had gotten drafted into the NBA when he was eighteen, which should have been a high school senior's wet dream. Except he'd also gotten custody of his eight-year-old brother.

Wes wanted Deacon to stop seeing him as a burden so they could just be ordinary brothers, but he didn't even know what that would feel like. Deacon had always taken care of him. Nobody took care of Deacon. Maybe he didn't need anything.

After about five minutes of staring at the TV screen and not even noticing what was on, Wes had grabbed a room key and gone for a walk. He figured he could scope out the facilities and be back in the room before the pizza showed up.

The small gym in the lower level of the hotel was so hot he couldn't stand it, but the attendant told him there were outdoor basketball courts. She signed a ball out to him and he pushed through the door. He'd grabbed his iPod before leaving the room and he turned it on, but realized he'd accidentally grabbed Deacon's. The driving beat of some club song he didn't recognize throbbed through the headphones. He hadn't known Deacon listened to club music. Wes didn't feel like shooting around, so instead, he lay on his back, his legs lifted straight from his hips, a ball balanced on his sneakers. He used his feet to juggle the ball, slowly and then faster. He watched the ball and listened to the unfamiliar song and wished there wasn't so much he and Deacon didn't know about each other.

Before Deacon had turned pro, they used to work out complicated routines, dribbling patterns and trick shots. His brother had told him they'd try out for the Globetrotters as soon as they were old enough. Wes had really thought that would happen. As a kid, he'd have believed they were going to live on the moon if Deacon has said so.

Wes lowered his left leg, leaving the ball balanced only on his right foot. He gave it a quick bounce and it landed in his hands. He flicked it from his elbow to his forearm and then up to spin on his index finger.

With his other hand, he got out his phone and called his roommate, Oliver.

"You know what's strange about this phone call?"

"Wes?"

"Who did you think it was? Don't you have caller ID?"

"It never hurts to confirm."

Which made sense for a guy like Oliver, who'd probably experienced more than his fair share of prank phone calls in middle school.

"I realized I need to figure out how to talk to my own brother and I called you."

"You're lucky my parents didn't take away my phone. They're quite upset that I've been suspended from school."

Wes winced and dropped the basketball. Oliver had called him a few days ago to say he was suspended for the semester but would be allowed back in January. He said he wasn't upset about it, but that didn't mean it didn't suck. Wes was used to being a screwup, but this was uncharted territory for his roommate.

"I wish I hadn't gotten you involved in this mess."

"I don't hold you responsible. My mother tried to convince the dean that I was suffering from peer pressure. That I wouldn't fit in if I didn't write that essay. After I mentioned I haven't ever fit in anywhere, she had to abandon that argument. I do know how to say no to bad ideas."

Wes figured that was the truth. He still felt bad, but he let the issue go.

"Anyway, don't you think this is proof of how messed up things are with Deacon? I mean, I called you to discuss my problems with a *human* relationship. You're terrible at human relationships."

"I am."

"I'm not. I'm good at human relationships. But for

some reason, I don't know how to talk to my brother. It's so bad that I'm turning to you for advice."

"It's because you have a power differential."

"Power differential? You learn about that in physics?"

"No. My mother's romance novels."

"You read romance novels?"

"My parents' camp is on an island in Canada. One year my bag fell off the water taxi on our way over and all my things were lost, including the books I'd brought to read. My father refused to return me to the mainland to replace my library. I think he hoped I'd learn to fish."

"Did you?"

"My father and I have few areas of overlap in our understanding of how best to spend vacation time."

"So, no?"

"My mother has stacks of romance novels in the camp. I was bored and they use a lot of the same tropes as fantasy literature. Plus, they have sex." Oliver coughed. "I was thirteen. It was educational. In many of these books, the relationships are in jeopardy when one person has more power than the other."

Wes scratched his shin. This was exactly why he liked Oliver. The guy was nuts, but whatever came out of his mouth was his real thought. He didn't have the filters that helped other people hide and pretend.

"I don't want to have sex with my brother, Oliver."

"Of course not," Oliver said. "That's disgusting, Wes. But you owe him what seems to be an insurmountable debt. He's had a heroic journey and that image of him as all-powerful imprinted on you when you were young. He swooped in and took you out of foster care. He played in the NBA and gave you every-thing he never had for himself. He literally saved you."

When Oliver put it like that...*insurmountable* didn't even start to cover it.

"We're living back there. In Milton. He accepted some coaching job so I can do my community service."

"In the romance novels, the bad boy frequently goes back to his hometown to atone for his sins."

"Deacon doesn't have any sins."

"No. But you do."

"I'll talk to you later, Oliver."

"I'll check my mom's romance collection. Maybe I can find something that will be helpful to you."

"You know there are magazines that will give you just the sex—you wouldn't need to read the whole book."

"Pervert," Oliver said. "I don't read them for the sex."

"That's what they all say."

After Wes hung up, he stuck his phone back in his pocket, flipped onto his stomach and did a few push-ups.

Oliver was right. He owed Deacon. He hadn't asked for anything—hell, he'd been a little kid—but he'd been a burden on his brother his whole life. Going to college hadn't changed a single thing. How could he confess that the only thing he'd learned since he'd started at State was that he wasn't nearly as good at playing ball as he'd thought?

All those years of being too young to do anything for Deacon. When he got to college, he was finally going to redeem himself. Deacon never got to play col-lege ball, but he'd made sure Wes could. All he'd ever asked was for Wes to stay in school and play hard.

Then Wes got to campus and things went wrong right from the start. He sucked in practice and Coach got down on him. He hated the classes he was stuck in and he messed up even more. He couldn't make things work, so he did what he'd always done—caused a distraction. If he was suspended because of the car, no one would ever know that he hadn't been good enough to start on the team.

Coach was right when he said Wes was a dead weight. That's exactly what he was to the team and to Deacon…it was what he'd always been. If only he didn't have to go back up to that room and see his brother, knowing Deacon had turned his life upside down again just to help. Wes couldn't take it.

DEACON HEARD THE door in the other room open, then the sound of a glass bottle being set down on the bar in the kitchen area. He went to the doorway. His brother had an open beer in his hand. He was across the room and up in Wes's space, confronting him, before he'd thought through what he was going to say.

"Pour that out."

"You're joking."

"Pour it out right now or I will."

Wes must have finally noticed how furious Deacon was, because he stopped smiling. "Hey. You're my brother, not the police."

"Damn right I'm your brother. Which means you're going to pour that beer out and you're not going to pick up another one as long as you're living under my roof."

"I'll be twenty-one in three years. You won't be able to say anything about it then."

"We'll see about that in three years. Right now I'm telling you to pour it out."

Wes lifted the bottle to his mouth and Deacon, who had never even raised his hand to Wes, knocked it away across the room. It landed against the door to the bedroom, but thankfully, it didn't break. Wes stared as the beer foamed out the bottle's neck onto the carpet. The hiss of the beer was the only sound.

"You're insane." Wes shook his hand as if it stung. He tucked it under his other arm. "It was one beer. What's your problem?"

Deacon pointed his finger at his brother. He needed all his self-control not to touch him, to shake some knowledge of what exactly alcohol had done to his childhood into him.

"My problem is you. You don't take anything seriously. Everything is a big joke to you. It's as if you think consequences don't apply. You know who else lived like that? Dad. And that scares the crap out of me. He didn't care about anything. He didn't accept responsibility for anything. And he died, drunk and high, in the snow because he was too wasted to get himself four more feet into the freaking house."

Wes stepped backward.

"Dad didn't just die, Wes. He died stupid. And Mom paid for it. And I paid for it. And you paid for it."

Deacon wished his brother would say something, but he was mute.

He felt like a complete jerk when Wes turned away and picked up the beer bottle from the floor. His brother drained the dregs of the beer into the sink and put the empty into the recycling bin. He got a towel from the bathroom and threw it over the wet spot near the door.

Wes spoke quietly. "All this time I thought Dad had a heart attack and you're telling me he what?"

"Froze to death. Right next to the back steps. Mom found him."

"You never told me that part of the story, Deacon. You know that? I mean, I knew he drank, but I didn't know...I never knew...how he died." Wes lifted his hands and let them fall back to his sides. "I was just having a beer. It didn't mean anything."

"There are blankets in the closet for the pullout."

Wes nodded. "I'm sorry about Dad. I can't imagine what that must have been like for you."

"Honestly?" Deacon swallowed back the sick feeling the stench of spilled beer raised in his throat. "After a while, I didn't miss him. I'm not saying I'm happy he died, but I hated what he did to my life. The way he made everything complicated just because we never knew what he was going to do."

"Still..." Wes said, but then he stopped.

Yep. That was about it. There wasn't really anything else to say about their family.

Deacon went into the bedroom and shut the door. The stench of beer permeated the other room and he wanted to escape. The last thing he wanted was to drag out their family history and pick through it, but how else would Wes learn? Deacon had said he was taking his brother home to Milton, but he'd built a fat buffer when he'd parked them in this hotel forty minutes up the highway. If he was going to do this thing for Wes, then he really had to do it. He dialed Julia's number. She answered on the first ring.

CHAPTER FIVE

JULIA RENTED THE top half of a duplex on a quiet street just off Main Street. Her landlady, Jessica James—who didn't think it was funny to be called Jesse—lived downstairs. When Julia had first moved in, she recruited Henry and her mom to help her paint, and each room was a different clear, fresh color. The living room had one citrusy-yellow accent wall, while the others were striped in fat bands of subtle yellow and cream. Bookcases lined every wall, lending warmth and interest to the room.

She was in her bedroom, already tucked into bed with a book she'd told the tenth-grade English teacher she would review. The teacher wanted to use it for the after-school book club, but she was concerned it might be too adult for some of the kids. Julia said she'd give it a read and offer her opinion. She'd been sucked in and had been reading all night.

When her phone rang and flashed Deacon's name, she instantly panicked. Was he calling to tell her he'd changed his mind about coaching? She answered right away.

"Hello?"

"Julia?"

As he said her name, she shivered. His voice was low and gentle, with a hint of roughness. It reminded her of the lead singer's voice in her ex-boyfriend, the drummer's, band. That voice had been almost as hot as the drummer's arms. Deacon was like a whole sexy rock band wrapped up in one guy.

"Yes?" She was suddenly conscious that she was in bed wearing only a short nightgown.

Please don't say you changed your mind about helping.

"I decided to rent a place right in Milton while we're here. I wondered if you know a real estate agent."

She sat up, the white eyelet comforter falling to her lap. She hadn't said anything to Deacon, but she'd been disappointed that he was staying in a hotel so far from Milton. Her girls had problems, but they were smart enough to notice when they were being patronized.

This was the second time today Deacon had pleasantly surprised her.

"Tali's mom is an agent. She works up in the Jericho area now, but I bet she has local connections. I can get her contact information and email you."

"I don't have email. Just give me a call, if you don't mind."

"Is the internet slow in the hotel? That happened to me the last time I went on vacation."

"No. I don't have email at all—that's what I meant."

"Really?"

"I never picked up the habit."

"That's… Wow. How are you working while you're here?" He definitely had a business. She'd read about it before she'd called him and he'd mentioned it was flexible enough to accommodate his coaching.

"My business is fine," he said in the same tone someone else might have said "shut the hell up." She slid back down and pulled the covers back up, feeling self-conscious again. Deacon had more than his fair share of boundaries. What was he protecting? Something with his business? Why wouldn't he talk about it? Most men loved work talk.

"You build physical-therapy centers. Is that correct?"

"We have a string of centers in New York State and we're just working on our first New Jersey center. They're aimed at the serious amateur athlete—kids who play college sports, older folks who do marathons or bodybuilding as a hobby. We're seeing more and more younger kids looking for care, too."

Which was exactly the kind of work talk she'd have expected when a man was asked a simple question about his business. So his business wasn't the thing he was protecting.

"That's great, Deacon. I'm always looking for resources to educate the girls about their health. How would you feel about being our fitness guru? We can run a few short programs on the bus to away games—"

"I'm the financial backer for the centers, Julia, not the physical therapist."

"I know, but you must have some expertise—"

"In basketball. Coach Fallon, that's me."

She was stung again. Boy, was he prickly.

"All right, then. I'll see you tomorrow."

He made no effort to smooth things over, simply said goodbye. Julia yanked the covers over her head. He was so frustrating. She realized he hadn't mentioned the reason he was moving to Milton. She was quite sure the omission wasn't accidental. Deacon Fallon was nobody's open book.

She punched her pillow and rolled onto her side. Next time he called, she'd get out of bed to talk to him. She needed all her wits about her, and she most definitely did not need to be distracted by her body's reaction to his sexy rock-star voice.

At the end of the second day in Milton, Deacon told Wes they were going to look at some rental places with Tali's mom. Wes had a few minutes before he had to meet his brother in front of the school, and he was on a mission.

He wove through the hallways, barely sidestepping a boy crouched amid the pile of clutter he'd pulled out of his locker. Two kids were wrapped around each other, making out at their locker, and Wes regretted, not for the first time, that he'd gone to an all-boys high school. Not that he hadn't done his fair share of making out with girls, but his opportunities had definitely been limited.

So far he'd learned a few things about the team he would be coaching. Number one, they sucked. Number two, no way would they win that bet. He didn't much care in either case. He did care, though, about Deacon.

When his brother had told him how their dad died, Deacon's face had been so completely blank of emotion it scared Wes. After he'd started college and his coach began to call him out in practice, telling him over and over that recruiting him had been a mistake and reminding him his scholarship had to be renewed every year, Wes had been terrified he'd get kicked out. Now he was sure a letter would show up rescinding his scholarship and Deacon would look at him with that same lack of emotion in his eyes.

He could do nothing about his basketball issues at the moment. But he could coach those sad-sack girls and try to figure out who his brother was, who their family was.

He knocked on the partly open door of Julia's office and then stuck his head inside. She beckoned him in, holding up one finger while she wrapped up a phone call.

"What's up, Coach Wes?"

He smiled at that. He hadn't really thought much one way or the other about what coaching would be like, but he was having a good time. He and Deacon hadn't spent this much time together in years. Being Coach Wes was all right.

"I wanted to see if you have any old yearbooks."

"Not in here. The library has a full set. You looking for incriminating photos of Deacon?"

Julia pulled on her jacket and put her wallet in her backpack, which she slung over one shoulder.

"Sort of." He waited while she locked the door of the small office. "I moved a lot when I was little and I don't remember a lot of things. I thought I'd recognize stuff when I got here, but I don't. I guess I'm curious."

She led him across the library to a shelf in the reference section. "Here are the yearbooks. Let me pull out the one from Deacon's senior year." She ran a finger along the spines of the black-and-gold books and quickly found the one she wanted.

"Wow. You remember the exact year he graduated?"

"It was my first year teaching. That's how I remember." She flipped open the book to the faculty section and pointed to her picture. "That's me."

Her hair was pinned up, which made her look more serious. Other than that, she didn't seem to have changed much in ten years, though in the picture she appeared less self-assured.

"You look the same pretty much," he said. "Is Deacon different than you remember?"

"So different." She handed Wes the yearbook but didn't elaborate. He thought he'd heard something in her voice. He glanced at her face, but she wouldn't meet his eye.

"You can take the book. I'll leave a note for Mr. Daniels so he knows I checked it out. Just be sure to bring it back. You want to see the Deacon I remember?"

She hitched her backpack higher on her shoulder and led him back toward the lobby. "There he is."

She stopped in front of the large photo of Deacon. Something was going on between the Fallons. She didn't know what, but the whole situation seemed off to her. Deacon had all his walls up at practice and refused to talk about anything but basketball. Maybe she'd have better luck with Wes.

"You told the girls you graduated from high school, right?"

"Yep. I was going to State this year, but I got suspended."

Julia spun to look at him. Deacon hadn't said anything about Wes and a suspension. She'd done the state background checks on them that they did on all volunteers, but that wouldn't have turned up anything like…like— What exactly was she dealing with? Wes seemed like a nice guy, but she couldn't be too careful with her girls.

"You got suspended?"

"It was stupid. I'm going back in the spring. Hey!" He pointed to one of the pictures in the case. "That's me."

She leaned forward. Wes had his finger on a skinny, eight-year-old boy wearing a Tigers sweatshirt that hung past his knees. A woman with tight black curls was holding his hand as he strained toward Deacon, who was in the center of the photo, accepting a trophy from a trio of men in suits.

"Who's that with you?"

Wes narrowed his eyes to squint at the photo. "My foster parents. His name was Dave." He pointed to a burly guy in a denim jacket, standing slightly behind him. "I don't remember her name. Their last name was Jackson."

"I thought you and Deacon lived with Coach Simon's family."

Wes moved a few steps down the case, studying each photo. "We did for a while, but they couldn't keep me. I moved around to a bunch of families—four or five, maybe." He tilted his head to read the inscription on a game ball in the display. "I was hard to handle, I guess. I remember running away a lot. Getting in fights. Deacon used to tell me to settle down so maybe Coach Simon would take me back, but..." He didn't look at her. "It was better once he got drafted."

Julia couldn't believe the way Wes was casually tossing out these facts. Had she known the brothers were separated in foster care? Was it her memory that was faulty and made her think they'd both been with Coach Simon or had she never known?

"How long were you separated from him?"

"A while. I was two when my mom died so that means Deacon was twelve. He got custody of me when I was eight. I lived with him at his coach's for maybe a year? I don't know. Like I said, I have trouble remembering, and it bums Deacon out when I ask him questions, so I try not to." He lifted the yearbook. "Thus my research!"

She smiled, but she was upset. Deacon hadn't told

her Wes was suspended. He wouldn't tell her why he'd come back to Milton now when he never had before. He was keeping a lot from her.

"This haircut..." Wes pointed to the large photo in which Deacon was sporting a mangy buzz cut. "He used to buzz his own hair. I'd beg him to do mine, but he wouldn't. Can you believe I thought he looked so cool? The mustache is priceless. In fact..."

Wes took his phone out and lined it up to get a shot of the mustache.

"What are you doing?"

She hadn't noticed Deacon coming up behind them until he spoke from just over her right shoulder.

"Nothing." Wes snapped another picture. "Making a documentary about sorry-looking facial hair."

"That picture better not be the centerpiece of any kind of blackmail scheme."

"You can't have your picture taken with a scraggly caterpillar on your lip and not expect to get blackmailed." Wes snapped another picture, not even focusing. She suspected that one was just to bug his brother. It was what she'd have done. "Did you honestly believe that thing made you look cool?"

"Honestly?"

"Yeah," Wes said. "Honestly."

"I figured it would make me appear older. So I'd be respected. I'd have grown one of those handlebar things if I could have."

Julia couldn't help it. She gazed at the picture and she saw it then. Deacon's gaunt face held none of the brightness or even the angst she saw on the kids at school every day. *Desperate.* That's how he looked.

"I respected you, Deacon," she said.

He didn't meet her eye. Wes glanced from her to his

brother. "I've got to grab my bag before Tali's mom gets here," he said.

"You better delete that picture."

Wes stepped back and cocked his head, pretending to consider the photo of Deacon. "Does it really matter if I have one or two little snapshots on my phone, when there's this giant framed one in the lobby with a spotlight shining on it?"

Deacon glared at him.

"Didn't think so." He pocketed his phone, but then pulled it back out and held his finger over the touch screen. "You want to give me Victor's number? I have a message to send him."

Deacon reached for the phone, but Wes darted away, dodging a group of girls on his way down the hall. Julia turned back to Deacon. He'd changed clothes after practice and had on a lush brown sweater over a black-and-cream-striped shirt and a pair of camel pants. The sweater made her yearn to touch him it appeared so incredibly soft. A good thing the gym was too warm for cashmere. She'd never have been able to focus on practice.

"We have to talk, Deacon."

He raised his eyebrows.

"When we spoke on the phone, you mentioned that Wes needs a letter of recommendation for college. You did not mention he needs it because he was suspended."

Deacon scanned the hallway behind her and then said quietly, "He had some trouble at school this semester. He's completing community service and he'll be reinstated next year."

Why hadn't she followed up on the red flags sooner? Damn it. She was sharper than that. She really needed information. If Wes had been suspended for something serious, something that made it impossible for her to allow him to coach, she'd be devastated. In the two days the Fallons had been around, she'd become... attached to them.

"What was the problem?" she asked.

Deacon must have heard the seriousness in her tone, because he stiffened. He was so defensive about his brother. "Nothing you should worry about."

"I'm sorry, Deacon, but I can't just accept your word on that. He's working with students, so I have to have the facts."

"He's not dangerous. He's—" He swallowed whatever detail he almost gave her.

"It's not enough."

He took a few steps away from her and then paced back. "I'm handling it."

"Maybe I can help."

"I knew it," he said. "This is about you thinking you can fix Wes. He's my worry, not yours."

Tears stung her eyes, which made her angry. She didn't cry. She didn't want Deacon to have the power to hurt her. She wished she didn't care about him. But she *was* hurt. She helped people. And she didn't have as many chances to help as she'd like.

"Fine," she said. "You're right. I would like to help Wes—if he needs it. I counsel kids all day, Deacon, and I'm good at it. But if you don't want me to talk to your brother, I won't. That doesn't change the fact that I've hired you both to work with my team and I have a professional responsibility to know the details of his suspension since he's going to work with the girls."

As soon as she said the words, she held her breath. She hadn't thought them through, but she'd really just issued an ultimatum. Had she driven the Fallons away before her partnership with them really got started?

Deacon put his hands to his face and pressed his fingers into his eyes. He was obviously in distress, and she felt terrible, but this conversation was necessary. When he looked at her again, the expression in his eyes showed hopelessness.

"He cheated on a paper. He got caught drinking in a bar. He started skipping practice, even though he's on scholarship, and he and his roommate moved the basketball coach's car into the weight room."

He listed the offenses quickly, with no inflection. She had trouble following, but when he was finished, she felt relieved. An eighteen-year-old college kid could do a lot worse things. Still...

"The drinking. He's with the team on road trips—"

"You wanted the details. You know them. Now you can decide if you'll let us stay. Is Wes a danger to your kids?"

There was danger, but it had nothing to do with Wes and the girls and everything to do with Deacon's haunted eyes and his deep concern for his brother. Her first impulse was to offer Deacon some advice. Had he been a parent in her office, she would have begun by reassuring him that Wes's offenses were pretty standard. But Deacon had made it clear he didn't want her help.

"Thank you for your honesty. I don't see any reason to change our current agreement."

She watched his expression. His blue eyes, so serious under the chunk of hair that fell across his forehead, were full of pain.

"Thank you, Coach Bradley."

"No problem, Coach Fallon."

"I, ah, have to go meet Tali's mom." She appreciated that he was making an effort to sound normal after their angry exchange. "Did you say her name is Marissa?"

"Why don't I introduce you."

Marissa was waiting out front, already talking to Wes. Tali's mom, as tall and slender as her daughter, greeted them and then handed Deacon a clipboard.

"I printed off the specs for some places I thought might work."

Before Deacon flipped the top page, Julia caught a glimpse of the first address. Hunter's Ridge, a very nice development just north of Milton.

He flipped through the other listings and then handed the clipboard back to Marissa.

"These places are a lot bigger than what we're interested in."

Wes appeared dejected. "That one place had a pool."

"It's almost November, Wes."

Marissa accepted the clipboard and drew out a lightweight laptop. "All right. You tell me what you're looking for and I'll pull up new options."

"Two bedrooms. In town. We want to be able to walk places. Or at least Wes does. I have a car."

Wes rolled his eyes. Marissa waited for a few seconds and then pursed her lips as she studied the screen. She glanced over at Julia. "Where are you living these days, Ms. Bradley?"

"I'm still on Orchard. Sharing half a house with Mrs. James."

"How about I take these boys to see that little place on the end of Briar? If they're determined to live in town, that's not a bad spot and they'll be right around the corner from you."

"Sounds good."

"Why don't you come? You can sell them on the neighborhood."

Julia was about to decline, but Deacon said, "We could use a tour guide. You can tell us how everything has changed since we moved away."

He wouldn't need a tour guide just to point out the closed businesses and run-down streets. He'd made his offer in an attempt to smooth things over and they both knew it. She wasn't exactly ready to be smoothed, but he was here because he was doing her an enormous favor. Her job had taught her that people were always much more complicated than they seemed. She could go along, work on repairing her relationship with Deacon and maybe get to know the Fallons. If Deacon had slipped up and revealed a personal detail, that was his tough luck.

She sat in the front of Marissa's spotless Taurus, and Deacon and Wes folded themselves into the back. Wes stared out the window and asked questions about everything they passed. Deacon didn't have much to say.

When they were a few blocks from her house, Julia said, "Tali's excited about the start of the season. Will we see you and her dad at the games this year?"

"Oh, I hardly have any time for those games."

Deacon spoke up for the first time. "Tali has a nice outside shot. Did you or her dad play ball?"

Julia couldn't decide if he was telling the truth or merely being polite. Tali did score more than most of the other girls, but Julia had always thought it was mainly because Tali was a ball hog and shot a lot. She'd encouraged her to pass more, particularly to Miri, who never seemed able to get a point on the board, but the lesson hadn't done much good.

"My husband. He used to get out in the driveway with her when she was younger, but he works nights now."

"Well, if you or her dad have a chance, you should come see her play. She'll be key to our offense."

"Tali?" Marissa appeared skeptical as she glanced at Julia.

"Come see," Deacon said.

Marissa pursed her lips again. "Maybe I will." She met his eyes in the rearview mirror and switched to sales mode. "You sure you don't want to check out something in Hunter's Ridge? Those places are gorgeous and I've got one sitting empty."

"Nope," Deacon said. "We want to be right in town."

She drove them past the elementary school. Wes's head swiveled as he stared at the school and the playground as they passed. He'd told her he didn't remember much. She wondered if seeing the town again was bringing memories back.

"There's nothing really nice in town anymore," Marissa said.

"That's all right."

They passed Julia's house, then made a right at the end of the block. Marissa parked in front of a small white house. She let everyone in the front door and Julia was sure she saw Deacon flinch at the musty smell that testified to months of a house empty of tenants. When she'd moved to Milton for her job, she'd had to adjust to a very different economic and social climate from the one in the college town she'd grown up in.

What did Deacon feel coming back to Milton after

being away for ten years? His current life was dramatically different from what it had been. He lived in an exclusive community near Lake Placid. This small house was nothing compared with what he must be used to. Wes was eagerly exploring, opening closet doors and peeking out all the windows to check out the neighborhood. Deacon was quiet.

He told Marissa he was heading to the backyard to see if the garage was okay for the Porsche.

"That Porsche would be happier out in Hunter's Ridge," Marissa said, making Deacon laugh.

Julia followed him outside, while Marissa and Wes stayed inside, counting cable connections. Wes was intent on getting the Xbox hooked up as soon as possible.

She waited until the back door closed behind them before she said, "Was what you said about Tali true?"

"True? Let's call it optimistic," he said. "She's not a bad outside shooter. We only have two kids who appear capable of generating any kind of offense, so she'll be key whether she likes it or not."

"Well, it was nice of you to say it."

He shrugged. "You bet that you'd make States and you'd turn up some boosters. If the kids' own parents don't come to the games, how will you get boosters?"

"You're devious."

"I didn't make the bet, but I did tell you I'd help. You've got to lure people into the gym somehow, and I'm not about to bake cupcakes to entice them." He kicked at the edge of a hole in the driveway. The asphalt, however, held. "If they come out to see their kid be a star, at least they're in the gym."

She'd been worrying about the team by herself for such a long time, even before the bet, that she was surprised at how relieved she felt to know he'd signed on to help with the whole package.

"Maybe we could give away bobbleheads, or something like they do in minor-league baseball."

"I can just see the look of utter disgust on Trey's face if he's ever confronted with a bobblehead doll of his sister."

They walked toward the garage.

"Can I ask a question, Deacon?" she inquired.

He glanced down at her and his eyes were wary behind his glasses. He shrugged.

"You beat it out of here as fast as you could and you've never been back. Now you're here to coach and you want to live in this run-down little place." She faced him. "What are you doing?"

He didn't miss a beat. "I'm renting a house."

She waited and wished he'd explain, but he didn't. He opened and closed the garage door and tried the lock.

They went back to the house and he told Marissa the place looked fine. She handed him the rental paperwork and he immediately passed it to Wes.

"What's this?"

"Assistant coaches handle the paperwork, too."

Wes rolled up the forms and stuck them in his back pocket. Julia hoped he wouldn't lose them. Marissa must have been doubtful, as well, because she said, "Make sure you drop the signed forms off tomorrow, and we'll get you a key."

WHEN THEY GOT back to the school parking lot, Marissa let them out near Julia's parked car. Deacon thanked the agent and reminded her that she'd said she'd try to make it to one of Tali's games.

The parking lot was mostly empty and the lights were on to battle the quickly falling dusk. Wes had said he wanted to walk back to the high school, so Deacon was alone with Julia.

He'd been angry with her earlier. She was such a dedicated person, so true to what seemed her mission in life—helping people and solving problems. But if he didn't know what was going on with his brother, how could she? She'd attempted to steer Deacon toward college ten years ago, which would have been a disaster all around.

No, better that *he* handle Wes, even if a part of him really wanted to ask for her opinion.

"So it seems we'll be neighbors."

Julia leaned on the bumper of her car. She was a lot shorter than him, but she had great legs. When she stretched them out, he couldn't help noticing the smooth curve of her calves, or the enticing outline of thigh visible against her skirt.

"You should let me take you and Wes for dinner on Saturday," she said. "We can go to the Pond and I can embarrass you by telling your little brother everything I know about Deacon Fallon's high school days."

He wanted to say yes. In fact, he wanted to know what talking to Julia, just the two of them, would be like. Two single adults without all his worry about Wes and her questions, or the terms of the bet hanging over them. He liked Julia. The trouble was, the rest of their lives did exist and it kept everything between them complicated.

"The Pond is still open?"

The small restaurant and bar was famous for its Friday-night chicken dinners. It made sense, he guessed, that a place like that with roots sunk so deep into local lives would manage to hang on.

"Still there. I don't think they've made a single change to the menu." She paused, and when he still didn't answer, she said, "If you're busy—"

"I'll think about it."

He never went on a date with a new person without thinking about it first. Restaurants, menus, unfamiliar places, they all held hidden traps for him. That was why he always made careful plans in advance, choosing restaurants where he knew the menu or calling in advance to find out if there'd be specials he could order without reading. He was successful at concealing his issues from people, but it took work.

He didn't want to do that with Julia. Vic was right. For the first time, he felt dishonest. Julia cared too much about people. He didn't want her to get involved in his life, but he didn't want to be the one who hurt her. Caring wasn't bad—he just didn't want it focused on him. He and Wes had enough issues to work out. He couldn't afford to have his secret exposed, but he didn't want to lie to Julia, either.

THE HARDWOOD FLOORS in the living room and hall of their rental house were desperately in need of refinishing, and the old-fashioned double-hung windows let in generous amounts of cold outside air along with plenty of light. The kitchen appliances, although clean, were old, and there wasn't a dishwasher. The linoleum near the back door was buckled, probably from a moisture leak somewhere. It was a decent house in a neighborhood that hadn't been decent in a while but hadn't completely given up, either. Despite their real estate agent's misgivings, the house was quite a bit nicer than any place Deacon had ever called home when he was living with his parents.

The house was unfurnished, but Tali's mom had given them the contact information for a company that rented furniture.

"You want to go online and pick out the furniture?" Deacon asked Wes. "Tali's mom said there's a website."

"Are you serious?"

"Someone has to be here for the cable guy and somebody has to get groceries and stuff," Deacon said. "Since you're sitting around here, you might as well be useful."

"If you leave your credit card, you know I'm getting a gaming chair. I bet they have the ones with built-in coolers."

Deacon snorted. Allowing his brother to choose the furniture meant the house would be furnished in a style that resembled Early Playboy Mansion or maybe College Beer Den with High-End Electronics. It didn't matter, since they wouldn't be living there very long.

While Wes was debating leather sofas with cup holders or without, Deacon drove an hour back toward the hotel they'd been staying in, to the nearest mall, and stocked up on dishes, sheets, towels and the other necessities that would get two guys through the day—a coffeemaker, a dartboard and a grill.

Deacon stopped at a grocery store, loaded the car with food and headed for home.

The furniture wouldn't be delivered until the next day. Neither of them wanted to go back to the hotel, so they wound up bunked down on the floor of one of the two small bedrooms upstairs. Wes made a pallet from the new bath towels and laid his sheets and blankets over it. Deacon wasn't quite so comfortable on a layer of sweatshirts and the stadium blanket he kept in the trunk of the Porsche, but he wasn't about to complain since he knew his brother would just tease him for being a girl.

He hadn't shared a room with Wes since they'd lived with Coach Simon. He'd forgotten how irritating trying to fall asleep with someone in the room asking obnoxious questions was. He was exhausted. Ever since they'd gotten to Milton, he felt that people were watching, attempting to figure him out. He was used to the simplicity of living alone.

"You're gonna have to do something about your spare tire if you want to get with the pretty coach," Wes said.

Deacon closed his eyes. He wished Wes would be struck dumb. "Don't say 'get with.' It's disrespectful."

"Yes, sir." Wes must have turned over, because a board in the floor squeaked. "I was merely suggesting that you cut back on the cheesecake if you want Julia to notice you in a sexual way."

Now he wouldn't get to sleep at all. Was that all it took? The word *sexual* coupled with Julia's name and all of a sudden his mind was full of images of her legs, those gorgeous eyes, what it might feel like if he put his arms around her and stroked her hair. Freaking Wes and his questions.

"I have a fantastic body. Anyone who notices me in a sexual way will be one hundred percent satisfied."

"Whatever you say, D. The thing I find interesting is your denial of the spare tire, but not the interest in Julia. What did you guys talk about while you were 'inspecting the garage' yesterday?"

"You're supposed to call her Ms. Bradley."

"Another deflection. Admit it. You like the coach."

"Shut the hell up."

Miraculously, Wes was quiet for about five minutes. The room was hot. With the low ceilings, all the air seemed trapped inside. They could use some of the cold that came in through the windows downstairs. Deacon missed his climate-controlled, programmable thermostat, but he hoped Wes was getting a taste of how most people lived.

He had tried to open the windows, but they only went up partway. The bars on the outside didn't block the air from entering—he knew that logically—but it felt as though they did. He hated sleeping with bars on the windows. Deacon gave up on sleep and started running plays in his mind—trying to work out how best to use the two kids he'd seen today who could shoot. When Wes called his name, his voice was pitched low and quiet, as if he almost didn't want to be heard.

"Deacon?"

"Yep."

"Is this what it was like?"

"What what was like?"

"Our place. When we were little."

"No."

Wes was quiet again, but Deacon was on alert. He knew his brother's silence was a trap, not a prelude to sleep.

"What was it like?"

Awful. Dark. Cramped. Worse when his dad was home and his parents were fighting. After his dad died and his mom checked out, when the baby cried, Deacon used to bring him into the bed, knowing his mom wouldn't respond, and he'd whisper over and over, "It'll be okay." He didn't know if he was reassuring himself or his little brother. It didn't matter anyway, because nothing had been okay. Not until they got out, at least. Not until he signed his contract and bought that house for Wes far away from Milton and all the crappy memories Deacon Fallon had stored up in eighteen years of living.

"Different from this," he said. "It was a trailer. We never had a house. The kitchen counter was always sticky, no matter what Mom tried. Beat-up carpet everywhere. Dark. Damp. The walls and doors were thin, so you could hear everything that went on."

He could feel how much Wes wanted to ask another question, though it didn't come. Deacon had intentionally buried his memories of Milton and their family. But he had Wes here now and he needed to deliver.

He rolled onto his side and groped on the windowsill for his glasses. He'd become used to his house in the woods, and the light pollution in this neighborhood surprised him, but at least it meant he could see Wes lying on his back, arms crossed under his head, his eyes open, the thin light from the street lamps making them glint.

"In the trailer we shared a bedroom. My buddies thought I should be pissed because I'd been an only child for ten years and all of a sudden I had to share my stuff with a baby. But I was alone a lot. I liked having you around, even if you were a baby."

He hadn't known how lonely his life was until Wes was born. He'd often wished the two of them could run away together; he'd never wished his little brother wasn't around.

"I'd been bugging Mom and Dad for a dog. I guess a baby was the next best thing."

"We never had a dog?" Wes asked, turning to him. "I thought I remembered a dog."

"Coach Simon had a dog. A big Lab. Totally out of control and aggressive. Maybe you remember her."

"This dog was small and white. Fluffy."

Deacon didn't recollect any white dogs. "Maybe one of the families you stayed with had it."

"Maybe." Wes straightened out so he was facing the ceiling again. "When it was just you and Mom and Dad, was it better, though?"

"What?"

"Was it easier for them with one kid?"

"Mom loved you. She wasn't the same after Dad died, but she loved you the way she loved me." Haphazardly, with love that surfaced randomly and hardly ever amounted to much.

"I didn't mean that. I meant, if they were poor, maybe an extra kid was the reason—"

"Shut the hell up, Wes," Deacon said. This was exactly why he never talked about their lives in Milton. Everything had been so royally screwed up that no way could a kid come out of it without thinking stupid thoughts like that one. "Being poor wasn't the problem. Not the way you're thinking. Dad was a drunk. He couldn't hold a job and he was always so freaking volatile. Mom couldn't get ahead with him dragging her down. She should have left him, but she wouldn't. Who knows why." Deacon was angry all over again, the same impotent anger he felt when he'd lived with his parents. "One kid, two kids, fifteen kids—their lives would have been the same."

"We got lucky, huh? The way everything turned out so different for us."

"Lucky, sure," Deacon said. "Lucky in our DNA and lucky that Milton is nuts for basketball. But more than luck, I worked hard to get the life we have. You can't expect luck to last. You have to work for what you want."

He wanted Wes to look at him again, but his brother kept his eyes fixed on the ceiling. It was hard to tell what he was thinking. Deacon took his glasses off and lay down again.

When he was a kid, he'd been scared a lot. Anxious about school, worried about his parents and then his brother. That last year in high school, he'd spent most of his time terrified something—an injury, a bad game, Julia's intervention—would derail his shot at the draft.

Now was different. Sharing this stuff with Wes had been difficult, but now he felt relieved. He wasn't sure yet what he thought about that.

And Julia. She noticed everything, put in her ideas and wanted to be part of his life. If Julia found out he couldn't read, she'd want to fix it. She put too much value on education to ever accept that he just wasn't going to get it. She'd look at him differently—she'd see him as less than other guys. If she knew, Wes would find out and then everyone would know. He had to hope she wouldn't figure it out. Maybe while they were here, he could pretend to be the kind of guy she'd want.

CHAPTER SIX

JULIA WENT OUT to Jericho for the evening. She drove
past the Fallons' and told herself she was just being
a good neighbor. If she'd seen them outside moving
boxes or planting perennials, she'd have stopped to
chat the same way she did when her landlady was out
in the yard.

If Deacon happened to be outside chopping wood
with his shirt off, well, she could have offered him a
glass of water.

Or something.

The front of the house was dark, but she saw a light
on in the back, probably the kitchen.

Maybe he'd be chopping wood tomorrow.

She and Henry and her mom had a potluck family
dinner once a month. She was pretty sure they each
thought of it as a charitable deed for the others—she
and Henry thought their mom needed company. Henry
thought she needed to eat better. Her mom thought both
her children worked too hard and needed enforced re-
laxation.

None of them ever mentioned these motivations to
the others. They just showed up once a month with
their potluck fare and enjoyed themselves.

Tonight Henry provided pulled pork; her mom
contributed fresh hard rolls and homemade coleslaw.
Julia stopped at a small farm market on the outskirts

of Milton and picked up a still-warm apple pie and a pint of whipping cream.

As Julia finished her last bite of tart apple filling, she reminded herself that living in the boonies had definite advantages. Farm-fresh produce chief among them.

"So you want to write a recruiting letter for your new boosters group and send it to the mailing list you got from the existing group?"

"Bingo," Julia said. The day after she'd made her bet with Ty, she'd signed up for the Milton Sports Boosters. If she was starting her own group, she decided it was smart to see what the competition was offering. Once her membership packet arrived, she threw away the letter that Coach Simon had signed, filed the car-window decal and had a great idea when she saw the membership booklet loaded with the names and addresses of folks who'd already spent five dollars to support Milton High School sports. She hoped some would willingly spend another five when they got her letter.

People in Milton were upset about the cuts to the sports program. She prayed they'd rally around her girls once they knew of the need and the opportunity.

Julia opened her laptop. She wanted her mom and Henry to review the letter and brochure she'd put together, because they both had more experience fundraising than she did.

"Can you believe they mailed me those names? I was half expecting to be blackballed when they saw my name on the application, and instead I got this little book of potential gold."

Henry and her mom exchanged a glance. As the youngest child in a family of high achievers, she was familiar with the glance. It was the one they used whenever the baby of the family was about to fall flat on her face.

"What? Why are you looking at each other?"

"Because you can't use that mailing list, Julia. If it's not illegal, it's definitely unethical, and positively against the terms of your membership in the boosters," Henry said.

"Oh." She sank into her chair. "No chance you're misinformed?"

When her mom nodded, backing Henry up, she knew for sure her brilliant idea was for naught.

"Nothing is ever easy, is it?"

"Let's see the letter anyway," her mom said. "You can't use the mailing list, but a mailing is a great plan. You'll have to build your own list, that's all."

"How much money do you have to raise anyway?" Henry asked. He and her mom were leaning forward to look at the screen.

Her budget for the tournament included a bus for the team, hotel rooms and meals for the girls. Not a single dollar lay set aside for extras, but she thought they could manage.

"Five thousand seven hundred and fifty dollars."

"Man, Julia, why don't you just get Geoff to pay it? You've got him cold on music trivia. Make a bet, beat him and take his hard-earned money."

"As tempting as that scheme is, Henry, the girls need to see the money coming from their community. This is about us showing that we make a difference."

If push came to shove, she might be forced to ask her siblings for donations, and she knew they'd come through for her, but she wanted to earn the money her own way. She didn't want another reminder that her brothers and sister were moving ahead fast in the world—at least by mainstream yardsticks like earning power, savings accounts and granite countertops in their kitchens.

Her mom got up and went to the kitchen. She returned with the pot of coffee that had been brewing. "The first thing you need to add to the letter is a message. You have to hook people in with some slogan so they want to be part of your group."

Julia recalled standing in the gym, watching Deacon make up his mind about the girls. She'd known the second he'd decided to agree. She'd seen it on his face when he said, "My Tigers."

"I've got the perfect thing."

They worked over the letter for another forty-five minutes, until her family was satisfied it was perfect. Henry said that if she wanted to print her slogan on some gear to sell at games, he'd front the initial costs.

His hands were full with his slow cooker and a plate of leftover pie, but she put hers on his cheeks and pulled his head down so she could kiss him. "Thanks, Henry. I appreciate the way you believe in me."

He rolled his eyes. "It's not about you, remember? It's the team."

When he was gone, her mom smiled at her. "That was nice."

Julia was feeling so satisfied that she said, "Brothers are nice."

"Ha!" her mom said. "I wish I had a recording of that."

They started to clear away the last of the dishes, stacking the coffee cups and dessert plates and then carrying them into the kitchen to the dishwasher. "How are your new assistant coaches? Everything working out with them?"

"Good," Julia said, but she must have hesitated just enough to raise her mom's suspicions.

"Good, but?"

"Good, but…I don't know. I guess I didn't really think about how much Deacon would have changed in ten years. I was kind of expecting a slightly older version of the teenager I knew."

"And instead?"

"He's a… Well, he's a man, for one thing." *A man, for sure.*

Her mom lifted her eyebrows. "An attractive man?"

Julia nodded slowly. Her mom had no idea and she wasn't about to enumerate Deacon's many fine points, but the list was long and full of words like lean, strong and sexy. "Yes. He's attractive. But he's so guarded. He… Well, he's complicated. I found out he took the coaching job because his brother needs to do community service as part of a discipline agreement. He got suspended from college for the semester."

"Suspended?"

"I practically had to threaten legal action to get Deacon to give me the details."

"Well, he's not your student any longer, so he doesn't have to tell you his problems. I imagine he'll open up more as he gets to know you."

"I realize that, but I can help Wes—if Deacon would only let me."

Her mom handed her the piece of pie she was taking home. "Julia, I love you and I respect you. You know that."

"But?"

"But you don't have to solve everyone's problems. Sometimes you can just be a friend."

Julia left a few minutes later. On the way home she thought about what her mom had said. Obviously she couldn't solve everyone's problems. Every year she counseled kids who quit high school or worse. But that didn't mean she should stop trying to help.

Besides, if Deacon couldn't trust her, how would she ever mean anything to him?

THE NEXT DAY, Wes was on Facebook on his laptop when his brother came through the living room in a pair of workout pants and sneakers on his way out for a run. Wes made another spare-tire joke, which was pretty darn funny until Deacon told him he was considering salad for dinner that night instead of the steaks he'd promised for the grill. That was the last of the fat jokes, Wes decided. Some things weren't worth it.

Once Deacon was out of the house, Wes called Oliver.

"If you were on Facebook, we could chat and I wouldn't have to call you all the time."

"Is that you, Wes?"

"Caller ID, man. I swear I will not mess with you via the phone-display screen."

"Facebook is a terrible idea. Why would you want to place a record of your life into the hands of a corporation intent on monetizing data?"

"Because you like to see pictures of your buddies from college doing keg stands?"

"Do you ever get tired of making my points for me?"

"I live to serve."

Wes went into the tiny kitchen and opened the fridge. He could make a sandwich, but he wasn't really in the mood. Maybe later he'd make a run to the grocery store for some frozen pizza. If Deacon let him drive the Porsche, he'd be sure to find a grocery store as far away as possible.

"I haven't seen you log into Master Command," Oliver said. "Did your brother restrict your Xbox privileges?"

Wes laughed. "No. We moved out of the hotel into a house. The TV is arriving today."

"Why did you move?"

A joke about being tired of room service was on the tip of his tongue, but he didn't make it.

"Did I ever tell you my dad died when I was a baby?"

"Not exactly. I knew your brother raised you."

"Yeah. He died. I was really little, like a couple months old, and I always thought he had a heart attack. Which doesn't make sense, since he was only about thirty. But you know how sometimes you learn stuff when you're little and you just never notice that you should be questioning it?"

Wes grabbed his jacket and went out the front door. A basketball sat on the porch—he'd grabbed it out of the trunk of the car the day before—and he picked it up and started dribbling down the street.

"I'm sorry about your dad, Wes."

"Don't you want to know how he really died?"

"It wouldn't be polite to ask."

"He was drunk and he came home, but he passed out in the snow and died of exposure. Right outside the back door." Even if the story hadn't concerned his dad, it would still have gotten to him. How incredibly sad that someone could get that close to home and die.

When Wes spotted a beat-up hoop at the end of his block, he tossed the ball in one-handed.

"That's a terrible story. I can see why someone would want to keep the details from you when you were a child. Who told you finally?"

"Deacon." Wes stopped moving and focused on keeping his voice steady. He could not cry on the phone with Oliver because he wasn't twelve and he wasn't a girl. "Deacon said, and this is a quote, 'He didn't just die—he died stupid.' And then he told me he didn't feel anything about him. You should have seen his face, Oliver. He meant it. He has no feelings for our dad."

"He's been holding on to that story for a long time."

"Yeah. He has. Want to know why he finally told me?" Wes spit the next part out fast, trying to keep it from hurting him all over again. "Because I remind him of our dad. He said I don't understand consequences. He thinks I'll turn out like our dad."

"Wes—"

"What if he's right? Not that I don't understand things, but that I'm useless and my life is useless."

"Wes, your brother doesn't know you."

"He's tired of taking care of me. He basically inherited a baby when he was twelve and he busted his ass to move us out of Milton. I have to get back on the team. I can't make Deacon responsible for me anymore."

"I'm not a basketball expert, or even very adept at understanding people, but it's possible Coach Mulbrake is wrong about you. Just like your brother is."

"I have to stop making him worry."

"Maybe if he knew how you feel…"

"Feelings aren't really part of Deacon's life. Paying him back with money or something would be so much easier."

Oliver had an enormous brain full of all kinds of useful information, but even he was stymied. After hanging up, Wes ran through dribbling and shooting drills for an hour. He'd get a second chance to play for State, and this time Coach wouldn't find fault with his skills.

ON SUNDAY, JULIA got up early and went to the local soup kitchen, where she served breakfast every weekend. She recognized a few of her students as they came down the line, but didn't engage with them unless they spoke to her first. Dignity was hard to acquire for most teenagers and even harder when eating at the food pantry. If they wanted to look through her and pretend they'd never met, she was more than willing to supply them that small grace.

When she was finished, she walked back to her neighborhood. She hadn't heard from Deacon since Friday. Not that she'd expected to, but... Okay, she'd hoped she might run into him. After talking to her mom, she'd told herself she should butt out. Whatever was going on between the Fallons wasn't her business. If Deacon wanted his brother to live in a run-down house while Wes did his community service, that was his business.

The trouble was, she'd failed Deacon once already. When he was a kid, she'd let the men in the boosters, Coach Simon, all of them, take advantage of him. Now that he was coaching with her, doing her this huge favor, she owed him, right? She was an excellent guidance counselor and her professional instincts told her the Fallons might need guidance. She couldn't ignore that. She'd bought Deacon and Wes coach's whistles, which was the perfect excuse to drop by their house. They'd like to have the whistles for practice on Monday, right?

She didn't let herself hesitate outside the house, but when she rang the bell, nobody answered. They hadn't put any curtains up, so she could see that they'd gotten some furniture. Two huge leather recliners and an equally huge TV were crammed into the tiny living room. She shook her head. She read Wes's taste in the set, but Deacon had gone along with it.

Disappointed at missing them, she started back down the walk, when she heard the thump of a basketball. Shading her eyes with her hand, she made out a lone figure shooting baskets at the end of the block. Tali's little brothers used the hoop, she knew, and a few other kids from the neighborhood, but she'd never seen an adult there.

The sun glinted on the man's hair, and when he turned, she could make out his tall lean frame, and the light reflecting off his glasses. Deacon. Her stomach flipped and she tightened her grip on the bag with the whistles.

She walked down the block toward him.

He didn't notice her, so she took the opportunity to watch him play. He was gorgeous—graceful, fluid, in control. He put the ball behind his back and dribbled fast for the basket. Pulling up suddenly, he shot. The ball arced in a clean line up and then down with a smooth dive through the hoop. The metal rim was bare of a net, but she easily imagined the swoosh.

He chased the ball down, his long legs covering the ground in smooth strides. He was wearing jeans and work boots, but he looked every inch an athlete.

When he turned to dribble back up the street, he saw her.

Tucking the ball under his arm, he came toward her.

"Did you have glasses in high school?" she blurted before she could stop herself. She hoped he wouldn't realize she asked because she was becoming slightly obsessed with their geek appeal. A delicious shiver ran through her. She'd fallen asleep on her couch last night and had the most vivid dream of him in which he leaned over her on a bed and then slowly took off his glasses. After that dream, she couldn't even remember what the drummer's forearms looked like, let alone why she'd ever noticed them.

"Julia?"

She snapped out of the dream. "What?"

"You seemed to be drifting."

"Sorry." She shifted the bag with the whistles to her left hand and wiped the sweat on her right hand off on her jeans. *Get a grip.* "I just don't remember seeing you with glasses in any of the pictures around school."

"I got them later. After I quit playing, actually."

"Oh."

A beat of silence followed.

"Are you looking for me?"

"Right!" she said. "I was. You and Wes."

"He's at the store. Apparently I got the ratio of fresh food to frozen pizza wrong when I shopped."

"Well, I'm sure you'll do better next time." She smiled. "I bought you a present." She lifted the bag.

He smiled. He had a very nice smile. It started slowly, one corner of his mouth turning up, then his lips pursed before the smile spread and at last reached his eyes, where little laugh lines made sexy crinkles. Oh, yes, it was a very nice smile.

"You didn't have to get us a present."

She shrugged and held out the bag.

"It's not a big present."

He took the bag and reached inside. When he pulled out the whistles, he appeared surprised.

"There's one for Wes, too. I wanted you to feel official, you know?"

"This kind of power will go to my head," he said.

"Pass it to me," she said. "Now lean over."

She had to take a deep breath. He was so tall and strong, but when he bent his head, she could see the vulnerable strip of skin where his hair didn't cover his shirt collar. Something about his submitting to her made it hard to keep her hands steady.

She slid the whistle over his head, and if her hands accidentally brushed the silk of his hair, well, she never said she was above temptation.

He straightened and she patted the whistle where it lay against the soft fabric of his jacket. His gaze followed her hand and then he lifted his eyes to meet hers. Her satisfaction surprised her. It was the same as when she sorted out some problem and found the perfect solution. In a way, she had. Deacon had her whistle, so that meant he belonged to her. Or at least to her team.

"Thanks," he said. "It's exactly my size."

"I was watching you play," she said. "You're amazing."

He gave the ball a quick dribble. "I've been playing for more than twenty years. I'd better be good by now."

"Is your shoulder all healed?"

"I did more rehab on it than you can imagine, but it just never came all the way back. It's good enough." He rolled his shoulders and she immediately wished she could think of another excuse to put her hands on him. She wanted to run her hands all over his shoulders and back. If she did, she knew she wouldn't feel a flaw or weakness, just pure, athletic perfection.

"You look incredible. Playing, I mean. You looked good when you were playing." She tried to keep her tone even, but wasn't sure she succeeded. He tilted his head and held her gaze for a beat.

"I do all right," he said. "Let's see you take a shot." He held out the ball.

"I'm awful, Deacon. You can't imagine."

He bounced the ball on his fingertips. "Take a shot."

"There's no point."

He put the whistle in his mouth and grinned at her around it. "Don't make me get all authoritative with you, Coach Bradley. Show me your shot."

She accepted the ball and squared up to the basket, but then she paused. "What do I get if I make it?"

"What do you mean?"

"If I let you see how bad I am, there has to be some reward. What are the stakes?"

"Shouldn't you have learned your lesson about betting on basketball?"

"Not funny," she said. "If I make it, you and Wes have to come to dinner with me at the Pond on Saturday."

"Okay." He gestured at the basket. "And what if you don't make it?"

"I don't know. What do you want?"

"If you miss… I really am drunk with power. If you miss, I want an I.O.U."

She was confused. "For what?"

He stepped closer and lowered his head toward her. "Whatever I want." Damn, if he didn't have the sexiest voice. "Once I decide what that is."

She sucked at basketball on a good day. With his

voice humming through her brain, no way would she make her shot. She wasn't even sure she wanted to. Dinner at the Pond would be fun. Being held hostage to Deacon's desire? That would be...exceptional.

She turned back to the basket as she once again imagined him leaning over her in bed, but this time, after he took off his glasses, he said, "Whatever I want, Julia."

She closed her eyes and flung the ball. A clang and a thump and it went through the hoop. She watched his face as the ball came down. Was there a hint of regret that he'd lost? She thought so.

"Saturday, Deacon."

He nodded. "All right." He picked up the ball. "I might ask for a rematch on this bet, though. Fair warning."

She walked home, letting the winter sun warm her face as she thought about what he might want from her and how much she'd enjoy losing that bet.

MONDAY WAS THEIR third official practice. Over the weekend, he'd determined that a total of four people associated with the team could play basketball. Two of them were named Fallon.

Another was Tali, though despite what he'd told her mother, she was so undisciplined he couldn't count on her unless she stepped up her game.

The fourth was the blonde girl who'd made that shot the first day. The sweet baseline jumper that convinced him to stay. That kid had a lot more natural talent than Tali and had practiced hard the first day but then hadn't shown up the second. He'd need more commitment than that from her.

He'd decided his first order of business that day was

to talk to the blonde girl and Tali because they'd have to carry the team. The question was, were they up to the work?

"Wes, I'm going to pull two of the girls aside to speak to them about what I need from them this year. You keep running the passing drill with this crew and then in ten, switch to the fast break."

Wes blew his whistle, held it away from his mouth and grinned at it. Julia was so pleased with her gifts, but Deacon, with his more complete knowledge of his brother's personality, had a more jaded outlook. Wes's delight in that damn whistle pretty much guaranteed he'd blow it some early morning when Deacon was sound asleep. Most likely in proximity to his ear.

"Julia, I need a picture of each of the girls so I can start making lineups. Here. Take my phone and get them over against that wall. Have them write their name on a piece of paper and hold it up. Just their first name. Tell them to write big so I can see it, okay?"

Even though he intended to make Wes do the paperwork for the team, he'd memorize the names so he could pick them out on the score sheets if he needed to.

"Yes, Coach," she said with a little salute. She was mocking him. First she'd given his brother a whistle and now she thought she could mock Deacon. He decided the assistant coaches were going to run laps with the girls once he finished talking to those two kids who actually knew how to play. "I'll just run to my office for a notebook and markers. Be right back, Coach."

She smiled at him.

"Better hustle, Coach. We don't have all day," he answered. She sauntered away, deliberately walking more slowly than he'd ever seen her move. He let himself enjoy the sway of her hips while he thought about their dinner date on Saturday. He still wasn't sure if he should've agreed to the date, but somehow, when she'd been right there close to him, challenging him to the bet, he couldn't remember all the reasons he should say no. He'd slept in his rental bed last night, but falling asleep hadn't been any easier than the previous night, when he'd slept on the floor. He'd lain awake for hours, remembering the feel of her hand on his chest and how her eyes had widened when he'd said he'd tell her what he wanted. He'd fallen asleep eventually, but not before he'd imagined scores of dirty sexy things he wanted to do to her or have her do to him.

When the gym doors closed behind her, he blew his own whistle. "Hey, you." He pointed at the stocky blonde girl just finishing up the passing drill. "Get out of line. We have to talk."

He retreated to the side of the gym farthest from the rest of the team so he could get a little privacy. He didn't want the other players to overhear what he had to say to these select kids. Julia was all about self-esteem, which was fine, but someone needed to think about winning.

He assumed the girl was following him, but when he turned back, she was standing on the baseline watching him. The rest of the team had stopped, too, and even Wes was giving him an odd look.

"Where's Julia?" Wes asked.

"She left on an errand. You're supposed to be running a drill."

Wes eyed the girl at the baseline, who still hadn't made a move toward his brother, and then Deacon. The kid was wearing the most expensive basketball shoes of anyone in the gym, including him and Wes. He thought this girl was the key to both winning and fundraising, but how would he know if he couldn't even get her to talk to him?

"You want to wait till she gets back before you have this meeting?" Wes asked.

He needed to send his staff to coaching training. He blew his whistle again and waved his arm impatiently. The kid finally started to jog his way. Compared with the speed she'd shown in the warm-ups, she was practically going backward, but at least she was moving.

On the upper end of weight for the girls on the team, her blond hair caught back in a ponytail that left some pieces to straggle around her angular face, she barely looked old enough for high school. But even with the extra weight she was carrying she was fast, and she could dribble. She'd made a bunch of deep perimeter shots when they were horsing around before practice and he'd observed her make fifteen free throws in a row last week. He hadn't seen her do much passing, because the other girls tended to avoid her, but he knew talent when he saw it, and she had it. His Tigers didn't have much to recommend them, but he had a point guard. Put this kid on the court with Tali and teach at least one of those other girls how to dribble, and the team had hope.

She stopped about three feet away from him and folded her arms across her chest. Wes was still eyeing him, and Deacon gestured for him to get the drill going. His brother shrugged and blew that damn whistle again, but he moved so he was facing Deacon, and was barely paying attention to the drill behind him. Deacon decided to ignore whatever was bugging Wes and focus on the kid in front of him.

"What's your name?" he asked.

No answer. Maybe something was wrong with her. Was that why the others on the team weren't paying attention to their drill?

"Listen," he said. "You're the best player on the floor and I'll have to lean on you if this team is going to make any headway on Ms. Bradley's bet. We need to work together, right? So start with the easy stuff. What's your name?"

She rocked backward on her heels, a flush sweeping across her cheeks and neck. He had no idea why. Sure, he'd blown the damn whistle, but he didn't think he'd done anything worthy scaring someone.

"I'm not a girl," the kid said. "My name is Max Wright."

Deacon wondered if everyone in the gym heard the same thud he did when the girl opened her mouth and turned into a boy. How had he missed that? Every single other person in the gym, including his brother, he realized, must have known. Even with the truth in hand, Deacon thought the kid looked like a girl. Like this team didn't have enough problems. Now they'd have to deal with whatever this was?

"You're not a girl," he said, his irritation at feeling foolish making him snap out his words.

Max flinched. "No, sir."

"Yet here you are in the gym, practicing with the girls' team. Am I missing something, or is this the slightest bit strange for you, too?"

When Max's arms tightened around his chest, Deacon felt like an ogre. Honest to God, he didn't know what the hell was going on here. Still, he shouldn't be taking it out on the kid.

"Ms. Bradley said I could practice with the team."

"But you're good, Max," he said. He hoped the compliment reassured the boy, got him moving toward an explanation, and besides, it was the truth. "Really good. I mean, why not go out for the boys' team?"

"I did. I got cut, sir." The flush on his cheeks deepened, and Max looked down.

Deacon had seen what this kid could do with a ball. Unless Milton High School had somehow enrolled an entire team full of basketball prodigies, no way should this boy have been cut from anyone's team. Deacon studied him for another few seconds, a sick feeling building in his stomach.

Not one masculine trait showed on Max's face. Deacon would bet his last dollar the kid wouldn't need a razor for another couple of years, and he wasn't even making the slightest attempt to combat his feminine appearance by cutting his hair.

Deacon had been around enough youth coaches in his time to know that some were saints and others were bastards. Unless Coach Simon had changed an awful lot in the past ten years, he fell into the latter category. Deacon had seen more than his share of Coach Simon's worst tendencies because he'd once lived with the man. When Deacon had watched Julia's team playing, he'd seen a gifted girl player. What had Coach Simon seen when Max had vied for a spot on the Tigers' roster?

Deacon had played on Coach Simon's youth basketball team, and at his mom's funeral Coach promised him that he and his brother would be looked after. Coach and his wife had enrolled in a certification program to become foster parents just so they could take Deacon and Wes in, but they'd tossed Wes out nine months later. Deacon had run away, determined to find Wes, or at least to get away from Coach and his wife. After they caught up with him, Coach told him that when kids his age couldn't be placed in foster homes, they got sent to a regional facility over an hour away from Milton. Deacon would never have seen Wes had he gotten sent away. He stayed with Coach Simon and played for him and hated him every single day.

When he was older, Deacon realized Coach had used him, first to make his rep as a youth coach and then to secure a position on the high school staff. He'd been an assistant coach when Deacon left, and promoted to head coach shortly after. Coach Simon's name did not appear on the list of people Deacon respected.

"You have any idea why they cut you?"

Max shrugged a shoulder noncommittally. Deacon was sure he had some theories.

"You have a bad day at the tryouts?"

Max shook his head.

"Maybe you were nervous. Got messed up. It happens to everyone." Not many kids showed up to tryouts in expensive shoes if they were expecting to get cut.

"I wasn't nervous. I didn't mess up." The boy wasn't willing to speculate about Coach Simon's motivation, but he also wasn't about to let Deacon think he'd done poorly. Nice to know the kid had some confidence under that soft exterior.

"Because you're pretty darn good, in my opinion. And I once sat on the bench next to Mr. Shaquille O'Neill, so my opinion is worth something." That got Deacon the hint of a smile. Just a slight twitch of the lips, but he'd take it. He went on more seriously, "I wouldn't have cut you."

"Thank you, sir."

"You don't have to call me sir all the time."

"I won't, sir."

Deacon tried to figure out what to say next, but Max

surprised him by offering, "When Ms. Bradley told me I could work out with her team, I said no." Max shook his head as if to emphasize that point. "I mean, I want to try out for the Tigers again next year, and if Coach Simon and the guys saw me going to the girls' practice—well… Plus, Ms. Bradley—I mean, Coach Bradley—isn't much of a coach. Her team stinks even though Tali's pretty good and Cora and Iris aren't terrible. But Mrs. Bradley's drills are about, like, feeling good, not getting better. Miri still uses two hands when she dribbles."

Max looked him full in the face for the first time, and when Deacon saw the humor in the kid's eyes, he decided Max had a lot more going on than was apparent from the outside. Coach Simon was looking like an idiot at this point. Leaving this kid on the sidelines was a mistake.

"Coach Bradley does have her challenges."

Clearly. And he was getting sick of looking stupid because she left out details like the gender of the team he would coach, or that the best player on the court happened to be of the opposite gender. For Pete's sake, did she think he wouldn't eventually notice that the only kid in the gym qualified to be his point guard was a boy?

"Anyway," Max continued, "after Ms. Bradley said you could be the girls' coach, I asked if I could practice with the team."

"Why?"

The kid gave him a look that clearly said he'd just asked a moronic question. "You played in the NBA." He enunciated each letter. Reverently. "Plus, when my dad finds out I got cut, I can tell him I'm working out with Deacon Fallon. Sir."

Every time Deacon thought he had a handle on this conversation, the kid made another statement like that one and the whole conversation slid sideways.

"Your dad doesn't know you got cut? Where does he think you are every day?"

"Basketball practice." Max held up the first finger of his right hand. "Which is true."

"In only the broadest sense," Deacon said. "He's going to find out."

"I know," Max acknowledged resignedly. Deacon looked carefully, but he didn't see signs the boy was scared. Only embarrassed.

"He'd have wanted to come in and complain," Max added. "Then I'd never be able to make the team. This way I can maybe tell him I'm working out with you on purpose. As long as he thinks I picked this, he won't complain."

Deacon peered at those expensive shoes. Someone either cared a hell of a lot about this kid or had money to burn. Maybe both. He wouldn't second-guess the boy's understanding of his own family, but he also wouldn't be surprised if the dad showed up to complain anyway once this flimsy cover story fell apart. It's what he'd have done.

"You know you can't play in games. We can't roster you on the team."

Max was silent. Now, when Deacon could have used a clue or something, the kid had quit talking again.

"So you're okay with just practicing with us?"

"Yes, sir." Max nodded enthusiastically, his ponytail swinging around his ears. "Thanks. Really. Thanks. When you said you needed to talk to me, I thought you were going to kick me out."

"Why would I? Maybe you can teach Miri to dribble

with one hand at a time." Max gave him a real smile then. "I don't guess you have any sisters who know how to play...?"

"Only child."

"Figures."

Max started to jog back to the drill, but Deacon put a hand on his shoulder. "I was serious about what I said, Max. If I'd been coaching those other Tigers, you'd have made the team, no question. Coach Simon is an idiot."

"Thanks, Coach."

The smile never left Max's face for the rest of the practice, and Deacon realized that as much as he'd joked about being on a power trip, his words meant something to these kids. He'd signed up to coach basketball. He thought the rest of the stuff Julia talked about would be up to her. He hadn't intended to get involved in any of these kids' lives, but putting that smile on Max's face felt a lot more satisfying than anything he'd done with his business in the past few years.

CHAPTER SEVEN

JULIA LOOKED FOR Deacon and Wes after practice, but they were nowhere in sight. Tali's brothers were running for the door when she grabbed Trey.

"Coach Wes told us we could help him bring the car around," he said.

"He's going to let me beep the horn," Shawn added.

"And me. Two times." Trey shoved at his brother. "I call shotgun."

She let them go and they went out the door, jockeying for position the whole way.

She hurried through the school toward her office. She had two phone calls to make to parents and she'd promised the technology teacher that she'd get him the contact information for a small web design firm interested in setting up an internship program for a student on the technology track at Milton.

She was reviewing her plan on how to tackle the conversation with the first mom, settling on her main points and working through the objections that might be raised, so when she opened the office door, she didn't notice Deacon sitting in her extra chair. He stood up and she stepped backward fast with a little shriek.

"My God, you scared me. I had no idea you were in here."

He didn't apologize.

He waited until she set her gym bag down, and then he said, "Sucks to get caught off balance, doesn't it?"

Her pulse had jumped when he'd scared her, but it didn't settle down when it should have. Instead, she was intensely aware that she was alone in her office with Deacon. In jeans and a khaki work shirt he'd put on over the T-shirt he wore to practice, he was looking masculine. His shirtsleeves were rolled up past his elbows and the lean strength in his forearms took her back to that daydream she'd had on Sunday. He moved closer, leaving her scant room to breathe, let alone move. Feeling trapped put her on the offensive.

"Has something happened that left *you* off balance, Coach?"

"Besides getting tricked into coming here to run a girls' team, finding out that most of the girls can't play and yet they're supposed to win the state championship game, and, finally, discovering that the only good player in the gym is a boy and therefore ineligible for the team?" The cords in his neck stood out by the time he got to his last point, but somehow he wasn't shouting. "Other than those few things, no. Nothing has been unexpected in the slightest."

"Oh. Max. Right." She straightened a stack of folders on her desk, trying to appear nonchalant. "But can I just reiterate that we don't have to win—"

"Don't even think about quibbling over the terms of the bet."

"Why are you so angry?"

"Because I shouldn't have to *find out* things out about my own damn team. Why wouldn't you tell me?"

"How was I supposed to know how you'd react?"

"What in the hell are you talking about?"

He seemed taken aback, honestly surprised that

she'd worried about his reaction. Was he really not like Ty and Coach Simon at all?

"You *lived* with Coach Simon. You were one of them, Deacon. Back in high school, all you cared about was the Tigers."

His jaw tightened. "I was never one of them, Julia. You have no idea."

"I was there."

"Yes, you were. You were there. But you aren't me." Deacon looked grim. "There's a lot you don't know about me."

Now *she* was taken aback. This deep anger was something new between them.

"Maybe if you'd talk to me, I'd have a better understanding of things."

"Okay, how about this? Coach Simon did something seriously wrong to Wes when he was a little kid, and I would never have brought my brother here if I'd realized he was still around. When you called me, I assumed he was gone since you were reaching for a coach for the Tigers. I wouldn't have agreed to come had I known the truth, and not because I didn't want to coach girls."

She was at a loss for words. "I'm sorry, Deacon. I should have been up front with you."

"Yes. You should have. I deserve to make my own decisions." He crossed his arms. "I don't want to 'find things out,' Julia. I want to know in advance."

"You're right," she said. "I should have trusted you. Max is vulnerable and I put my worries for him first."

"Vulnerable?"

"When you talked to him, did he tell you they cut him without one word of explanation?"

"As a matter of fact, he did."

"Well, we both can guess why he wasn't allowed on the court with the Tigers."

"He told me he didn't know."

"Oh, please. He got cut because he looks like a girl. I wouldn't be surprised to find out they think he's gay," she said, irritated with him for making her state the obvious. "He wants to play basketball. He needs this. He never should have been cut from the boys' team, but at least this way he has an outlet for his love of the game."

"I have serious doubts about whether he needs to spend his afternoons playing with people who won't challenge him to improve his skills, but the fact is, the league doesn't care about what kids need. There are rules, eligibility standards, bylaws, all that stuff, and the people who run the league take them seriously." He leaned toward her. "For all you know, you're jeopardizing the team's eligibility by letting him into practice."

"Don't be ridiculous. I'm sure no one minds. It's not as if he's on the roster—"

"So you can't say if it's against the league rules? Have you even read the handbook?"

"You know what, Deacon?" She couldn't believe he'd be caught up in an issue like this, when the important thing was giving kids like Max a chance to do what they loved. She stalked around her desk and opened the bottom drawer, where she kept her coaching files. She grabbed the plastic ring-bound book containing the league rules and threw it to him. "If you care so much about the rules, why don't you read them?"

He caught the book and held it, but he didn't so much as glance down. He was glaring at her. He shook his head impatiently, flicking the strands of dark blond hair out of his eyes.

"We both got into this coaching 'partnership' for selfish reasons. You want to win your bet with Ty and I have Wes to deal with. But if we're going to do this, if you and I are going to pull these girls together and make something out of the season, we have to have each other's backs. I can't keep walking into ambushes because you didn't see fit to give me the whole story. You have to trust me and vice versa. If we're partners, we're in it together."

A professional woman would have stepped back. Maybe put the desk between Deacon Fallon's intensity and the sizzle of connection she felt when he'd said the word *together*. But Julia didn't feel professional just then. In fact, she was wondering how being together would feel with Deacon on an extremely unprofessional plane.

That she hadn't told Deacon about Max because she wasn't sure how to approach the subject was true. The kid was an odd duck and didn't quite fit in at Milton. She'd been glad to give him a place with the other kids she'd collected. When Deacon had taken him at face value, she'd lost her heart to Deacon just a little bit. Since the board cut the guidance staff, she'd been on her own in the office and she hadn't realized how lonely she'd been or how much sharing her worries for the team with someone else would mean.

She licked her lips. Her voice when she spoke was low and husky. "I'm sorry I didn't tell you about Max."

He nodded. "So there's nothing else? Nobody on the team who's not enrolled at the school or secretly has alien blood or anything?"

"Well, we haven't run the alien-blood tests yet," she

said. "But I think we're good. Everything's out in the open now."

"Okay. Thanks."

After he left, she thought about the one or two more things she maybe could have told him. Like the fact that she was really interested in seeing more of him out in the open, and that she wouldn't turn down an invitation to be his partner off the court. She couldn't wait for Saturday.

ON TUESDAY, THE gym doors opened halfway through practice and Ty and Coach Simon walked in. Julia's heart sank. As soon as Deacon saw the men, he immediately scanned the gym, searching for Wes.

Once he located his brother, safely at the opposite end of the gym working with Cora on rebounding, he strode toward the men. She hurried after him.

Ty's smile was as open and welcoming as if he'd been friends with Deacon all his life.

"Deacon!" Ty said. "Coach Simon's been asking about you. We figured we'd come by to say hi."

Deacon and the coach nodded at each other. "Hey," he said as he took Simon's outstretched hand. The handshake lasted a hair too long, moving fast from nice-to-meet-you to I-can-dominate-you-with-my-powerful-grip.

Julia suddenly realized just exactly how much of a miracle it was that any peace talks in the history of the world had ever ended without bloodshed. This was just a group of guys meeting in ostensibly friendly circumstances on the side of a basketball court and the posturing and testosterone were unreal.

"We have a proposition for you, Deacon," Ty said. "Coach here thinks that with your NBA experience, you'd probably be able to help the Tigers get tuned up for the season." Ty clapped a hand on Deacon's shoulder. "Not that they're not already in great shape. But it seems a shame to waste your time here in Milton."

A stray ball lay on the floor and Deacon put the toe of his sneaker on it, and rolled the ball back and forth under his foot. "I saw them practicing the other night. Looked like they need work on the fast break."

"That's exactly the kind of thing we'd love to have you teaching them," Coach Simon said. "Your brother and Ms. Bradley should be able to handle the girls' team. You could join us as an assistant while providing high-level oversight to this team."

"By high-level oversight you mean…?"

"Conferencing with the coaches. Maybe stopping by practice one or two times a week."

"You want me to work with you guys and leave the girls' team to Wes and Julia?"

Coach Simon looked over their heads to the side of the gym where the team had gathered. "It's not much of a team, son. Smart money says you're wasting your time on them when the Tigers are headed back to States."

Deacon put one hand on the back of his neck. "Well, one thing I've never been accused of is being smart."

Coach Simon's eyes glittered with anger, but he kept his tone level when he said, "That's your final word?"

"Final word," Deacon echoed. "These girls are my Tigers."

"You're being a bit unreasonable, right?" Ty said. "No reason we can't all get along."

Deacon's hands balled into fists.

Julia saw Wes starting over. Deacon saw him at the

same time, and turned his back to block his brother from Coach Simon's view.

"I'm getting along. I'm getting the girls ready for States and I don't have time to take on any more volunteer work." He waited a beat and then blew his whistle. Turning away from the men, he yelled, "Line up at half-court. I want to see you guys scrimmage."

He started to walk off, headed for the girls.

Ty handed Julia a piece of paper. "Handle this. The maintenance crew is coming in on Saturday."

Coach Simon called after Deacon. "You know, I would have expected a little loyalty, son. I took you into my home and you have never said thank you."

Deacon was back across the gym and up in his old coach's space before Julia had time to react. "My practices are closed to the public. If you want to come back, submit a request to Coach Bradley."

He crossed his arms and waited until Ty and Coach Simon left the gym. When the door closed behind them, he glared at her. As he walked away, he muttered, "Freaking thank you. Jackass." Then he blew his whistle and waved the girls into a huddle.

Julia had almost forgotten Wes was there until he said, "He makes it sound like he did us a favor." She was surprised at the anger in his voice. In the time they'd spent together, she wasn't sure she'd heard him say a serious word. "He used D. Used him and didn't care who got hurt when he did it."

"Wes?"

"People say Coach Simon did Deacon a favor. Some favor."

"Wes!" Deacon admonished. "Let's go."

"Donny Simon rode my brother's talent from a volunteer job in the youth league all the way to the head coach's job here at the high school. If anyone owes anyone, it's Simon who owes my brother."

He jogged back to the game before Julia had a chance to ask him anything else. She was floored by the fierce protectiveness that had flared up. From the things she'd seen and the way Deacon talked about Wes, she didn't think the boy had a serious bone in his body. She knew how devoted Deacon was to his brother. It looked as if that feeling went both ways.

She glanced at the note Ty had given her. It was a memo from the facilities team that they would be reconfiguring her office space that Saturday afternoon. She was losing four feet off the right side and a foot off the front. She hadn't heard one peep about any other building changes being made. She imagined that Ty only delivered this note because Deacon had refused to abandon the team—he'd had it prepared, and had held it in reserve to punish her should he not get his way. She'd been thrilled to hear him picking her girls, but now she wondered what else they'd be expected to give up.

THE TEAM PRACTICED hard the rest of the week. No one saw much improvement, but Max did get Miri dribbling with one hand. It was a start.

The boy Tigers opened their season on Friday night. Deacon and Wes actually drove to the high school and parked the Porsche in the lot out back. They watched the crowds streaming in, but neither of them made a move to get out.

Finally, Deacon looked at Wes. "You want to drive on the way home?"

Wes nodded and got out to switch seats with him.

They didn't go home, though. Instead, they tuned the game in on the car radio.

Wes stopped outside Julia's apartment and Deacon ran up the steps to the porch. When she answered the door, she was wearing a pair of jeans and a Milton Tigers hoodie.

"Coaches meeting. In the car."

They parked down the street from the Fallons' under the streetlight near the old hoop.

Wes didn't protest when they exiled him to the tiny backseat. Julia forced him to let her have the driver's seat and none of them said much as they listened to the game. It started off tight, and the Tigers kept it close as they battled their perennial rivals, the Westview Wildcats.

Westview was down by two in the last few minutes and their hotshot point guard got fouled on a fast break. When he made both sides of a one and one, Wes whispered, "Way to go, Wildcat." Milton pulled ahead again in the last thirty seconds, and then the game was over.

"We're up next week," Julia said.

"The girls'll be ready."

She tightened her lips and nodded. "I hope so."

She said she didn't know how to drive a stick shift, so Deacon drove her home. After she went in, he saw a light go on in the front of the top-floor apartment and he wondered if that was her bedroom.

Earlier that week when Donny Simon had walked into the gym where his team was practicing, where Wes was working, there'd been a second when he'd felt the old powerlessness. But the confrontation had gone down and he'd come out unscathed. He wasn't the kid he'd been when he was in the center of Tigers basketball. Working with Julia was helping him see that. She counted on him—not to win games, but to lead her team.

They were going to dinner tomorrow, and he still wasn't sure it was a good idea. He glanced up at that lit window again. He wasn't backing out, though. There was too much he wanted to know about Julia and about himself to miss this chance.

LATE SATURDAY MORNING, Julia got a call from the district maintenance supervisor that they'd finished work on her office. The supervisor, a woman named Nina, mentioned that Julia should put in a request if she needed any help getting her belongings back in the office. Julia told her she was sure everything would be fine because she'd arranged with Henry to meet at the school and put it all back together. She got to her office first, and when she opened the door to the space, she saw everything wouldn't be fine.

Technically they'd taken only a few feet off either end of her space, but somehow it now looked incredibly small and cramped to her. Maybe this was an optical illusion or maybe it was because her heavy metal desk was now angled out away from the wall into the middle of the room. She could scrounge up a tape measure to confirm, but she was pretty certain just from eyeballing the area that the desk would no longer fit against any of the walls.

She pulled the door shut, counted to three, then opened it again. No change. Ty's note had been so specific about the new dimensions of her office, she had to believe he'd known this would be the result. Had he measured her desk just to be sure he'd leave her completely out of luck?

A few seconds later, someone knocked on the door. She yelled, "Come in."

Henry took one look around and said, "I hate what you've done with the place."

Julia let out a sharp laugh. "No kidding." She lowered herself to sit on the floor. "I'm starting to think my principal may not like me."

"What in the world gives you that idea?"

Julia crossed her eyes. "I'm getting a voodoo doll. He'll be sorry when he develops a mysterious case of pin in the forehead."

Henry set his back against the wall and slid down to join her. "You're funny when you're scary." He lifted his knees and rested his wrists on them. "You want a hand bringing the stuff from outside back in here?"

"I don't think that's a good idea," she said. "Until I figure out what to do about the desk, moving anything else is just busywork." She ran her hand over the thin nap of the carpet. "Remember Dad's office? He had that big old-fashioned wooden desk and those tall windows. I used to crawl up on the window seat and close the curtains to make a hideout."

"Yeah. I used to love drinking out of the triangle cups he had for the watercooler."

"Remember he had that intercom on his desk? The one he used to communicate with his secretary? He had a woman sitting outside his office who typed his forms, filed his triplicates and made sure he had time to do things like guide. And counsel. I've never had an office that had real walls, and now I can't even fit my stupid desk inside this cubicle. If I didn't deal with confidential stuff, I bet they'd take away my door."

"You picked the wrong era to work in the public schools."

Maybe the wrong era had something to do with it, but as Julia sat in the midst of her office and thought about all the things she had to do just to keep her head above water with the paperwork and district requirements, she wondered if she wasn't in the wrong job entirely. Lately, the best part of her day was practice. And not just because she liked looking at Deacon's arms when he demonstrated things with the basketball.

She kicked the closest leg of the desk. "I would put in a request for a new desk, but my principal is liable to decide I don't need one at all. Or maybe he'll just lop a few feet off either end of this one and call it done."

"You could begin a trend for tripod desks."

"Maybe parents would start showing up for their meetings if there was the constant threat of my desk collapsing on me."

She kicked the leg of the desk again on the off chance it might suddenly condense, accordion fashion, and become a smaller, more convenient size.

"You know, I haven't made this offer since Paulie Grant blew you off and went to see the Patriots game instead of going to the Sadie Hawkins dance with you, but, well, if you want me to beat Ty up, I will."

"He played high school football, Henry." Julia knocked her shoulder against his. "Don't get me wrong, I appreciate the offer, but I don't want to see you killed."

"Hey!" Henry spun around so he was facing her. "'Played high school football' doesn't intimidate me. I work out."

"You're right," Julia said. "I'm sorry I insulted your masculinity. You're quite strong." She patted his knee. "And generous. The second I decide I'd like Ty beaten up, you're the guy I'll call."

Henry nodded. "Damn straight." They were silent for a couple of seconds. "Maybe if we empty a couple drawers in the filing cabinets you can consolidate and get the rest of your stuff back in here."

"The desk will still be sitting in the middle of the room, right?"

Henry sighed. "You want me to buy you a new desk? We could go to Staples and see what they have."

She stood and brushed off the seat of her jeans. "That is sweet. But I'll leave it like this for now. I'm having dinner with Deacon and his brother tonight, and I'm going home to relax until it's time to go. Sorry I got you down here for nothing."

"It's not for nothing. Now I know you're having dinner with Deacon, and I can plan to casually drop by. Where are you eating, the Pond?"

"Why would you do that?"

"Because Mom told me there's something going on between you and your new assistant."

Julia sighed and rolled her eyes. "Mom needs to learn not to take me seriously. Nothing's going on."

"You're sure?"

She nodded.

Before he left, Henry shoved the desk as close to the wall as it would go.

Julia stood in the library for a minute, looking at the contents of her office—a mishmash of unmatched filing cabinets, an old conference table, various lamps and a collection of four chairs, two with duct tape around the joints in the legs.

This was where she did her professional work. *Way to depress yourself, Julia,* she thought.

Maybe Henry had a good idea. She could probably cull some of her papers. Not that this would make the desk any smaller, but the office would feel less cramped with fewer filing cabinets.

Her oldest filing cabinet, standing right outside the door to her office, had five tall drawers full of paper. She opened the bottom drawer. There she kept the files of the kids she'd lost.

Deacon's file was in front of the drawer. He was the first kid she'd let down. She'd wanted so much to get him into college. All these years he'd been in her filing drawer, and now he was back, about to meet her at the Pond.

She yanked the drawer open the whole way and pulled out the stack. There weren't many files. A few each year—thirty or forty. It felt like a lot, though, when she held them all at once.

She hardly ever looked at the notes about these kids, but she was unable to give them up. Even after all this time, she still held on, hoping she could make a change for one of the kids.

Stupid.

How could she help them now? None were in school anymore. They'd all moved past the limited reach of her increasingly limited office. She set the stack of files off to the side. She wouldn't bring them back into her office. The space was small enough now without shoving all these regrets in with her.

CAUGHT UP IN her thoughts about the kids she'd been unable to reach over the years, she didn't notice the Fallons when she walked into the Pond. She finally heard Deacon say her name in a tone that made her realize it wasn't the first time.

"Hey," she said. "I was..."

"Ignoring us?" Wes finished with a grin.

"Impossible," she said.

"We got a table," Deacon said.

They ordered two pizzas, one for Julia and Deacon and one for Wes. After the waitress took their order, Wes disappeared and she figured he'd gone to the restroom, but he reappeared at their table a few seconds later with a basket of the soft bread sticks the Pond was famous for.

She put her straw in her soda and stared as he ate a bread stick in one enormous bite.

"What? I'm hungry." He picked up a second bread stick. "And these are delicious."

"You're rude," Deacon said.

"No, it's not that," Julia said. "Watching Wes makes me realize how unfair it is that I've never once experienced life with the metabolism of a teenage boy."

"Yeah, but you also never experienced the frustration teenage boys feel when—"

"Wes!" Deacon drew a finger across his throat. "Cut it out."

Wes grabbed another bread stick and muttered, "She works with teenagers. She knows—"

"She doesn't want to talk about it at dinner."

"She is listening to every word you say."

Julia had a sip of her soda, pursing her lips demurely around her straw.

Deacon glared at his brother. "What was all that prep school tuition for if you didn't learn anything about polite dinner conversation?"

"Wait," Julia said. "You went to prep school? Like a boarding school?"

Wes nodded.

"Huh. What was that like?"

He glanced at Deacon and shrugged. "Fine. Good."

Just that suddenly, the conversation ended in an uncomfortable silence. The Fallons were the kings of not talking when she hit on a subject they weren't interested in exploring. She was surprised to hear that Deacon had let Wes go away to school. He seemed so protective.

"So when you left here, you went to boarding school?"

"When he turned twelve." Deacon grabbed the basket of bread sticks and took the last one for himself. "I was on the road with the team and he couldn't travel with me, despite a highly persistent campaign of begging. He stayed at home with a nanny and I came home when I had breaks."

"Oh." She'd put her foot in it again. "I'm sorry for being so oblivious. Of course you needed help."

Wes glanced up. "Constance wasn't just help. She was family. Really hot-and-sexy family."

"She sounds, um, great. How did you find her?"

"Deacon picked her up in the grocery store."

"Wes, that's not true."

"Sure is. My first nanny was named Mrs. Smith. You had to call her Mrs. Smith whether you were eight or eighteen. Even the person who wrote her checks had to call her Mrs. Smith, which bothered him a lot."

"Wes, this is such ancient history."

"Deacon set her up with her own apartment in the lower level of the house. We could hear her, you know, moving around a lot at night. Sometimes she'd go out at weird times."

"Not so weird that you'd pry into her personal life," Deacon said. "I never had a nanny, so I didn't know what was normal."

"Deacon thought she was a bird-watcher."

Julia sat fascinated as they filled in pieces of the story, playing off each other. "But she was really a madam?"

"Drug dealer."

She spit out her water and Wes grinned as he took another huge bite of pizza. "I love telling this story."

"You don't have to look so happy, Wes. The poor lady went to jail."

"The poor lady was growing and selling weed out of your nanny quarters. Plus, she smelled funny, and not like pot—like a wet diaper. Double-plus, if Mrs. Smith hadn't gotten hauled off to the pokey, you wouldn't have picked up Constance in the grocery store." Wes's triumphant grin was infectious. "Constance smelled lovely."

"Wes had a crush on her."

"She only had eyes for Deacon."

"Okay, buddy. Enough."

"I'd love to hear about the grocery store," Julia said, even though she'd already decided she hated the nice-smelling Constance. If only Mrs. Smith had made better life choices.

"We don't need to dig into that history."

She knew the history itself wasn't the problem, but her presence. Trying to cut off this story was more of Deacon's stubborn unwillingness to let her in.

"He ordered a cake for my birthday, and when he got to the store to pick it up, my name was spelled W-E-S-T. I was sitting in the car, waiting for him and he was trying to get the bakery people to change it, but they wouldn't help."

"This is such a boring story," Deacon said.

"So don't listen. Anyway, Deacon is arguing with the bakery people and getting nowhere. Constance comes along, picks up a spatula, and just obliterates the letter *T*. She was an apprentice baker, but we didn't know that at the time. D just thought she was a random shopper.

"Anyway, they started talking and she got fired right in the middle of it, and she wound up coming to work for us the next day. She stayed until last May when I graduated."

"I thought you went to boarding school."

"There were breaks. The summer. When Deacon was home, she'd make him cinnamon rolls and stuff."

Constance wasn't real. She was barely the idea of a person and Julia hated her. She wondered how serious she and Deacon had been.

"Okay, you know what?" Deacon said. "I'm finished talking about Constance. We needed help. She helped. Move on."

They did move on then, sharing their pizza. Afterward, she and Deacon ordered coffee, while Wes had an ice-cream sundae. She sneaked a spoonful of the sundae and Wes pretended to be outraged before he pushed it closer to her side of the table. She resisted it, but she appreciated the gesture. He was a sweet kid. Impulsive, sure, and he had some goofy tendencies, but he'd grow out of a lot of that, she imagined.

Deacon wouldn't let her split the bill or leave the tip. She was getting ready to be irritated with him, but he opened the door for her and held it, his T-shirt stretched tight across his chest and the strong muscles of his forearm flexing. She carried herself carefully as she passed him so she wouldn't brush against him.

Outside the Pond, Wes said he was going to walk home.

"It's November. You'll freeze."

"It's not that far," Wes countered. "Besides, I want to call Oliver to see how he's doing."

Which left her and Deacon alone.

"I'm on foot, too," she said. "I parked at the high school and walked over."

"Let me give you a ride, then."

She said yes. She'd had fun with him and Wes, but she wanted to be alone with Deacon. Just to see what it felt like.

"He loves to get a rise out of you, doesn't he?" Julia said.

"He's the definition of irritating." Deacon's slight smile took the bite out of his words.

She wondered if he knew how hard Wes worked to keep his attention. She doubted it.

He opened the car door for her and again she slid carefully past him. When he was settled in his seat, she said, "You don't have to open the door for me all the time, you know."

"Yes, I do."

"Why?"

"Good manners," he said. And she knew he meant it. With Deacon, some things were just true. Good manners. Honesty about the things he was willing to discuss. And a whole lot of secrets he wasn't interested in sharing.

"Did Constance like you to open doors for her?"

He shook his head. "Wes needs to learn to shut the hell up. She was the nanny, not the girlfriend. The last three years she lived with us, she was getting her nursing degree. Her boyfriend shared the nanny apartment with her. Wes and I are both invited to the wedding next March, and he knows it."

Julia settled into her seat more comfortably. She

even had the generosity to feel sorry for Nanny Constance. Imagine living with Deacon for ten years and never getting to cross the line into an inappropriate employer-employee affair. Constance must have had willpower of steel.

"I have a question," she said, "and it's not about Constance. It's about Coach Simon."

"You're not my guidance counselor anymore."

Based on what she was learning, she hadn't been much of one back then.

"I'm your friend, Deacon. I thought I knew you in high school, but I was wrong."

"Fine," he said. "What's the question?"

"Wes told me Donny Simon sent him away. Why did he change the placement?"

"It was all a long time ago, Julia." He pressed his lips together as if he were holding back other words. He didn't ask for things, but he was so clearly asking her to let this drop. She wouldn't torture him just to find out what else she'd missed back when his file had first come across her desk.

The ride back to the high school was a short one, and she stayed quiet, watching the light and shadows from passing car headlights streak across his face. He looked different in profile. With his strong nose and sharply defined jaw, he was all masculine power from this angle, but she knew that if she could see his eyes, she'd find humor and caring and hurt lurking there. Nothing about Deacon was uncomplicated.

He pulled his car in next to hers. "Thanks for dinner," she said.

"No problem. You have your keys?"

"I'm actually heading inside. My office was 'reconfigured' today and I have to start sorting my stuff."

Deacon glanced at the dashboard. "It's almost eight o'clock on a Saturday night and you're going back to work?"

"What will you do when you get home?"

He rolled his eyes. "Play Xbox with Wes."

"Liar. Anyway, as you know, my office wasn't that big to begin with and now it's practically a closet. I have to do something about the mess before Monday. If I don't edit my stuff, it won't fit back in."

He turned off the engine.

"You're not helping me."

"Do you have to move furniture?"

She pictured herself trying to shove her heavy metal desk across the carpeted floor on her own. "Are you sure you wouldn't rather go home to your overgrown recliner?"

He leaned in close and said, "I'm sure." She swallowed. *Okay then.*

CHAPTER EIGHT

SHE'D BEEN IN the school after hours plenty of times, both in crowds for events and on her own. Sometimes she sat in her office for several hours after dinner, making phone calls to parents unavailable during the day. Tonight, though, the halls seemed smaller, or maybe Deacon just had a way of filling up space.

They walked together down the hall to her office, and she was so conscious of him next to her. The hairs on her arms felt as if they were standing up and reaching for him. She was electrified, and if she brushed against him, she'd explode. She was very, very careful not to brush against him.

"Those are the things that won't fit," she said, gesturing at her small conference table, the two medium-size filing cabinets and several boxes of books. "I have to sort out the books and see if I can condense the files." She ran a hand over the wood-veneer tabletop. "Even though this thing is ugly, I'll miss it. Sitting at the table seems to help set parents at ease, which doesn't happen if I'm behind the desk."

"What can I do to help?"

"Well, I have a second problem, less easy to solve than this one."

She unlocked her office door so he could peek in at her desk.

"Are you aiming for avant-garde with this placement, Julia?"

"I don't know what else to do with the desk. I think Ty measured it, then designed the new space to be sure it wouldn't fit."

Deacon studied the desk and then slowly turned in a circle, eyeing every inch of her small office. He knocked on the partition at the back of the cubicle.

"You have a tape measure?"

She shook her head.

He put his back against one wall.

"How about a pencil?"

She picked one out of the ceramic mug a student had given her several years ago.

"Mark off my height. I need to know how high the partitions are."

He stood erect, his heels against the wall, looking straight ahead. She got up next to him, but kept a bit of distance, not trusting herself if she touched him. She went up on her tiptoes and held the pencil flat against his head to make a mark on the wall. His hair was as thick and smooth as she remembered from the day she'd given him the whistle. She held the pencil too tightly and when the tip broke against the wall, the pencil skidded out of her hand and she overbalanced. She clutched his shoulder with her free hand to keep from crashing into him. He didn't flinch, his muscles and balance combining to keep him rock steady as she gathered herself.

"You okay?" he asked, his voice low and much too close to her ear. She nodded, the pencil forgotten as she breathed in his scent, and let herself touch him for one or two seconds longer than necessary, sliding her hand through his thick hair, deliberately this time, relishing the combination of soft silk and hard muscle in his shoulder. His right hand came up and rested gently on her hip.

"I'm fine." She backed up, giving herself space and trying to settle her nerves. "My mom used to measure us like this on our birthdays. The marks are probably still inside the front-hall closet."

He rubbed his thumb against his lower lip and she turned her back on him, manufacturing urgency around finding the pencil, to keep herself from touching his lips. When she faced him again, he was studying the wall where he'd made his mark.

"I'm a little over six foot two, so that means..." He cocked his head and examined her bookcases. "You need to swap the bookcases so they're vertical, not horizontal, for starters. Then if you..." He reached behind the tall filing cabinet and flipped something that sounded like a metal latch. He went around to the left of the cabinet and repeated the move. Then he lifted the top section off the cabinet. Apparently those three drawers were one unit while the bottom three drawers were another. She had no idea they came apart. "Move these over against the wall. Now you can get your conference table in here."

"Where?"

"Trust me."

She'd thought about her office space when she was at home. She'd even tried to use an online interior-design program to draft a floor plan, but she'd gotten hopelessly lost in the tiny grids and the square-footage calculations. Deacon appeared to have a plan and she had nothing. She stepped back and gestured at the office. "It's all yours."

He paced off the dimensions of the cubicle, then

went out into the library to view the exterior walls. When he came back, he looked delighted. His mouth turned up with that full-on smile that brought the laugh lines out around his eyes.

"I had a thought. I can work with the space in here and I'm positive we can fit everything back in. Or I can put the walls back where they were."

"You can move the walls?"

"They're not real walls, Julia. These modular things are all mounted on tracks. Whoever shifted yours left the old tracks in place. If I snap the walls out and slide them back into the old slots, how much do you want to bet no one notices?"

She clapped. "You can really do that? Ty's sneaky plan will be totally thwarted?"

"Absolutely. We'll make sure to move everything around in here anyway so it will appear different."

"I'm in awe. You're a genius. An evil genius, but that's all right by me."

Before he started, he rolled the sleeves of his shirt up and she licked her lips. He stood on one of the chairs and reached overhead to lift the ceiling tiles aside. His shirt rode up, partially exposing the waistband of his boxers. She spent a few minutes utterly mesmerized by the hollow at the base of his spine until he snapped his fingers.

"You want to help me with the turn bolts?"

They loosened the bolts on the partition supports and then Deacon muscled the panel back a few feet. They repeated the process, and her office was back to normal size.

She started out helping him shift the belongings, but realized that even though he wouldn't tell her to butt out, she was definitely more of a hindrance than a help. She hopped onto her newly positioned desk and sat cross-legged while he tugged and lifted and worked his magic.

He was a wizard, she guessed. Either that or he had a secret identity as a professional organizer on one of those do-it-yourself shows. If he did have a TV job and she was watching his show, she'd be tempted to send him fan mail. Maybe even the kind of fan mail the studio would confiscate because the contents weren't exactly G-rated. There was something about a strong, competent guy in jeans hanging just right that got her motor running and made her think thoughts she really shouldn't.

The interplay of his brain and his brawn mesmerized her. His spatial skills were remarkable. He took her office apart and made it infinitely more useful. He saw combinations and angles that, once he'd maneuvered her furniture into the new alignment, made total sense, but that she'd never have figured out on her own. He kept her belongings so orderly and organized that even though she had the same amount of stuff, the space felt much more open. He even maneuvered the desk flat against the back wall, a tight but perfect fit in a spot that made much more sense than her original one.

"You're all set," he said as he settled her extra chair under the end of the conference table. "You can get back to solving all of Milton's problems bright and early Monday morning."

She slid to the edge of the desk and stood. "I can't thank you enough for this, Deacon. I would never have been able to fit my office back together."

"Not a problem." He put his hands in his pockets. "I'm glad Ty didn't win this one."

"My brothers and Allison keep getting bigger and bigger offices, partnerships, raises, and here I am, ten years into the job, and I've got walls closing in a little tighter around me. Thank you for saving me from that."

She must have sounded more bitter than she'd intended.

"You all right?" he asked.

"Just wondering what life will be like at the end of the next ten years, you know? Nothing to worry about."

She crossed to the door and held it open, one hand on the light switch, ready to flip it off once he was out. He went through the door first but stopped and pointed to something just beyond her line of sight. "Is that yours?"

She leaned out and saw the stack of files she'd culled earlier. "Oh, it is. Thanks."

He bent and picked up the stack, prepared to hand it to her. She saw the instant he registered that his file sat on top. He lifted one hand, put his finger under his name on the file tab and traced it across. Then, without looking at her, he dumped the other files into her arms and strode out of the dark library, the folder with his name on it under his arm.

"Deacon, wait."

He didn't answer. She flung the files onto the floor inside her office and then fumbled for her keys to lock the door before she raced after him. She was horrified that he'd seen his file. He was so private. Who knew what he was thinking?

HE COULDN'T BELIEVE she'd been looking at his file. What the hell did she even have it for? If she was storing files for kids who graduated more than a decade ago, no wonder she couldn't fit her furniture in her office. He should have made her sort everything out herself, because maybe then she'd have had to recycle some of the junk she was hanging on to for no god-damn good reason.

He felt the thick manila folder sliding under his arm, and he grabbed it and held it in his right hand. How was he supposed to work with her knowing she'd looked at that stupid thing and seen a laundry list of everything wrong with him, every failure and unhappy moment laid out in black and white?

He heard her calling him, but he didn't stop. She caught up with him in the parking lot near their cars.

"I don't want to talk about this," he said. He was mad, and he didn't care enough even to hide it.

"Deacon, I'm sorry," she said. "I was sorting out some things today and I came across your file. I had that stack set aside to recycle. I didn't open it."

He held the file up. "I am *not* this kid anymore."

"I know."

"What's in here doesn't have anything to do with me." He sounded childish and he knew it, but he couldn't make himself stop protesting. "All the stuff that's written in here, it's over. Got it?"

She wasn't the kind of person who backed down from a fight, especially when she thought she had something to contribute.

"If you were completely past it, you wouldn't be so angry right now. Your childhood was horrible, Deacon. Maybe if you deal with some of those memories, you *could* actually put them to rest."

His temper was a physical thing. He could taste the anger and was so angry he wanted to spit or yell or punch something. No matter what he did, his past was always on him, dogging him, shaping his life.

"Wes told you some story about the Simons and you think you know something about us now, is that it?" he said. "Wes was eight years old when we left Milton. He doesn't remember half of what went on and some of it he never knew. Whatever he tells you is probably fiction or as good as."

"So what's the real story? Deacon, I should have known what was happening to you."

"Why?"

"Because I was your guidance counselor."

"Julia, I didn't need a guidance counselor. I needed to get my little brother the hell out of foster care."

She looked so stricken. He was still angry, but he knew that most of what was wrong with him was shame. His school file was a story of failure. If that was the place she thought she'd find out more about him, well, he was screwed in her eyes.

"Deacon, please."

"Please what? You've been working in Milton for ten years. Haven't you seen more kids like me in that time? I'd think you could guess what our life was."

"I've met a whole lot of kids, you're right. But I want to know about you."

"Fine." He'd tell her. She wanted to know this stuff, so he'd share it with her. "This is between you and me. Whatever Wes thinks is enough for him, and I do not want you to tell him what I tell you."

"Okay."

"When my mom died, Wes and I went to live with Donny Simon and his wife. He was my basketball coach in the youth league we all played in before we got to high school. I was twelve and Wes was two. Donny hadn't ever had foster kids before and he only took us so he could keep me on his youth league team.

I didn't know that. All I knew was my mom was dead and this guy who'd always been decent to me said he'd keep me and Wes together. Wes was little. He was confused and he didn't understand all the rules the Simons had. I went to school all day and he was alone with Mrs. Simon, who wasn't very keen on raising a toddler. Donny's daughter moved back home with her baby after some guy knocked her up. One day while I was at school, Wes hit the baby with a block. He was moved to a new foster home before I got home from practice."

Julia put her hand over her mouth. "Deacon, my God."

"No one would tell me what happened or where Wes was. They knew I'd try to get him back. I ran away the first night, but the cops picked me up. Finally, my social worker arranged for me to visit Wes on weekends. He got moved four more times after that. Once on Christmas Day. I never knew what was happening with him. Nothing was in my control.

"Later on, when I started getting scouted, Coach Simon came home with this agent. He made me sign a contract. Coach kept the signing bonus. He said I owed him. He offered to take Wes back if I'd pay him maintenance."

"The bastard," Julia said. "Who would prey on children like that? Why didn't you say something?"

"Because the only thing that mattered was me getting Wes the hell out of here. Coach Simon held the ticket to my playing time and that was my ticket to the draft. I did what he said and kept my mouth shut." Deacon's smile was tight and sad. "Even Mrs. Smith, the pot farmer, was better than what we had here."

"But if I'd known…"

"You'd have messed things up. I promised my mom

I'd take care of Wes and I did. The situation wasn't the kind a guidance counselor can fix."

"I would have tried."

There was no use going on with the conversation. She wouldn't let the issue go because that wasn't how she was built. She cared too much and tried too hard. She wanted to help everyone she met. Who was he to show her the ways kids like him couldn't be helped?

"I'll see you on Monday," he said. He went around and got into his car but didn't pull out until she'd turned out of the parking lot. He was going back to his rental place to build a fire and burn his file. Then he would try to forget that she'd seen it again.

HE MANAGED TO avoid being alone with Julia that week. He ran the girls hard at practice and stayed up late struggling to find some way to use the kids he had effectively. The boys won again on Friday night.

He and Wes tripped over each other all morning the day of their first game. Both of them were wound tight with pregame energy and neither was willing to admit how much he wanted his own win.

Eventually Deacon went for a run. When he got back, there was a note from Wes that he'd taken Trey and Shawn down the block to play ball. The little boys had started hanging around the old hoop with their buddies from school, and Wes was teaching them some of the Globetrotters routines he and Deacon had memorized when they were younger.

They left for the game an hour earlier than they needed to. Deacon remembered similar jitters from his playing days—his insides feeling as if they were carved out, leaving a hollow center of nerves and drawing his focus in so that nothing mattered but the game.

Wes carried the score sheets, the lineup cards for the other team and the binder full of health releases and emergency forms for their players. He'd gotten everything neatly organized in plastic sleeves with color-coded tabs.

Julia was already in the locker room when they arrived. She looked sheepish. "I had paperwork to do for next week," she offered as an explanation, despite sitting in the empty locker room without a pen or paper in sight.

He and Wes stepped out of the locker room when the girls got there to change. They'd have their pregame meeting in the weight room across the hall. Deacon almost opened the door to the gym, but he decided he wanted his return to the Milton gym—alive with game night excitement—to be with his Tigers behind him.

Julia brought them into the weight room. Max stuck his head around the door and she waved him in. "You belong here with us," she said.

Max winced and Deacon once again thought he should talk to her about what she was doing with the boy. He was a great kid, but where he belonged was on a competitive team where he would actually get to play.

"First game of a new year," Julia said. "We have new coaches, a new attitude, and we're going to have great success. So let's get out there and play our game to win!"

Tali led them down the hall and through the double doors into the gym. Deacon waited for the crowd to roar, but nothing came. No one was there. The Westview team had half the bleachers full, but on the Tigers' side of the gym, the bleachers were practically empty.

Trey and Shawn were present. He was surprised to see Victor. An older man sat near the top of the stands, but Deacon thought he might have come in just to get warm. An older woman and a guy around Julia's age waved to them from a spot halfway down the court. That was it.

He turned to Julia. "Where is everybody?"

"Welcome to Tigers basketball," she said.

The game was grim. Tali took as many shots as she could, but once the Westview team figured out she was the only one with any ability, they double-teamed her all night. Miri might as well not have been there, for all the support she offered. Cora got a couple of rebounds and made her foul shots, but when the game ended, the final score was Westview 34, Milton 6. Victor could barely meet his eyes as he stuffed a hundred-dollar bill into the coffee-can donation bank they passed around after the game.

Julia was in the locker room with the girls when the woman and guy who'd watched the game walked up to him.

"I'm Carole Bradley," the woman said. "This is Julia's brother Henry. You must be Deacon."

He blinked. The woman was about sixty and still pretty. He could see where Julia got her eyes and her smile. Henry, the brother, openly appraised him, but Deacon didn't read any aggression in his gaze.

"It's nice to meet you both," he said. "Sorry the game wasn't more exciting."

"Oh, that was actually a big game in Julia's career. I don't remember a time when they've scored more than six points."

Carole probably thought she was being polite, but Henry closed his eyes. "Mom, you'll scare him off."

"Well, it's the truth isn't it?"

"I know what we're up against," Deacon said. "We'll work it out."

"Ringers?" Henry muttered.

"The thought has crossed my mind."

"We're going to stop and see Julia, but we'd love to have you and your brother for dinner. Set up a time with Julia and let us know."

Deacon nodded. They seemed nice. He could see how a person like Julia, confident and generous, would come from a family like that. No doubt the Bradley family's school files were slim, well organized and full of the letter *A*.

DEACON AND WES had a lot of free time. Plans for the Jersey center were moving ahead full-steam and he didn't have a lot to do with the work now.

During weekdays before practice, they spent a fair bit of time messing around at the basket at the end of their street. Wes had moved a couple chairs onto the grass for any of the neighborhood kids who used the hoop, too, and Deacon decided a new net was needed.

On Sunday afternoon, he brought the net down to the hoop. The little boys were there and an older woman sat in one of Wes's chairs.

"Hey, Shawn," he called when Tali's brother ran up. "You guys have an audience today?"

"That's my grandma."

"Introduce me."

Shawn led him over to the woman, struggling out of her chair, but he crouched in front of her.

"Grandma, this is Coach Fallon. His brother, Coach Wes, has the superfast car. He's the one who let me beep the horn."

The Reader Service — Here's how it works:

Accepting your 2 free books and free gifts (gifts valued at approximately $10.00) places you under no obligation to buy anything. You may keep the books and gift and return the shipping statement marked "cancel." If you do not cancel, about a month later we'll send you 6 additional books and bill you just $4.69 each for the regular-print edition or $5.44 each for the larger-print edition in the U.S. or $5.24 each for the regular-print edition or $5.99 each for the larger-print edition in Canada. That's a savings of 15% off the cover price. It's quite a bargain! Shipping and handling is just 50¢ each in the U.S. and 75¢ each in Canada. You may cancel at any time, but if you choose to continue, every month we'll send you 6 more books, which you may either purchase at the discount price or return to us and cancel your subscription.

*Terms and prices subject to change without notice. Price does not include applicable taxes. Sales tax applicable in N.Y. Canadian residents will be charged applicable taxes. Offer not valid in Quebec. All orders subject to credit approval. Credit or debit balances in a customer's account(s) may be offset by any other outstanding balance owed by or to the customer. Offer available while quantities last. Please allow 4 to 6 weeks for delivery.

If offer card is missing write to: The Reader Service, P.O. Box 1867, Buffalo NY 14240-1867 or visit www.ReaderService.com

NO POSTAGE
NECESSARY
IF MAILED
IN THE
UNITED STATES

BUSINESS REPLY MAIL

FIRST-CLASS MAIL   PERMIT NO. 717   BUFFALO, NY

POSTAGE WILL BE PAID BY ADDRESSEE

THE READER SERVICE
PO BOX 1867
BUFFALO NY 14240-9952

Get FREE BOOKS and a FREE GIFT when you play the...

LAS VEGAS GAME

Just scratch off the gold box with a coin. Then check below to see the gifts you get!

YES! I have scratched off the gold box.
Please send me my **2 FREE BOOKS** and **gift for which I qualify.** I understand that I am under no obligation to purchase any books as explained on the back of this card.

▲ DETACH AND MAIL CARD TODAY! ▲

☐ **I prefer the regular-print edition**
135/336 HDL FNRR

☐ **I prefer the larger-print edition**
139/339 HDL FNRR

FIRST NAME | LAST NAME

ADDRESS

APT.# | CITY

STATE/PROV. | ZIP/POSTAL CODE

Worth TWO FREE BOOKS plus a BONUS Mystery Gift!

Worth TWO FREE BOOKS!

TRY AGAIN!

Offer limited to one per household and not applicable to series that subscriber is currently receiving. All orders subject to credit approval. Please allow 4 to 6 weeks for delivery.

Deacon held out his hand and she grasped it between both of hers. Her fingers were bent sideways, twisted by arthritis, but her palms were strong. "Your brother let these two make a ruckus with that car," she said. Wes had driven them home from practice the other day.

He started to apologize, but she laughed. "Little boys love a ruckus, don't they?"

"My brother sure seems to," he agreed.

"What's in the bag, Coach Fallon?"

"A new net."

He removed the net from the package and walked over to the hoop. Trey and Shawn and three other boys all crowded around. He'd forgotten until it was too late that he didn't own a ladder. He wasn't about to buy one just to put up the net, plus he'd climbed enough playground poles when he was a kid that he'd assumed this one would be a piece of cake.

"Let me shinny up, Coach. You're too big!" Trey said.

Deacon shook his head from his perch partway up the pole. He didn't like the looks of the rust on the pole or on the bolts for the backboard. No way would he let one of the little boys climb up there and he didn't trust it to hold his weight, either.

He climbed back down and gazed around. "I need somebody to hop onto my shoulders and put the net up."

Every hand went up and he realized he would have to pick one of the eager little volunteers and disappoint the others.

"Coach Bradley!" Trey yelled. "Check it out! Coach Fallon bought us a new net!"

Julia strolled across the last few yards of sidewalk.

"Hello, Mrs. Sedai," she called to Trey's grandma. "What's going on?"

He held up the net and said, "I'm just choosing a volunteer to help me hang this, but everybody wants to help." She read the plea in his words and held out her hand for the net.

"Okay, this has fifteen hooks and there are five of you. What's the fair way to split this job?"

"Oldest gets to do them all," Trey said. Shawn lowered his head, but Deacon grabbed his shoulders.

"Shawn, you behave," his grandmother said.

"We can each do four hooks," one of the other boys said.

"Four?" Julia held the net up so they could see the hooks. "Does that sound right?"

"Three," Trey corrected. "But I still think I should get extra, 'cause I'm the oldest. Shawn probably won't even be able to do it."

"Well, why don't we let him go first and we'll find out," Deacon said.

Julia bit her lip to keep from smiling at Trey's expression of outrage. "Always one step ahead of the ten-year-olds, aren't you, Deacon?"

"You got it."

He crouched and held his hands over his shoulders. Trey slid his feet across, grabbed Deacon's hands and squealed as he straightened. Julia was behind him, one hand on the back of his shirt and one supporting Trey until she was certain he was stable.

"Ready?" Deacon asked.

"Ready."

Trey did just fine with his section of the net, so Shawn only got to do three hooks. The boys were delighted when they finished the job and immediately began a fierce half-court game pitting Trey and Shawn against the other kids.

He and Julia retired to the chairs. Mrs. Sedai was on her way back to her house to get her roast on for Sunday dinner, her black purse hanging over one shoulder. "Tali tells me you're raising money to send those girls to the state tournament," she said. "I'll give you five dollars today. I might have a little bit more at the end of the season."

Julia pulled a membership card out of her backpack and carefully wrote it out for Mrs. Sedai.

"Is your team all full up?" she asked.

Deacon shook his head. "No, ma'am. You want to play?"

She swatted his arm. "I taught Tali's mom to play. If I were a few years younger, you'd be happy to have me. No. I have a great-niece. Naya. Her mom and dad drive her to Jericho to play on a team over there, but maybe she'd play here if she knew Deacon Fallon was coaching. I'll tell her."

"Great," Julia said. "We're in the gym every day at three."

After Mrs. Sedai had gone, Deacon said, "How'd we do last night?"

"Well, with your friend's hundred dollars and my mom and brother kicking in again, we're close to eight hundred bucks."

He kept his eyes on the kids as he said quietly, "I can pay for the trip, you know." He hated to flaunt his money, but not much use in having it if he couldn't spend it when he wanted to. The budget for the trip would hardly bankrupt him.

"That's so generous, but wouldn't it mean more, not

just to the girls but to Milton, if we did this with help from everyone?"

"I knew you were going to say that."

"You know what you could do with five thousand dollars, though? If you have it lying around?"

"What?"

"Fix up this little park. Give the kids a nice place to play, with some seats for the older people." She patted the arms of the plastic lawn chair. "And I include myself in that group."

Deacon gave her a high five. "That's a brilliant idea. Maybe we'll call it Coach Bradley Memorial Park."

He immediately phoned Victor.

"Hey," he said.

"Hey," Victor answered. "How are the Milton Lady Tigers?"

"They're not the Lady Tigers, just Tigers," Deacon said. "And they still stink. We're willing to hire WNBA players if you can find a few to pass as high school girls."

"Got it. What's up?"

"Do we have any money in our charitable-gifts budget at the business?"

Julia flashed him a thumbs-up.

"We don't have a charitable gifts budget."

"Well, if we made one, could I get some money out of it?"

"What are you gifting?"

"A little pavement. Some posts." He turned so he could see the rest of the area. "A couple benches. Maybe some bushes. A fence."

"Are you building a hot tub?"

"A basketball court. Half-court, really."

"Now you don't just need players—you're building your own court?"

"Not exactly."

He explained the situation and Victor was all over the idea, just as Deacon had expected he would be.

"I'll find out who we need to talk to in Milton about permits or permissions or whatever and get everything sent to me."

Deacon felt the familiar stab of embarrassment and quickly shot a look at Julia to be sure she hadn't overheard. Victor didn't think anything of it. Of course he was the one who'd deal with the paperwork; after all, he was the one who could read. Confronting his own stupidity made him impatient. He wondered how Vic had stood it all these years.

He recovered as they went over the details, and by the time they'd finished, he was pumped in a way he hadn't been since they'd opened their first rehab center.

He hung up with Victor, and without thinking about it, he put his arm around Julia's shoulders. As soon as he touched her, he realized what he'd done. She was warm and soft tucked against his side, and her hair was cool and silky where it touched his wrist. She stiffened at first, but then relaxed into him.

He shouldn't have hugged her, but since he'd gone this far, he let himself bend his head to kiss her hair. "Thank you," he whispered. "That was fun."

Her arm snaked around his waist. He bit his lip when he felt her fingers tug on his shirt. She felt the way he'd imagined, and at the same time like nothing he'd ever expected. Her size and shape weren't surprising but the prickling awareness of her that ran up and down his side, his thigh, his chest, his arm, anywhere she touched him, was nothing he'd ever felt.

"I really didn't look at your file, Deacon. I wouldn't do that."

He bit his lip. "Okay."

She shifted her weight and her thigh pressed tighter against his side.

"Julia," he murmured. "Please."

He didn't know exactly what he wanted from her, but she faced him and that was right. He drew her tight against him, feeling her arms around both sides of his waist now.

He lowered his head, his lips finding hers waiting for him. Her lips were firm and warm and he kissed her with a ferocity he hadn't anticipated, nipping her bottom lip between his teeth, holding her steady before he released her to kiss again.

He brought his hands up between her and him. She was wearing a zip-up jacket, and if he could unzip it and get his hands inside—

"Yeah, we owned you, baby!" Trey's shout of joy when his team won the game woke Deacon up. He broke off the kiss and stepped back. Julia's eyes were unfocused and she shivered at the loss of his warmth.

"I don't know what that was. I…I was just happy," he said. "About the court. And you. Giving me the idea. I was happy about working together."

"Working together? I should go. Thank you."

"Thank you?" he repeated.

"You're the one who said 'working together.'"

"I apologize."

"Then not thank you. More, um, wow." Her face lit up. "Wow. Like fireworks. Yep. That's what I meant."

CHAPTER NINE

THE KIDS ALL had to head home for dinner, so Deacon
was alone at the court, thinking about fireworks and
Julia, when Wes walked up, on his cell.

"I don't care what anyone says," Wes said into the
phone. "Our deal hasn't changed."

He glanced at Deacon, lifting his chin in acknowledgment.

"If I go, you go, man." Wes sounded angry. "I'll take
care of it."

Wes turned his shoulder slightly, seeking a measure
of privacy, maybe subconsciously. Deacon fetched the
ball out of the bushes to give him some room.

"When I get back, we'll handle it," Wes said into the
phone. "I promise."

He spoke for a few more seconds, then shut off the
phone.

"Was that Oliver?"

Wes didn't look as though he was going to answer,
so Deacon tossed the ball to him to distract him. His
brother took two steps backward and then shot. The
ball bounced off the rear of the rim and Deacon ran
after it.

When he pivoted to pass it back to Wes, his brother
was crying.

Not crying crying. But his eyes were red and he
was... Oh, hell, he was crying.

"Wes?"

"Goddamn it." Wes spun around and slammed his hands over his eyes. When he spoke, his voice was muffled. "It was Oliver. They're kicking him off the basketball floor in the dorm. By the time I get back, he'll be living in one of the regular freshmen dorms."

"He should have been in one of the regular dorms from the start," Deacon said. "He's not on the basketball team."

"I liked living with a guy who wasn't on the team," Wes said. "But thanks to me, he's now suspended and homeless."

"You're blaming yourself because he accepted money to do your work?"

Wes pivoted back around and he wasn't crying anymore. "I'm not blaming myself for anything. I'm stating a fact. Thanks to me, Oliver is suspended and homeless."

"He wrote your paper. Nobody forced him to." Deacon paused. "Did they?"

"Are you serious? You think I forced him to help me?"

"I don't know, Wes. None of this makes any sense to me."

"Deacon, we weren't cheating. It was a joke." Wes crossed the pavement and grabbed the ball. He dribbled back to the center of the road and shot.

Wes kept shooting and rebounding for himself. Deacon watched him work, understanding how the physical release would make it easier to talk.

"The homework he did was a paper for my sports literature class. I was supposed to write a three-paragraph 'essay' describing my personal reaction to the movie *Rocky*."

Wes stopped speaking, looking to him for a response, but Deacon was unsure what to say. No chance Wes had been covering up some problem with school all this time, right? He didn't need Oliver to do his work for him?

"I don't get it. You're a decent writer. Did you run out of time?"

"No. I told you. It was a joke. The assignment was a joke. The class is a joke. Who knew they'd care who wrote the damn paragraphs about *Rocky?* Deacon, it's a literature class and all we did was watch sports movies. After *Rocky,* they're watching *Slapshot.*"

The classic hockey movie was one of Deacon's favorites. Paul Newman was outstanding in that one. Wes saw Deacon start to grin and cut him off.

"I was pissed because the class was constructed to give the sports teams an easy English credit. I know I'm no Einstein, but I can read a stupid book in my stupid literature class, can't I?" Wes tossed the ball at the basket, and when it missed, he grabbed the rebound and stuffed it. "Oliver and I were joking around about what some of the guys might write, and he did this priceless imitation of Canoski, the third-string center. I dared him to write it up, and then as a joke I handed the paper in with my name on it."

Wes grabbed the ball and threw it with a sidearm pass toward the bushes behind the basket. It hit the pole instead and rebounded toward them, then rolled to a stop near Deacon.

"The only reason they added it into the suspension is that Coach wanted Oliver off the floor. I can't believe that paper is the reason he's getting kicked out of our room. When I go back, I'm going to be alone—the class is such a farce, Deacon, that I swear you'd get an A."

Deacon felt as if Wes had slapped him. His emotions must have registered on his face, because Wes said, "I didn't mean that the way it sounded. I just meant because you haven't been in school in a long time."

"Of course not." Nobody ever meant it when they made jokes about GEDs or SAT scores or high school dropouts in front of him. They didn't think about him that way. Deacon Fallon skipped college on purpose for the NBA. Who cared if he'd barely passed English, or had been excused from his foreign-language requirement entirely, or had taken two separate shop classes senior year?

He picked up the ball from the street and started for the house. "Find out if Oliver wants me to call someone for him. Doesn't sound like he should have been suspended."

"Deacon, I said I didn't mean it," Wes said. "I'm sorry."

"I know," he said. "I get it." He did get it. All too well. There would be things people like Wes and Vic and Julia—hell, Trey and Shawn—could do that he couldn't. All kinds of ways they'd never be able to connect. He got it. And he hated it.

ON MONDAY AFTER practice, Deacon unlocked the front door while Wes flipped open the mailbox.

"Hey look, Deacon," Wes said. "A letter for you."

His brother tossed the black envelope to him with a little flick as he went past him into the house. Deacon let the front door close so he could open the letter in private. If Wes were there, he'd want to know what it said.

It wasn't a letter, he thought as he pulled the white card edged in yellow and black out of the envelope. It was an invitation. The Tigers logo in the top-right corner told him it was from the school. He held it up, focusing on one line at a time as he pieced together some of the words.

He was invited to a boosters party. He got that much. When he'd been in school, they always had a midseason event at Coach Simon's house. Deacon guessed they'd carried on the tradition.

He saw the phone number on the RSVP line. No way in hell he wanted to go. He'd decline the invite, but it was a little late to call a stranger's number tonight. He'd take care of it tomorrow.

Inside, Wes was sitting on a stool at the kitchen counter. He had his own invitation open in front of him. "You going?" he asked.

"Absolutely not," Deacon said.

"I bet Julia's invited, and I bet she makes you go," Wes said.

"First, Julia can't 'make' me do anything." Wes snorted, but Deacon ignored him. "And second, why would she want to go to a boosters party? She hates the boosters."

"If she goes, she can rub you in their faces. They stole her funding and she got Deacon Fallon to come back to Milton and coach. She won't miss parading you around that party. I guarantee it."

"I bet she's not invited in the first place," Deacon said. But Wes was right—Julia would not want to pass up that chance. "From everything I've seen, Ty would happily murder her."

"Any chance you'll go if she doesn't force you?"

Deacon shook his head.

"That's why they'll invite her."

His little brother could be some sort of master spy. How did he understand so much about the underbelly of human motivations?

Before he had a chance to counter Wes's points, his phone rang. Julia's picture popped up on the display. "Hello?"

"You brought a suit with you, right?"

THE BOYS' TEAM showed up at practice the next day. Their workouts in the gym didn't begin until her time ended at four o'clock. Before that they lifted or did conditioning in the machine room. They didn't come into the gym ever until after the girls had gone.

She didn't notice them, didn't know they were there until Max dropped a pass and she heard mocking laughter behind her.

"Way to go, Maxine!"

"Look out, or you'll get cut from this team, too."

More laughter rang out as Max scrambled after the ball, his face red. The boys were standing bunched up in a group near the doors, every one of them in a black Milton Tigers warm-up outfit. She knew most of them and even had a good relationship with a few of them as individuals, but she'd seen the psychological damage the Tigers inflicted when they moved as a team on some victim—a boy who'd crossed them, some kid with a defect or difference, or a girl they had decided to single out.

Max recovered the ball and faced the team.

"Hey, Tali, why are you hanging around with Maxine? I thought you had better taste."

Max glanced at Tali but then away when she tossed her hair forward and refused to meet his eye.

Julia started across the gym, intent on telling the boys they had to leave.

Deacon caught up to her just as she reached the group.

"I'll handle this," she said.

"I'm right with you." Deacon blew his whistle. "Tigers, take five."

The girls stopped their drill, but they didn't leave the gym. Miri, Max and Cora edged toward them. Wes jogged over and halted next to his brother.

"What do you need, guys?" she asked the group.

Neil Reuss, a tall, muscular kid with an outsize ego and a poor understanding of boundaries, said, "Coach Simon told us Deacon Fallon was running the girls' team, but we didn't believe him."

"Coach wouldn't lie to you, would he?" Julia smiled.

None of the boys acknowledged her.

Deacon smiled at them, but then said, "This is a closed practice. I told Coach Simon folks require written permission to attend."

"You're really Deacon Fallon?" Neil asked.

"I really am."

There was a stalemate. The boys' team obviously hadn't thought through their plan and they were at a loss. Julia hoped they would decide to leave on their own.

"I'm really his brother," Wes said. "Isn't that really cool?"

Seth Farris, a tall, skinny freshman, snorted. He shrugged when Neil glared at him.

"You guys want autographs? I can put a word in for you."

Neil crossed his arms, but a couple of the guys inched away from him, Seth in the lead. Apparently more than one of them just happened to be carrying a Sharpie and a basketball.

"Line up here," Wes said.

Julia looked at Deacon, but he lifted his hands to indicate he had no idea how to control his brother.

"Coach Bradley, will you hand these young men a booster membership after they fork over their five-dollar donations? Max! Tali!" Wes yelled. "You stand here." He pulled Max over next to Deacon, making it physically obviously that they were in collaboration. "Collect the money. Tali, you stand next to him and make sure everyone pays."

Neil stormed out of the gym and slammed the doors behind him. Most of the rest of the team lined up where Wes told them. They stepped forward one by one, handing their money to Max—which Tali counted—getting a booster card from Julia, and passing their basketballs over to Deacon to sign.

Seth, the first in line, asked Deacon to write "To Seth" on the ball, but Deacon said firmly, "No person-alizations. We have a practice to run."

She watched him sign for each boy, his signature messy and basically illegible, but nevertheless satis-fying to the Tigers.

After the signing, Wes told the boys that now that they were official Milton Girls Basketball Boosters, they were welcome to attend the last fifteen minutes of each Friday practice for a little instruction from Coach Fallon, and that they were expected to show up for the home games.

The boys' team lit up when he mentioned the time with Deacon, but didn't look so happy about the game attendance. She gave Wes points for creativity, though.

Once the boys had left, Julia drew him aside. "You're brilliant, Coach Wes. Thank you."

The smile he had for her could only be described as sunny.

He blew his whistle and got the girls back to work. Deacon scowled at his hands, which were splotched with black ink.

"Your brother just made us another fifty bucks. Evil genius, it seems, runs in the family."

That wiped the frown off his face. He watched Wes, who was blowing his whistle repeatedly at Tali as she sauntered back from the water fountain. "He's all right, isn't he?"

"Yep." In fact, they all were. At that moment the whole ridiculous team was doing a-okay.

THEY GOT A win against Carlisle Academy, the weakest team in the league, who couldn't guard Tali well enough to stop her from scoring fourteen points. Cora bagged another four and the hapless Carlisle Academy Flippers went down.

The next week, they lost again. Deacon was pretty sure that was the nail in the coffin of their season. The season wasn't that long, and he had enough information to predict the outcome of almost every game.

On the Sunday after their second loss, he poured himself a third cup of coffee and got out his board to see if he could figure out some small, statistically improbable but nonetheless viable way they could still get to States.

"What is that?" Julia inquired.

He wheeled from his board, startled that she'd walked in without him hearing.

"Wes told me you were back here in the kitchen. He said it was okay if I came in."

"It's fine. You just surprised me."

She peered around him. "Did you make that?" she asked, pointing to the large sheet of poster board.

He nodded. He thought better when he could touch information and move it around. On the board, he'd placed the logos he'd printed out for each team in the league and lined out the schedules. Each team had a color dot associated with it.

"It's the season, right?"

He stepped back and let her view it more closely.

"What do the colors indicate? Red, yellow, green? Oh, I get it…if we have a chance against them or not."

Deacon nodded anew. "We needed that win on Friday, Julia," he said. "Without that one…" He stared at the board, unwilling to look at her as he gave her the bad news. "I don't see a way for us to get to States."

"We can beat Carlisle Academy again," she said.

"But they're going to lose both games against Leeds. It won't help our record."

"We're not even halfway through the season," she said. "You can't give up on them."

"I'm not," he snapped. "I'm trying to plan, that's all."

"Planning to lose."

"I'm not planning to lose, Julia. I'm looking at this season realistically and maybe readjusting the goals to see what we can make of it."

"Readjusting the goals how?"

"Maybe thinking about a different way to measure success. We started out with the bet and we both have plenty of reasons to show Ty up, but maybe States is not in the cards for this team this year."

She pressed one of the logos back on the board. "We can win this," she said. "I know we can."

"And I'm telling you it's looking really unlikely from a mathematical, logical point of view."

She shook her head. "You're not allowed to give up on them," she said. "Don't even think about it."

"I'm not giving up on them," he answered. "I just want you to be sure you're clear about who wants to win this thing and why. Because from where I'm sitting, this is about you deciding what success is for this team, and maybe that's not the only way to look at it."

"What?"

"You're so stubborn, Julia. And that's a good thing. But you are so sure you're right and you keep poking at people to make them change. To make them be the way you want. Maybe that's not fair to the kids. That's all I'm saying."

"That's *all?*" She emphasized the last word, and he heard the hurt in her tone.

"Julia, listen…"

"No, you listen," she said. "I'm good at my job. You had an experience with me a long time ago. I was new. I was young. I'm not even sure I was wrong."

"For me, for my life? You were wrong."

She shook her head. "We're going in circles here, Deacon. I'm taking off."

DEACON PUT HIS suit out on the bed and then checked his black dress shoes. He'd go over them with a rag before he left, but they didn't need a polish. He'd attended to that earlier.

If it had been up to him, he'd have skipped the boosters party, but since Wes had been right and Julia was making him go—scratch that, he'd decided to go because it mattered to Julia—he had to admit he was looking forward for one reason.

The last time he'd been to this midseason party, he'd been a gangly, punk-ass high schooler with no money, no security and no power. He'd needed the boosters and they knew it. Sure, they needed him, too, but the relationship hadn't been balanced at all.

Now he was going back there, to Coach Simon's house, to face those same people, and now he had something they didn't: he'd made it. Up and out and into the NBA, and who cared if his career had lasted less than five years. Every guy he met at the party would know he'd lived their dream. No one could take that away from him.

Even better, this time he'd have Julia Bradley on his arm. The only thing left to work out was convincing his brother to stay home. He wouldn't be able to enjoy rubbing his success in anyone's face if he was worried about Wes.

Twenty minutes later, the Fallons completed negotiations. In exchange for a solo excursion to the boosters party, Deacon would purchase a round-trip plane ticket for Wes's friend Oliver to visit them. He'd do the laundry for the next month. (What Wes didn't know about the fluff-and-fold service wouldn't hurt him.) And he'd give Max Wright a one-hour private ball-handling lesson.

After they shook on the terms, Deacon said, "I'd have given Max the lesson for nothing. He just needed to ask."

"That's all right. I called in my 'no' response for the party as soon as I opened the invite."

"You were never planning to go?"

"Nope. But Oliver will be psyched about the plane ticket."

Wes barely dodged the pillow Deacon threw at his head.

His little brother was a devious twerp, but it didn't really matter. Deacon was going to the party with Julia. It would be just the two of them. Exactly how he wanted it.

JULIA HAD CONSULTED about fashion with a friend of hers who used to be in the boosters before she got transferred away from Milton. Her friend had recommended something totally sexy. The guys in the boosters were basically cavemen, she said, so while Julia might want to be so cool, sophisticated and elegant that they'd be intimidated and awed by her, that look would go right over their thick heads.

Julia unzipped the storage bag where she kept the dress Allison gave her last year for her birthday. Her sister was the queen of the "I want you to have *this*" gift. She didn't care what *you* wanted because she was convinced *she* knew better. Her success rate with such gifts wasn't as high as she liked to believe, but Julia had to admit, Allison had a phenomenal eye and she did get her choice right fairly often.

Julia pulled out the dress and held it up in front of her full-length mirror.

"Oh glory be, Allison. I'm surprised this thing didn't set my closet on fire!"

Allison clearly did not believe in hiding one's assets. The dress was like a sin right on the hanger.

Julia stripped off the gray pants and black top she'd worn to work and shimmied into the dress. It was red, but a deep shade close to violet. The halter top left her back bare and sat daringly low. When she'd first tried the dress on, she'd been surprised that the shantung silk fabric, while structured, also managed to cling to her curves, skimming her breasts and accenting the flow of her waist and hips.

She'd decided that as she was already putting up with the boosters, she might as well go for the total head-to-toe torture. She slipped on the peep-toe booties she'd bought on sale earlier that week.

She did a quick spin, checking herself in the mirror. The boosters wouldn't know what hit them.

She and Deacon hadn't discussed their kiss. It was as if it had never happened. Except, it hovered between them every second they were together.

No one, not the drummer, not any of her boyfriends, had ever set her off balance with a kiss. Deacon did. She'd almost let him put his hands inside her clothes right there in plain view at the basketball hoop on Briar Street with Trey and Shawn and a whole bunch of other elementary school boys watching.

She did not do things like that. Yet with Deacon she did.

When she walked into the boosters party tonight, she'd have both the Fallons with her, one on each arm. She was delighted at this. It would be tremendous. She'd be the focus of so much envy she wouldn't be surprised if someone developed green spots.

Yet a tiny part of her wished she could go with just Deacon. Not that she didn't love Wes. She just wanted to know what might happen if she and Deacon and the sin dress spent the evening alone together.

THE MINUTE SHE opened her front door and he saw what she was wearing, he needed all his self-control not to push her back against the wall and strip the silk dress right off her.

He did kiss her. He couldn't help himself. He put his lips on hers and lingered, smoothing his tongue across her mouth, sucking and nipping and savoring each taste while he let the tips of his fingers skim under the fabric of the dress. He already knew from her backless dress that she wasn't wearing a bra. Her nipples stiffened and she moaned into his mouth.

"Deacon. Please."

It was what he'd said to her at the park.

Neither could say what they wanted. They just knew they wanted it from each other.

He cupped her breasts outside the fabric, leaving his thumbs underneath, gently pressing with his nails into her soft flesh. He wasn't hurting her, but she knew he was there. She felt his need.

She was the one who managed to disengage.

As he drove to Coach Simon's house, he kept his hand on her knee.

Coach and his wife had moved since Deacon had lived with them, so he wasn't walking back into a familiar home, but it sure did feel as if he'd been sucked into a time warp. So many of the same names and faces at this party as ten years ago when he'd played for Milton. Coach Simon's wife gave him a kiss when he came in, but the kind of air kiss he hated. If you didn't know someone well enough to give a real kiss, lip to skin, what was the sense in this fake air kissing? He managed to get away from her without having to really talk to her.

She knew he blamed her for sending Wes away and he knew she blamed him for making her a foster parent in the first place. The less time they spent in each other's company, the better.

Julia was killing it in her dress and heels. He and Julia had gotten separated when they walked in and he kept getting waylaid by people who remembered him, so he hadn't been able to catch back up with her. But he saw her. The dress set off her pale skin and warm brown hair perfectly. The majority of the women at the party were wearing black, and they probably all wanted to kick themselves for not choosing the kind of bold color Julia had. She didn't understand halfway. That excited him—and terrified him, too.

He took a glass of water from a passing waiter and sipped it as he looked over the crowd to where she was standing with several older guys. He admired the gorgeous V of skin that insane dress exposed, and remembered what it felt like to put his hand on her bare flesh. He wondered how it would feel to tug on the crossed ties at her neck. If he undid them, there would be nothing between him and—

"Deacon! I heard you were back, but I didn't believe it."

"Cory Miller," Deacon said. "Man. Good to see you."

"Ten years," Cory said. "That's a long time."

Cory hadn't changed much since high school. His dark red hair still stood on end in a bristly buzz cut and his pale skin was still freckled. Maybe there were a few lines around his eyes and mouth, but Cory was such a good-natured guy Deacon figured they were mostly from smiling, not age.

"So you're a booster now?"

Cory shrugged. "You know how it is. You stick around Milton, this is what you do. Of course, you

didn't have the chance to be one of our fine supporters while you were off in the NBA."

"Couldn't have done it without my number-one re-
bounder," he said. Cory had been the closest thing he
had to a friend in high school. They hadn't actually
hung out—he hadn't hung out with anyone. But the guy
had such enthusiasm for everything he'd managed to
draw Deacon out of his worries and kept him updated
on the gossip on their team members and the scoop
about their opponents. He'd been a connection to the
real life the other kids at Milton were leading. "What
are you doing these days?"

He and Cory managed to find a semiprivate spot
in the hallway leading from the living room to the
kitchen. They were interrupted once or twice by a
guest edging past toward the powder room, but they
had time for Cory to tell him about his wife, a woman
he'd met in college, and their twin baby girls. He'd
moved back to Milton to work in his father's insurance
agency. Most of the guys at this party owned their own
businesses, were retired or worked long-distance jobs
that let them make money when so much of Milton was
poor. Cory caught him up on most of the guys from
their old team, and Deacon was amazed that their faces
came back to him so easily once his old friend mentioned a name. A few of them were apparently at the
party and he'd have to be sure to look for them.

"So I heard you pissed off Ty Chambers," Cory said.
"You're coaching the girls?"

"Ms. Bradley called me out of the blue and asked me
to come back." He almost told Cory that he'd thought
she meant the boys' team, but he held back. Cory had
been a decent guy back in high school, but even in the
short time Deacon been in Milton, he'd seen how much

anger Ty had about Julia. He wouldn't risk letting it get out that she'd tricked him. That was between the two of them. "My brother needed something to do before going back to school next semester, so I figured what the hell."

"What the hell, huh?" Cory took a sip from his bottle of Miller Lite. "Must be nice not to have to work."

Deacon shook his head. "I work. It's nice to have flexibility, that's all."

"Too bad you couldn't come back from your shoulder, though."

He knew there were still rumors that he'd quit, had been intimidated by the play in the NBA and not lived up to his potential. But Cory didn't seem to have an agenda. Deacon didn't sense any insincerity. "Yeah. Sucked." He looked around, but they were still semi-isolated. "Hey, listen, since you're the kind of guy who joins stuff like this, you want to join the girls' basketball boosters? We guarantee good seats at our games."

"That's because no one comes."

"It's only five bucks."

After he pocketed Cory's cash, he glanced around for Julia. She'd kill him if she knew he was checking up on her, but he'd do it anyway. This crowd was full of barracudas. He was about to take off, when he realized Cory might have the answer to something that had been bugging him.

"Can I ask you something on the down low?"

"What do you mean?"

"You know how things are at the high school. I need some information, but I don't want certain people to find out I'm asking. There's a kid involved who doesn't need any negative attention."

"Sure." Cory nodded. He'd always been a stand-up guy and no one else seemed willing or able to tell him what he needed, so Deacon decided to trust him.

"You know a kid named Max Wright?"

Cory gave a short laugh and shook his head. "Your instinct to keep his name out of the conversation at this party was a good one."

"What's the story?" Deacon braced himself to hear what he suspected, that the kid was gay and Coach Simon didn't want him in the locker room, but Cory's answer surprised him.

"Max and his dad moved here last summer. His dad is a producer from Hollywood and they have more money than they know what to do with as far as I can tell. They bought a bunch of acreage and built a place out near the state forest. Ty and Coach Simon must have thought fate had finally smiled on them again, because this talented kid with a dad rolling in dough just fell in their laps." Cory leaned in. "I heard Ty was getting set to accept bids for a new weight room. He was sure they were getting a big gift."

"And?" Deacon asked.

"They invited Max's dad out to schmooze him and the guy turned them down flat. Told them he wasn't interested in contributing. They moved here so Max could experience public school the same way everyone else in America did. He picked up the check the night they met at the Pond for drinks, but that's the last dime they've gotten out of him."

"They cut that kid because his dad wouldn't give them money?"

"They cut him because his dad humiliated them."

Man. He'd been psyching himself up to go to the mat for the kid over homophobia, and instead the problem was money and the egos of the stupid Milton boosters. They played with kids' lives and never took responsibility for the damage they caused.

A lucky thing he and Cory were sequestered in this hallway, because if Ty Chambers or Coach Simon had been in his sight just then, he'd have been tempted to punch them.

"Max is too good to sit out his high school career. What happened to the youth league?" Milton had always had a town league separate from the school teams. Most of the jayvee team played on a youth league team, too, while they were honing their skills before they made varsity. "When I asked Max about it, he said he didn't know anything about it."

"We haven't had the youth league in about four years. No money. Everything's been cut to the bone." Cory rubbed his thumb and index finger together. "Some kids go over to Jericho to play. How did you meet Max, anyway?"

"He's practicing with my team," Deacon said. When he'd said "my team," he'd felt a surge of pride, which surprised him. They might stink, but at least kids weren't turned away for no good reason.

"Shoot, Deacon. First Ms. Bradley forced them to fund her team because she threatened a lawsuit. Then she brought you back without a word to the big boys. Now she's aiding and abetting the basketball career of Max Wright in their gym, under their noses? She must have a death wish."

"Did you see her dress?" Deacon asked.

Cory nodded and had another sip from his bottle.

"I suspect she wore that on purpose to screw with them."

Deacon raised his water glass and Cory knocked his

bottle against the lip. "Go, Ms. Bradley," Cory said. They both drank deeply.

"I'm going to find her."

"Go, Deacon."

CHAPTER TEN

TY TOUCHED HER. He pretended it was an accident. He even looked over his shoulder to see who had jostled him and forced his thick-fingered hand into contact with her breast. But she knew he'd done it on purpose.

"Sorry about that, Julia. Lost my balance." He wiped his fingers deliberately on a cocktail napkin and she knew he'd not only done it on purpose but also wanted her to know it.

She wished she hadn't worn Allison's gift dress. She'd worn her sin dress to this party with Deacon to show the Milton sports bigwigs she had everything she needed and they couldn't take it from her, and Ty had found a way to shift the balance and make her feel trashy.

She wasn't sure what she would have said to him if Deacon hadn't suddenly been there at her side. "I was looking for you," he said quietly.

Ty put on his one-of-the-guys smile and asked him, "You having a good time? Got everything you need?"

Deacon's voice was flat when he said, "I do." Julia glanced up and his eyes had gone dark the way they had the other day when he found out she'd kept the truth from him about Max. He was furious about something, though she didn't know what.

Ty didn't seem to notice. He turned his head and then motioned to Coach Simon, who'd been talking to a group of women near the bar. As Coach made his way toward them, Ty said, "We've gotten off to kind of a rough start since you've been back, Deacon, and Coach and I want to make it up to you."

Coach Simon was wearing a black sport coat with a yellow pocket square and a Tiger Pride tie. "We want to take you out to dinner. This party isn't the place to talk, but we want to lock down a date when the three of us can get together and really connect. We have a lot of ideas and we'd just really like to get some one-on-one time with you. What do you say, Deacon?"

"I say no, thanks."

Ty's smile dropped faster than it would have if Deacon had punched him.

Deacon went on, "I get it. I do. You guys feel you helped me out…made me what I am…and maybe you did. But I don't owe you. You got what you needed from me when I played for Milton, and I got what I wanted. Now I figure I'm more of a free agent."

That piece of information settled among them like a stink bomb.

Coach Simon took off the gloves. "You were a punk when I met you," he said. "And now you're an ungrateful punk."

"As long as we all know where we stand," Deacon said. "Julia?" He gestured toward the door. "You ready to go?"

She'd never been more ready in her life.

She turned and he put his hand on her back. His touch was warm and firm against her skin, and within seconds it had obliterated all memory of Ty's unwanted advance. She moved through the crowd without seeing anyone; it was as if she'd been reduced to the spot of skin where Deacon's fingers rested. He reached past her to open the door and she leaned back slightly, wanting him to spread his hand, wanting to encourage him to explore further, maybe slide his hand around her side and under the silk of her dress.

He shut the door behind them and she missed the contact with his hand, but he turned back and this time he put his arm across her shoulders, pressing her against his side the way he had the day they'd kissed at the park. The fabric of his suit was rough on her bare skin and her nipples tightened in response to the touch of his hand on her bare arm.

She shivered.

"I don't suppose this dress came with any kind of coat," he said.

"No."

He pulled her closer still as they walked down the driveway toward his car. "It would have ruined the effect, I guess."

"I'm not sure it had the effect I intended, anyway," she said.

"Oh, it had the right effect," Deacon said. Then he stopped and drew her in front of him. He opened his sport coat and wrapped the sides around her. Her arms went around his waist and she was pressed against his tie, her senses full of the taste and feel of Deacon Fallon. "It was extremely effective," he said. "Trust me."

When she moved against him, she felt his erection and she couldn't help a wicked smile.

"I don't care about impressing the boosters anymore. There's just one old Tiger I'm interested in."

"Who are you calling old, *Ms. Bradley?*" he growled.

She laughed, lifting her face to his, ready for the kiss he brought. "Go, Tigers," she said.

THEY BARELY MADE it in her front door. As soon as she flipped on the lamp, he had his hands up under her hair and was tugging open the ties of her dress. He didn't let the halter top fall, though. He took his time, holding the ties with one hand behind and then ever so tenderly drawing them down, over her collarbones to the tops of her breasts, then down again until her nipples were just exposed.

He dipped his head to her right breast, licking and then suddenly pulling the nipple into his mouth. He tightened both hands on her breasts, testing their weight, letting his thumb rub over her left nipple while he kept teasing and tasting her right.

"Deacon. In the bedroom. I don't have curtains in here."

He followed her down the short hallway. Her bed was covered in white lace, with piles of white lace pillows, and a fluffy white rug lay on the floor. The walls were painted a pale, silvery gray and bookcases were everywhere, up both sides of the two windows and lining the low wall where the roof sloped. She had more books in one bookcase in her room than his parents had owned in their entire lifetimes.

He stopped in the doorway. He didn't belong here. He was an illiterate jock faking his way through life, and she was, well… She was Julia Bradley. If she ever knew the truth about him, she wouldn't want him anymore.

He tried to pull away, gently taking his hands off her, attempting to knot the tie of her dress until she raised her hands to hold it in place. "I should go."

"Deacon, no. Please. I don't...I don't want to be alone." She was holding her dress up and she looked so vulnerable and so incredibly gorgeous.

"I want you to touch me everywhere, Deacon. Please."

She let the straps of her dress fall and he saw her round, taut breasts, tipped with pink nipples that had felt perfect inside his mouth.

His body responded to her invitation. He forced himself not to think about anything but their two bodies meeting.

He kissed her neck while he followed the V of the dress down to her waist, then plunged his hand inside to feel the smooth skin of her naked backside.

A thin strip of fabric around her waist caught his thumb. He murmured against her lips, "Are you wearing a thong?"

When she nodded, he felt his erection straining hard against his pants.

"I can't... I have to..." He pressed against her and she understood. She unbuckled his belt and unbuttoned his pants. Soon enough she'd shoved them and his boxers to the floor. He stepped out of them at the same time as he dragged her dress down over her hips, leaving her only in a sinful, black thong.

He had to look away for a minute, to recover so he didn't embarrass himself.

"Deacon, you're beautiful."

She ran her hands up over his stomach to his chest, then followed the line of his shoulders, down his arms, and took his hands in hers to lead him to the bed.

He focused on her eyes, not letting himself think about anything else as she drew back the lace coverlet and they lay down on the sheets.

"Do you have something?" He didn't have a condom with him. He hadn't expected to wind up here. Luckily, she did. Once she'd pulled it on him, she rolled onto her back. He raised up over her, holding himself on his forearms.

"Can you take off your glasses?" she asked. "Just for a second. And then you can put them back on."

"I don't need them when we're this close," he said. He removed them and laid them on her nightstand on top of a dog-eared book lying facedown, waiting for her to pick it back up. He focused on her eyes again. She was there and he was there and nothing else mattered.

For the next few hours, nothing else did matter as they explored and learned each other's bodies. Finally, he was completely done in and she was lying sprawled across the bed, her gorgeous ass tilted up where one leg draped across his thigh and her head pillowed on his chest.

"I always said you were gifted," Julia murmured. "Nobody moves like Deacon Fallon."

He smiled down at her and kissed the top of her head. "This was a team effort, Coach. Don't forget your contributions." He let his hand slip down to her ass and squeeze. He didn't know where her thong had ended up, but he would never forget seeing it for the first time.

"So," she said. "That happened."

"Yes, it did."

"What are we going to do about it?"

Forgetting it ever happened seemed like the safest choice, even if it was impossible.

Talking about it and figuring out what it meant made him feel queasy just thinking about it.

They settled on doing it again to be sure it really felt as good as they'd thought.

This time when they were finished they both went straight to sleep.

He woke up just as it was turning light out and used the bathroom. He considered climbing back into bed with her, but he couldn't pretend anymore. He'd done his best last night to focus just on her body, on the moment in time. Now that he could see the outside world again, he knew he had to go. She didn't wake up when he sneaked out and down the steps to his car.

Wes was asleep in his recliner when he let himself in the back door. His brother opened one eye and took in Deacon's half-dressed state.

"You and Coach Bradley?"

"You're having a nightmare, Wes. Go back to sleep."

His brother closed his eyes obediently, but then opened one to peer at him as he climbed the stairs. "I can tell what's real and what's not, D. Just so you know."

WHEN SHE GOT up, she wasn't surprised that he was gone. She'd half expected it, actually. He'd shared his body with her. She stretched and let herself savor *that* memory for a minute. But he wouldn't let her into his life that easily. She hoped he knew she had her own thoughts about what should happen next.

AT PRACTICE ON the following Wednesday, he had to admit it. The girls weren't getting any better. If it had been possible, he mused, they'd have gotten worse. Lucky for him they'd already been totally freaking awful when he'd come on board, so there was no way to get even worse.

He blew his whistle and waved Max off the court. "You go sit. They let you do all the work and then in the games when you're not there, they don't know what to do."

Max scowled, but he hit the bench. If Deacon had had a whole team of compliant, talented Maxes, he wouldn't have had an issue.

He did not have that kind of team.

"What is up with this craziness?" Tali scowled and then balanced the ball on her hip, tapping her perfectly manicured nails impatiently. "Are you benching my top scorer just to even things out with this little scrimmage? We're winning, Coach. Don't mess with that."

"You need to learn to score for yourself, Tali."

"Why do I need to learn that when I can pass it to my man Maxie and he scores for me?" Tali gave a high five to Cora. "That's called resource management. We learned about it in business studies."

"I'm thrilled you're paying attention in class, Tali, but Max doesn't count as a resource since he's not actually on...the...team." He didn't shout at her, which he counted as a win. However, he was boiling inside.

He blew the whistle again and got the girls moving, but they still stunk and he was still frustrated.

By the time the scrimmage ended, he was so mad he could barely see straight. The girls weren't trying. If they'd show up and play, he might be able to do something with them, but they had an attitude that said none of it mattered, and sure enough, it didn't. Not to them.

Julia paced the sideline next to him, tense and anxious. The season mattered to her, all right. On Sunday, he'd decided he would call her and tell her they should pretend that what happened never did. He thought they could go back to their former, nonsexual, cocoaching relationship. But she'd appeared on his front porch before he could phone, and somehow he'd ended up kissing her again.

She was a very good kisser and her body had been right there. He liked her body. Liked it very much.

So it was Wednesday and they'd slept together two more times and he didn't know what to do about any of that, but he did know this basketball team stunk.

Maybe some good old-fashioned pain-then-shame drills would work.

"Line up on the baseline," he yelled. "We're running suicides. The team that won the scrimmage runs until I say stop and the losers do an extra five after that."

Julia glanced up at him, ready to protest, but she said nothing. Wes lined up next to Miri, and Max sprinted over to line up next to Wes, with Trey and Shawn right beside him. He almost yanked the four of them off the line since they weren't part of the team, but then he decided they might as well run, too. Max could use the conditioning, Trey and Shawn the energy release, and it was Wes's business if he wanted to be on the coaching side of the line or messing around, trying to be everybody's buddy.

Deacon whistled and they started. He watched his brother joking with Miri as she struggled to keep up. "If you cheat, even by an inch, I'm sending the whole team for another round."

They ran. Julia paced. She gave him a couple of looks that he interpreted as pleas for leniency, but he ignored her, and she let the drills go until he was ready to call them in.

He blew his whistle and Tali's team staggered to the benches. Cora lay flat on the floor, arms flopped wide. Tali put her head between her knees, hands crossed on the back of her neck. The gym was silent except for the sounds of panting. Trey and Shawn were lying on top of each other, totally limp. He'd never seen them so still.

He blew his whistle once more and sent the losing team off for another round. Miri let out a little sob, but she ran, Wes and Max pacing her on both sides.

When it was over, the team lay sprawled on the benches and floor. He gave them less than a minute before he strode over and stood in the middle of them. Looking at their faces, he doubted he'd be able to do it again, but he followed through on his original plan. They'd endured the pain; he owed them the shame. Maybe if he took what he'd said all the way, they wouldn't need another session.

He projected his voice when he spoke, not yelling but nevertheless filling the gym.

"We can't keep playing this way and expect to get anywhere close to States," he said. "You don't come to play. You don't put forth your best efforts. Tali, last game you missed a pass because your hair was all over your face. Real ballplayers pull their hair back. Cora, you downed an entire bag of chips during warm-ups on Saturday. That's not good for your body, but it *sucks* for our team. You can't play with grease in your veins. Every one of you needs to learn to take yourselves seriously, because if you don't, I guarantee you your opponents won't, either. I want you all to go home and think about what it'll take for you to bring a new attitude with you tomorrow. And then I want you to show up ready to work."

Wes raised his hand. Deacon ignored him.

Wes said, "Excuse me, Coach?"

Deacon kept ignoring him.

Wes tooted his whistle. He didn't even blow it properly, which might have had some proper lowering effect coming at the end of a shaming speech. He tooted it. As though he was being cute.

Deacon thought he might strangle his brother, but Julia jumped in. "Yes, Coach Wes?"

"I have a suggestion."

Julia and Wes both looked at him. It was a little late for them to be asking permission to interfere with the pain-then-shame approach, but he managed to sound fairly civil when he said, "What?"

"We need a dance."

"A dance?"

"Yeah," Wes said. "Like in sports movies—they all have dances. *Remember the Titans*." Wes did some goofy move that involved his arms. "*Glee* did 'Put a Ring on It.'"

"We're having enough trouble learning the fast break, Wes. This is a basketball team, not a dance troupe."

"Well, the basketball part hasn't worked out that great so far," Julia said.

Listening to this conversation, the girls were starting to shift around. The interest he saw on their faces told him he'd lost any momentum that might have been building toward shame. They were supposed to be contemplating their suckiness, not feeling better because their precious Coach Wes wanted to dance with them. Now for sure he'd kill his brother.

His brother dribbled under his legs, then tossed the ball to roll it down his arm behind his neck. "Remember you used to show me those Harlem Globetrotter moves and we'd make up routines?"

"Wait," Cora said. "Coach made up dances with you?"

"It was basketball, not dancing," he said.

"Right, so we'll do basketball in our dance," Wes countered.

Deacon gave Wes a look that he hoped would clearly convey both his opinion that his brother had lost his mind and his desire for his brother to shut the hell up.

"Like *High School Musical*," Julia offered.

"Exactly," Wes answered. "Just like that."

"You've watched *High School Musical?*" Deacon asked. He thought that made-for-TV Disney movie was strictly for little girls.

"Anyone who had a girlfriend in 2005 watched *High School Musical*, Deacon," Wes said. "It was an unavoidable phenomenon."

He turned to Julia, hoping she could help him get this conversation back on track, but she shrugged and said, "I didn't even have a girlfriend, and I watched it three times. It's actually a decent movie, and I rewound the dance scenes more than once. This might be fun."

"Fun is not something we're having trouble with," Deacon said. "We need basketball skills."

"That's what I'm saying," Wes said. "Watch."

He took the ball and did a set of tricky maneuvers, passing it between his legs, behind his back, dribbling it low and high, and ending by spinning it on his index finger.

The entire team was standing by the time he finished, and they exploded in cheers and whistles. "That was awesome," Max said.

The idea of coaching his basketball team using a dance routine lifted from a tween movie made him want to kick something. The girls shouldn't need this kind of distraction to care about the game. But he watched as his brother spun the ball again, and Wes's smile was genuine and happy—sunny, just as his teacher had said all those years ago. The girls watched him, a thousand times more engaged than they'd been in any of the drills Deacon had demonstrated for them. Julia clapped for his brother, her eyes sparkling as she circled her hips and started a cheer of "Go, Wes! Go, Wes!"

Deacon had no idea whether this would get them any closer to winning, but he'd take the joy he saw right here as a win for today.

"Fine," he said. "You show up on time for practice tomorrow. Each one of you runs the fast-break drill without a mistake. Miri makes at least two free throws. And then you can work on your dance." He blew his whistle. "Hit the showers."

They raced for the door, their exhaustion from the pain part of the program totally forgotten. He heard Tali tell Cora that they needed to get on YouTube immediately and check out some moves to practice. Miri reappeared in the gym a minute later, tugging Max by the elbow. Deacon couldn't hear what she said to him, but he guessed it was a demand for free-throw lessons, because the two of them lined up on the foul line and she started shooting.

Granted, she was still shooting far short of the basket, her balls landing with freakish precision four or five feet short of the net. But she was working on it, which was more than she'd done in the first few weeks of practice.

Wes was near the door, his arms crossed as he observed Max and Miri.

"This dance thing is your baby," Deacon said to

him. "You manage it. You keep them focused. You work it out."

"Thanks, Deacon," he said.

Wes went outside to get the car, and Julia, who'd been hovering nearby, approached. "This'll be great for them," she said. "They're not used to practicing the way you've been working them."

"I'm not the one who made that bet."

"I know," she said. "I'm not criticizing. I actually think you and Wes make a really good team."

"It's not teamwork if he undermines me every time I try to get something done."

"He's not undermining you," Julia said. "The girls need you to keep them honest and to push them. They need him to remind them that it's okay to be kids. You're a good team," she repeated.

That time he let the matter go, let the words sink in. Maybe she was right. Maybe he and Wes *could* work together.

"You heading out?" he asked.

"In a minute." She started toward the ball rack. "I have to count the balls. If we're doing this dance thing, we don't have nearly enough."

Of course not, he thought. Why would a basketball team need enough balls to give one to every kid at practice? How many times in her day did she run into this kind of tricky bullshit that made whatever help she was attempting to provide practically impossible to implement?

Another of Miri's shots landed behind him and he heard Max shout, "Keep your eyes on the back of the rim."

"I'll buy the balls," he said.

"I don't want you to do that," Julia said. "We're already taking advantage by having you coach for free. We can't expect you to pick up the tab for equipment, too."

"I want to," he said. "It's not taking advantage if I offer."

"Yes, it is."

He recognized the signs of extreme Bradley stubbornness kicking in. "Fine," he said. "I won't buy them."

"Good." She nodded and turned back to the rack of balls, squeezing each one to test its viability as a practice ball.

"I'm going to apply for a grant. My buddy Victor is affiliated with a foundation run by a former NBA player that funds small half-court playgrounds for at-risk youth and lazy women who like to sit on benches. I'm sure he'll be able to get the balls to me by tomorrow." Deacon put his hands in his pockets and adopted a thoughtful expression as he pretended to study the basketballs. "I think my grant application will specify pink balls. No. Pink and white stripes."

She spun back to face him. She was mad he'd gotten the best of her, but she couldn't tell him no. He gave her an innocent grin and said, "My Tigers are fond of the color pink."

"Your Tigers are fond of pink. You're…"

She grabbed his hand and tugged him around the back of the bleachers, out of sight of the free-throw lesson. Before his eyes adjusted to the low light, she reached up and pulled his head down so she could kiss him quick and hard on the mouth.

"You're impossible," she said. "Thank you." He didn't draw back, enjoying the way her small, warm hands felt in his hair, her right thumb sliding against his jaw.

She kissed him again and this time he was ready. He wasn't standing passive. He met her kiss, caressing her lips with his own as he brought his hands up to her hips, then settling his fingers at the flare of her waist. She took half a step forward and pulled him closer. Her hands were more insistent where they tangled in the hair at the back of his neck, and she trapped his lips against hers.

He opened his mouth and she responded. Her lips parted and she darted her tongue into his mouth. He stroked down, running his hands over the curve of her bottom, testing the muscles, all while he savored the kiss.

She broke away, moving back enough that he saw the sheen of sweat at her hairline and the moisture on her lips.

"Captain of the Tigers four years running and I never once kissed a girl under the bleachers," he whispered. "I was missing out."

"It was the mustache, Deacon. Even the most die-hard Tiger fan would have been put off by that scraggly thing."

"That mustache took me months to grow. It was misunderstood."

"It was tragic," she said. And then she kissed him again. When she pulled back the next time, she tilted her forehead against his chin and murmured, "Thanks." Then she backed away and left the gym. He wasn't sure where she'd gone, but he was afraid he'd need to find her. He'd felt the definite outline of a thong under her jeans and he couldn't let it go to waste.

HE WAS AS good as his word, but then, Julia had expected nothing less. Four cases of pink-and-white basketballs were delivered to the front office at noon the next day. Ty called her on the loudspeaker.

When she got to the office, he was standing in front of the balls with his arms crossed over his chest. "What's this? How did you pay for this equipment?"

"I'm not exactly sure," she said. "Coach Fallon arranged for them."

"Deacon bought balls for the team?"

"He said he was applying for a grant."

Ty's face was red. "Get them out of here. They're blocking the fire evacuation path."

Sweating to move the cases by herself was a small price to pay for the satisfaction she felt at upsetting the principal.

The girls met Deacon's conditions perfectly. You could have heard a pin drop in the gym when Miri went to the line to shoot her free throws, but after the second one went in, the entire place echoed with cheers.

Julia passed out the new balls, prompting a second round of cheers. Cora and Miri actually hugged Deacon, which made him look adorably uncomfortable. She'd like to hug him herself.

Trey and Shawn worked the iPod that they'd hooked up to a set of speakers, and the girls started planning their dance. She and Deacon leaned against the wall, observing as Wes demonstrated moves, and they did their best to copy him.

The door opened and a dark-haired girl slipped inside the gym. She watched the team for a few seconds. Julia leaned around Deacon and waved to her. "Hi. Can we help you?"

"Nothing...I thought this was going to be basketball

practice." She hesitated, squinting back at the dancing, but then noticed Deacon. "Oh. *You're* Deacon Fallon."

He nodded.

"You look better without that mustache." She jerked her thumb over her shoulder in the approximate direction of the lobby trophy case.

"Thank you," he said.

The girl glanced from him to the dancing on the court and back again.

"Are you looking for somebody?"

She took a deep breath. "Is it too late to try out for the team?" she asked. "My grandma said Deacon Fallon was back, and I want to play for him. It's, like, my dream come true."

"Oh! You're Mrs. Sedai's granddaughter. She mentioned you might come by. Sure," Julia said. "What's your name?"

"Naya Contini. I'm a senior."

Deacon got a better look at her. "You're not related to Freddy Contini, are you?"

"My cousin. I used to come to your games when I was very small. Freddy lets me watch his videos from your senior season. I've wanted to meet you for a long time."

"So you've been playing in Jericho?" Julia asked. "Is it possible you know what you're doing?"

She was joking when she said it, but Deacon said, "Freddy was pretty darn good. You got any of his moves?"

She held out her hands. "Just give me a ball."

They walked her to the opposite end of the court from the dance and Deacon put her through her paces. When she was finished and they'd told her she was a bona fide member of the team, she jumped and screamed.

Deacon introduced her to Wes. She got caught up in the spirit of the dance soon enough, and not only did she turn out to be their very first legitimate, experienced and gifted basketball player, she could dance.

As she was heading home that afternoon, for the first time in a while Julia felt hopeful about the season.

"THAT NEW GIRL is good," Wes said. "Where'd you find her?"

"She found us," Deacon said as he drove the car into the garage. "Apparently she used to come to my games way back when dinosaurs roamed the earth."

Wes put his hand over his mouth.

"What?"

"I'm holding in my old jokes."

"Ha." Deacon got out. The way Naya talked about his playing days as if they were ancient history, as if he was some kind of blast from the past, had been disconcerting. But that didn't matter in the long run, he supposed. If they got Naya and Tali working together, they were that much closer to putting some points on the board.

CHAPTER ELEVEN

AT THEIR NEXT GAME, several members of the boys' team filed in before the pregame warm-ups even started. Cory Miller turned up with his brother and their wives and kids. Naya's parents came. Her dad asked if it was okay for him to tape the game—he was putting together her highlight loop for colleges. Obviously, he had film from her other team in Jericho, but being complete didn't hurt.

Right before tip-off, Naya's cousin Freddy, who'd been on the team with Deacon and Cory, showed up. Freddy had a few of the other guys from their team in tow and Deacon shook hands all around.

The girls did their dance before warm-ups. Trey and Shawn were in the stands with a knot of their elementary school buddies and they all followed along. The Milton fans applauded enthusiastically and the girls even got a smattering of cheering from the Carlisle side of the gym.

Miri passed around the boosters' donation coffee can, and when it came back to them, it was heavier than it had ever been. Julia lifted the lid and peeked inside. The can was stuffed with bills. Before going out for the tip-off, Tali retied her sneakers and then, with a band she'd had on her wrist, pulled her hair back in a tight ponytail.

The game got off to a bad start, and she tried not to

think about how much worse it felt to lose in front of all these people—when they'd lost before, at least no one had been there watching.

But then, right before halftime, Naya and Tali started to click. Deacon leaned over to point this out, but Julia had noticed the new pace of the game, even if she didn't understand what had changed.

The Tigers were playing together for the first time, and that made a huge difference regarding how much the other team could focus on Tali. She made a couple of shots, but she also fed the ball to Naya as if they'd been doing it all their lives. Miri got fouled and she made both shots. Tali shot twice and dished Naya a gorgeous pass off the fast break. By the time Naya leaped over the head of the opposing center to tap in a rebound, they were ahead at the half for the first time all season.

They took a four-point lead into the locker room and didn't lose it. When the final buzzer sounded, their Tigers had put up a second win.

Deacon treated them all to ice cream at the Pond afterward. The restaurant was packed with fans, excited from the game, calling out to one another. She wondered if this excitement was what Ty or Coach Simon felt after one of their games. Was this energy the thing that made them care so much?

She stayed at the Pond until the very last fan had gone home. She didn't want to miss one second of the good times.

CHRISTMAS MORNING. A few days earlier, Wes had bought a small tree, which he'd propped up in the corner of the living room in a bucket of water. He strung it with blinking lights and put a star on top.

When he told the girls about his tree, they showed up the next day with an assortment of decorations—a box of candy canes, a ceramic sneaker, some plastic foliage Julia later told him was mistletoe and a basketball key chain that Max said would look exactly like an ornament once they stuck it on the tree. Max was wrong—it looked exactly like a key chain hanging on a Christmas tree, but Wes left it.

Deacon had never spent Christmas with a girlfriend and as he lay in bed with Julia, he thought about the day ahead. When they'd made their plan to volunteer at the soup kitchen in the morning before heading to her mom's house for dinner, spending the night together had made sense. Obviously. He enjoyed making love to her, but that was a given. The trouble was, the rest of the day struck him as a very bad idea. He still wasn't comfortable in her apartment here in Milton. Why did she think he'd fit in with her family in Jericho? Her brother and sister were coming from Manhattan and he had a really, really bad feeling about the whole thing.

He'd actually considered canceling, but his life and Julia's were so entangled now. How could he break up with her when he saw her every day at practice? He could ditch the team, but they had just hit their stride, and he didn't have it in him to do that.

Past experience told him that inertia was an awful reason for continuing a relationship, but that wasn't all he had with Julia. She was generous in bed and out. She seemed to love Wes and the way she thought about his brother was helping Deacon see Wes differently. Had she been anyone else, he'd be thinking of ways to keep her happy, rather than wondering if he should break things off.

But she wasn't. She was Julia Bradley. He knew her

and she knew him. She'd seen where he'd come from. She'd known him when he was a desperate kid. He'd yet to catch her giving up on a project or a plan for improving someone's life. All it would take was one slip and she'd know he couldn't read. Then he'd become a job for her and his new relationship with her, with Wes, everything would come crashing down.

She had her back to him at the moment, and the sheets between them were cold. Athletes ranked about as high as Italian grandmothers on the list of People Who Are Superstitious. He looked at the space between Julia and him and he didn't like it. It was a bad omen.

Instead of inching closer to her, he got out and walked around the bed. He put his head under the covers and lifted her nightgown carefully, then woke her up with his tongue. He savored her smell and taste and reveled in the powerful orgasm he gave her. At least here in bed, he knew exactly what he was doing.

Deacon showered and then got dressed in the early-morning gloom in his room while Julia took her shower. He put on gray flannel dress pants and a blue sport coat, even though she'd told him he didn't have to dress up. He rolled a tie carefully and stuck it in his pocket.

After Julia emerged from the bathroom, he crossed the hall and banged on Wes's door. He heard a muffled insult and he banged again. "Don't be rude to me, or I won't give you your present, you ungrateful twerp."

Wes's pillow hit the bedroom door and Deacon laughed. "Merry Christmas!"

He brought Wes's gift and Julia's downstairs with him and stuck them under the tree. Two gift bags already sat there, the tops stapled closed. His name was written on one tag and Julia's on the other.

He put coffee on to brew. Hearing the shower running again upstairs, he poured three cups. When he got back to the living room, Wes was sprawled on the couch, holding the box from Deacon on his chest. He was dressed in jeans and a button-down shirt, his dark hair curled damp across his forehead.

"Time to open my present?" he asked.

"Wait for Julia to come down."

"Here I am," she called. She had on a short red skirt and a black V-neck shirt that distracted him momentarily. Her breasts weren't huge, but they were perfectly shaped and sat up high.

"Go for it," Deacon said to Wes, then sat in the chair near the window and tugged Julia onto his lap. The leather was cool against his back from the outdoor air seeping in around the poorly sealed window frame, but she was warm and soft on top of him.

Wes ripped the paper off the box and raised the lid. He pulled out the warm-up jacket Deacon had ordered for him with the Tigers logo on the back and 'Coach Wes' embroidered in yellow script over the chest.

Wes lifted out the jacket, then turned it to see the front and back. Deacon couldn't tell if he liked it or not. Wes put it on and patted the front. "This gift is inspired," he said. "I couldn't have picked better myself."

His brother grabbed the gift bags from under the tree and tossed one to him. "Surprise."

When Deacon opened the bag, he found the identical jacket, but his said Coach Fallon and the embroidery was in block capitals, not script.

"This is hilarious," he said.

Wes handed Julia the remaining two gifts under the tree.

"You didn't have to get me presents," she said.

"If we hadn't, you'd have complained and you know it," Deacon said.

She opened the bag first.

"That's from me," Wes said.

"You did a fine job with the staples."

"Deacon's a peeker. You can't trust him."

Deacon smacked him on the back of the head.

She pulled the bag open and found her own warm-up jacket inside. "Perfect!" she said as she tugged it on. "I didn't want to say anything, but I was jealous that I didn't have a jacket."

Wes nodded. "Everyone will be jealous when they see our jackets."

"The other coaches will be demoralized before the games even start," she agreed as she tore the wrapping paper off the box.

"That's my present," Deacon said. "You can tell me later that you like it better than Wes's."

As soon as she opened the box and saw the second warm-up jacket, she grinned. "I feel like I'm coaching with the Bobbsey Twins."

"I can return it," Deacon said.

"You cannot. It's customized," she said, pulling on the first jacket, the one with the cursive script. "These jackets are mine forever."

She grabbed Wes and gave him a kiss on the cheek. "Thanks, Coach Wes," she said. When she turned to Deacon, his eyes gazed hungrily on her mouth. She put her hands on either side of his face and drew him to her, letting her lips linger for a beat too long. He drank in her smell and the taste of her skin. "Merry Christmas, Coach."

He leaned into her kiss and whispered, "Merry Christmas, Coach."

Julia got up to refill her coffee, and Deacon stood and crossed the small living room to look out the front window. The Tigers logo on the back of her jacket seemed to glow in the weak light coming in from the porch.

"How about us—having Christmas in Milton again."

"How about it," Wes said. "I don't remember a single other one from when we lived here. Isn't that weird? The first one I remember was after you signed the NBA contract and Mrs. Smith made that disgusting casserole thing for dinner."

"She probably saved the pot brownies for her real friends."

Julia sat down near the tree. She was wearing both jackets, one on top of the other.

Wes stretched out on the couch. "But I have this super-strange memory of spending one Christmas at the police station. It must have been a dream or maybe a movie I saw or something."

Deacon didn't have to tell him. He could keep it to himself and let Wes think he was remembering wrong. But he'd promised himself he'd see this through.

"That's a real memory," he said quietly.

"What? Are you kidding?" Wes faced him.

Deacon took a sip of his coffee.

"After we got split up, you were with a family who lived on Route 9, outside Milton. You were only five, but you were getting good at running away. So Christmas morning, I guess they weren't paying attention and you sneaked out. You made it about three miles down the highway before the police picked you up. You really don't remember this?"

"I remember being in the police car, but like I said,

I thought it was a dream or something. And I remember you were with me."

"I was. The social worker called me to see if I knew where you were and I made her come get me so I could help look for you. When they picked you up, I rode in the car with you to the station."

Deacon stood and paced the length of the room. He leaned against the window, gazing out again. "Not the worst day of my life, but it ranked right up there."

"So what happened?" Wes asked.

Deacon shrugged. "They sent us home. You were so pissed. You thought…you know…that you'd found me and that was that…we would be back together."

Wes shook his head. "Nope, I don't remember any of that."

"Good," Deacon said. "That's what I wanted."

He went into the kitchen. "How about eggs and bacon, you guys?"

"Sounds great," Julia replied. She came up behind him and leaned her forehead into his back as she locked her arms around his stomach.

"What didn't you tell him?" she asked.

That the foster mom showed up at jail and screamed that Wes was more trouble than he was worth and if they thought she'd take him back home when she was already looking after four other kids, they were mistaken. That Wes screamed right back at her, and Deacon was the one who ended up getting slapped when he stepped in between her and Wes.

That after she left, he and Wes played checkers with the police officers all day until the social worker found an emergency placement. Someone brought them chips from the vending machine and hot chocolate. At the end of the day, he went back home to Christmas dinner with Coach Simon, while his little brother got sent off to try to fit into yet another stranger's house.

"Just a bunch of stupid, sad details he doesn't need to know. I'll tell you something nobody knows." Deacon covered her hands with one of his. "I couldn't believe Coach wouldn't let him live with us. I mean, his daughter had a kid and the house was cramped, but he was five freaking years old. They had room for me, and I was tall and ate a lot more than Wes. Except I was useful to his team. Anyway, when he took me home, I went into the garage and broke his table saw. He never knew I did it."

"You broke his table saw?"

"I used a pry bar to split the arm right off it. He thought his daughter hit it with her car."

"That's awesome."

It hadn't felt awesome. It had felt weak. He'd been so furious with his parents for dying, with his coach for being selfish, with himself for not being able to bring Wes home. All he wanted to do that night was hurt the people who'd let his little brother down. Breaking the table saw hadn't done anything to fix the situation.

THE MORNING AT the soup kitchen passed quickly. Wes found a Santa hat and a set of jingle bells, which he put around his neck. He sang carols and spouted lines from Christmas specials in lieu of actual conversation. His goofy enthusiasm charmed the other volunteers and the breakfast visitors. Julia knew several of the people in the line, and she introduced Wes to some of them. He had a natural curiosity about people that smoothed any awkwardness arising from the difference in their situations.

When the jobs were assigned, Deacon opted to work

in the back. He sliced bread, cracked eggs, peeled pota-
toes and poured juice. Toward the end of the shift after
all the food had been prepped, he emerged from the
kitchen and joined Wes and Julia in the serving line.

An older woman with stringy hair and the deeply
wrinkled face of a lifetime smoker came through. Her
hands shook as she accepted the tray from Wes. Julia
noticed a large tattoo on the back of the woman's wrist.
It made her think of the logo of a band, but she couldn't
pull up the right name. Deacon supported the shaking
tray as he put a mug of coffee on it. He glanced at the
tattoo, then looked sharply at the woman's face.

"Reggie?" He sounded slightly unsure. The woman
nodded. He leaned toward her. "It's Deacon. Deacon
Fallon."

"Good God, Deacon. Of course it is. It's been years
since I saw you. You still look just like your mom."

He took her tray from her, hovering awkwardly
close to her as if he thought he should hug her but
didn't know how to go about it. "How have you been?"

Reggie coughed and eyed her ratty sweatpants and
winter jacket shiny with age. "About the same."

Deacon hesitated.

Reggie said, "How have you been? Life's treating
you good?"

"Good." He gestured to his brother. "Wes, this is
Reggie Carday. She was mom's really good friend.
They did practically everything together."

"Wes Fallon." Reggie smiled as Wes shook her hand.
"You're the spitting image of your dad." She held his
hand between both her own. "He was a handsome man
but didn't have an ounce of sense in him."

Wes looked down. Julia didn't like the implication
that Wes's physical resemblance to his father meant

anything about their personalities or gifts. "Wes and Deacon are coaching the girls' team at the high school this winter. They volunteered after the funding got cut."

"At Milton High School?"

Julia said, "We wouldn't be able to get along without them."

"You should have seen this one play when he was a kid," Reggie told Julia. "Tall like his dad, but his mom was the one who played basketball. Our team wasn't that serious, but she was way better than all the rest of us."

"Mom played ball?" Wes said.

Deacon appeared unsure. "I don't know."

A man and woman carrying two toddlers joined the line, and they watched impatiently as Reggie spoke to the Fallons.

"Okay," she said. "Off I go. Nice to run into you guys again. Nice to remember your mom. Take care."

Deacon's voice was a gruff whisper when he answered, "You, too."

He kept her tray and walked with her as she made her way to a table. He bent sideways so he could listen to something she said. Julia pivoted to assist the family with the toddlers get their meals. When she glanced up again, Deacon was nowhere in sight. She touched Wes's wrist. "I'm going to find your brother."

Wes nodded. "Meeting people who knew me back then is so weird. My memory is mostly blank and they fill in these things I never expected."

She forgot sometimes how young Wes had been when he lost his parents. "We have about ten more minutes. There are always stragglers, so call me if you need help."

She checked the kitchen but didn't see Deacon, so she ducked out the door into the parking lot. He was leaning against the building, his back against the wall, his face up to the morning sky. His hair and eyes, the perfect line of his jaw and neck, were beautiful to her. She'd never really noticed a man's neck before Deacon, but she had a real thing for his. The combination of strength and vulnerability, lean muscle and sensitive, smooth skin turned her on. She'd like to remember him in the pose he held now. But then she realized he wasn't admiring the clouds scudding high overhead; he was upset.

"What's going on?"

"Reggie was the prom queen or homecoming queen or Ms. Popularity or something. She and my mom graduated from high school together here in Milton. My mom had this picture of her and my dad at a dance—Reggie's in between them wearing some kind of little crown."

"She must have a hard life," Julia said. The woman eating inside had the face and posture of a seventy-year-old, but if Deacon was right, she couldn't be more than fifty.

"My mom was thirty-one when she died. I always thought it was a tragedy. She was out at a club and there was a fire. Reggie and the group they hung around with were all there, but Mom was in the restroom when it started and she got trapped. All these years and I never really thought about what would have happened if she hadn't died. What my life would have been. Or hers."

Julia wasn't sure what he was asking. "You can't know, Deacon. Guessing at things like that is a great way to make yourself crazy."

"Sometimes guessing's all you've got. I didn't even

know she played ball. Nobody ever mentioned it. I mean, she got pregnant with me when she was a junior, so she couldn't have played much, but still. I have this thing I do well and all this time it came from her."

He rolled his shoulders, lifting himself away from the wall. "We should get back in there and finish up."

He was so damn good at shutting down his feelings. She couldn't imagine how much he'd been hurt when he was a kid. Given his natural tendency to feel for people, the repeated losses and upsets he'd lived through must have left him reeling. It was a wonder he was still willing to risk new relationships. Yet he showed up every day, connecting with the kids, caring about them, being part of their lives...and hers.

A new crew of volunteers arrived to take over the breakfast cleanup. Reggie was gone. Julia grabbed her second warm-up jacket and stood near the door, waiting for Deacon and Wes to finish saying goodbye to the staff.

Someone banged on the door next to her and she opened it. A stack of boxes wobbled past. She caught a glimpse of a blond ponytail and then Max's dad was in the doorway, balancing his own stack of boxes full of groceries.

"Do you know where we should put our donations?" he asked. Julia didn't think he recognized her. They'd met only once, briefly, when Mr. Wright had registered Max at the beginning of the year.

"Straight down that hallway."

Boxes still balanced precariously, he followed Max toward the kitchen. She trailed along behind him. Mr. Wright was a taller, better-built version of Max. She wasn't a huge fan of long hair on men, but his blond ponytail gave him a slightly geeky look that combined with broad shoulders, warm brown eyes and slim hips, was very appealing. He had charmed her the one time they'd met—his intelligence and Hollywood charisma adding to the nice picture his good looks drew.

Max was stretching when they got to the kitchen, hands pressed to the small of his back. The boxes he'd been carrying sat on the table next to him.

"Hi, Coach...I mean, Ms. Bradley," Max said.

"Max," she said. "Good to see you. Are you here to help out?"

"We're on some cleanup crew or something."

Deacon and Wes noticed Max and joined them.

"Hey, Maxie," Wes said.

"I didn't realize you had so many friends here, Max," Mr. Wright said.

"You've met Ms. Bradley, Dad. She's the guidance counselor from school. And this is Deacon and Wes. They're my basketball coaches."

"A pleasure to meet you," Mr. Wright said. "Max talks about the team quite a bit."

"He's a good player," Deacon said. "Really good."

Max shifted his feet, glanced over his shoulder, then tugged his dad's sleeve. "We should get started. They're already partway finished."

Max and his dad were new in town, she remembered. And she'd already invited two strangers to her mom's house. Two more wouldn't be that much more work.

"Mr. Wright?"

"Please, call me Laurence."

"Laurence, then. Deacon and Wes are coming to my mother's house for the afternoon today. We'll have dinner and relax. You and Max are more than welcome."

When Laurence smiled, a deep dimple appeared next to his mouth. "I'm sure Max would enjoy that," he said. "I'd love to get to know you better." His gaze was steady and curious. "All of you."

Julia was driving herself to Jericho, and the Fallons were coming in their own car. On her way, she dialed her mom's phone. Her sister picked up.

"Hey," Julia said. "Will you tell Mom I invited two more people home with me?"

"What is this—the year of the stray?" Allison asked.

"No. And as a matter of fact, this guy I just invited is about your age, hot, single, smart and rich. You'll love him."

"You fixed me up on a blind date at my own mother's house on Christmas?"

"No. It's not a blind date. It's just dinner and the afternoon."

"Whatever, Julia. Keep him away from me and keep out of my business. I'm not one of your students."

ON THE WAY to Jericho, Deacon missed a stop sign and took an extremely steep curve at a reckless speed. His brother was never reckless. When he was little, other kids had always assumed he'd have fewer restrictions since his brother was raising him, but Deacon had been careful, controlled and cautious.

"Something bothering you?" Wes asked.

"No."

"Because if Mr. Laurence Wright gave my lady the once-over he did Julia, I would be pissed too, except I wouldn't endanger the life of my precious younger brother—"

"Wes?"

"Yep?"

"Shut up."

Wes wished it wasn't so cold. A ride this crazy in a car this fast was meant to happen with the top down.

"He's rich, as well. Tali told me she's hoping Max will fall in love with her because his dad is loaded. Although how she figures that will happen when she treats him like absolute dirt—"

"Wes!"

"Sorry."

He wasn't sorry, though. He liked needling Deacon. His older brother was entirely too serious and needed Wes's help to lighten up. When Deacon took another turn too fast, Wes decided to back off. If he wanted to make it alive to New Year's, maybe he should lay off the insults.

"Julia liked her jackets."

"She did," Deacon agreed. He glanced over his shoulder into the backseat of the car. "I bet Laurence doesn't have gifts for her family."

"How could he? They just got invited and it's Christmas. Nobody could get presents on such short notice when everything's closed."

WHICH WAS TRUE, of course, unless you were Laurence Wright, Hollywood producer. Then the laws of the universe didn't apply to you and you showed up with a beautiful, six-inch-square watercolor painting that Julia's mother loved because some guy named Jean Luc who not only had a show last year in a gallery in Manhattan she adored, but was also your neighbor in Hollywood, had painted it.

The Wrights appeared about half an hour after he and Wes did. Laurence handed Carole a small package wrapped in tissue paper and when she unwrapped the painting, Deacon's stomach sank. The boxes he'd brought in with him were piled under the Christmas tree next to the packages Julia and her family had wrapped for one another. He'd gotten Carole a box of candy. Granted, it was an incredibly nice box of candy, made by boutique chocolatiers in Lake Placid who used local, sustainable products, including mint grown in a New York City high school's garden. But it was still just a box of candy.

Julia's family home was comfortable, warm and plush the way places were when the families who lived there had been financially comfortable for a long time. The living room's two couches and several chairs were solidly built and upholstered in a mix of prints that coordinated without looking too overdone. The windows and polished wood floors were well maintained. Each room was full of memories—photos, art, beloved objects.

Julia's eldest brother, Geoff, offered them all drinks while they settled into the living room for hors d'oeuvres. Deacon had a Coke and Wes had sparkling water. Max asked for sparkling water, too.

Allison, who was taller than Julia and thin in a way that suggested hyperdedication to diet and exercise, announced it was time to exchange presents. It turned out that their family had a long-standing tradition of exchanging just one present. Books. Of course, Julia had made sure there was one for him and Wes.

She and Henry helped to distribute the wrapped packages to the right recipients. She apologized to the Wrights for not having one for them. Deacon's package was medium-size and heavy. Probably a hardcover. Julia had picked it out for him. What did she think he'd like to read?

A quick, deluded vision showed him tearing off the paper only to see a picture book, as if Julia knew all about him and would give him what he deserved.

That was ridiculous and unfair. Obviously she would never expose him in such a mean way. What the book was didn't matter much since he'd probably expose his own secret in a matter of minutes.

CHAPTER TWELVE

THE BOOK SAT cold and heavy in his lap while he waited his turn to unwrap it. His eyelids felt hot and itchy, and inside his head he had the odd but familiar sensation that his brain was unfocused. As if everything he knew, every competency he had, was evaporating. Once he had removed the wrapping paper and tried to read the title, the letters would dance and blur, the meaning slipping out of reach. Even if he recognized some of the words, he'd never be able to read them with any surety that he was getting them right.

Henry held up his book, which had a color photo of a baseball stadium on the cover. Deacon gripped his package a little harder, one finger nervously picking at the edge of the tape. Laurence leaned over to eye the book Allison had opened. He said something about the author, but the blood pounded in Deacon's ears and he couldn't hear.

Wes's book had a picture of a guy in a Yankee uniform from the fifties on the cover. Deacon was next up, and his skin went clammy with panic. He turned the book over while he gave one more look around the room, hoping for escape. Max was watching him, and Deacon had an inspiration.

"Here, buddy. You open it for me." Max tried to say no, but Deacon tossed him the book. "Kids should be the ones opening presents, not old guys like me."

Max tore the paper off and, as Deacon had hoped, held the book up and read out the title.

Julia scooted over to the end of the couch so she could touch his knee. "You haven't read this one, have you?"

"No," he managed to say.

Laurence took the book from Max and opened the cover to read the inside flap. "I read this last month. The review in the *New Yorker* intrigued me. It reminded me of Alan Furst," he said. Because if you were a freaking Hollywood producer with long blond hair and the build to intimidate anyone who thought about calling you a girl, of course you liked to read, too.

"I saw that review," Julia said. "That's probably what made me pick it up when I was shopping." She smiled at Deacon, open, honest and completely unaware of what a failure he was. "I hope you'll like it."

He couldn't sit there next to her, lying to her face. He didn't belong here. The rest of them, even Max, were all on the same path, doing the same kinds of things, and he was an outsider. Too stupid to belong with people like them.

Laurence handed him the book.

"I'm sure it's great," Deacon said. "Hey. I left my phone in the car and a good friend might call. I'll be right back."

He hurried outside and opened the car door. He tossed the book onto the front seat. Max had said the title was *Winter's Fury*. The picture on the front was a blur of shadowy shapes in the snow. He couldn't tell what the book might be about. If he left it in the car, he wouldn't have to discuss it. He could pretend to forget what it was about if anyone asked and Julia would answer...or Laurence, since he'd already read it.

Deacon had been irritated with Max's dad ever since the boosters party. He couldn't understand why the guy would throw his own kid to the wolves over his ideas about what sports should be. If Laurence had written out a stupid check, Max would be on the boys' team, where he belonged. Now that Deacon had met Laurence, he decided he didn't like him at all.

JULIA WENT TO the kitchen to help her mother bring the dishes to the table. She was surprised when Wes and Max appeared a few moments later.

"You guys don't have to help," she said. "You're guests."

"We're not real big on family holidays," Wes said. "This is fun for me."

"Me, too," Max added.

She handed Max an ice bucket and a pitcher of water, and he headed off to fill glasses. Wes hovered next to Carole, who was taking dishes out of the warming oven and passing them to him to place on the table. As she tossed some pine nuts into her roasted asparagus, Julia kept listening for Deacon to return, but he hadn't come in before she was finished. Maybe he'd gotten that call from his friend, or had received a message he needed to respond to. He'd seemed off while they were opening their gifts. She wished she knew what was wrong.

When her dish was ready, she followed her mom through the swinging door.

Geoff was at the far end of the table, with his girlfriend, Tamara, next to him. Carole sat at the near end.

She said it was good for the cook to be close to the swinging door to the kitchen.

There were two empty seats at the table, one next to Laurence and the other across the table between Allison and Max. Julia was certain Max would prefer to sit next to Deacon, so she took the spot next to Laurence.

Deacon didn't look at her when he walked in. He slid into the remaining empty chair and sipped his water, but his face was shut down. Maybe he was still upset about seeing his mom's friend.

Henry said grace before they ate. He remembered to ask for blessings for the Tigers and Julia muttered, "Especially the girl Tigers." When Henry had finished, he said she'd probably negated his whole prayer by affixing an exclusionary clause to it.

"She didn't exclude anyone," Max said. "Just clarified the terms."

Laurence said, "I didn't realize you were also a coach, Julia. Do the three of you share strategies?"

Good Lord! Laurence thought Max was playing on a boys' team coached by Deacon and Wes. She didn't know how to answer the question, but Wes saved her.

"We talk shop all the time," he said. "Did Max tell me you produced *The Last Good Spy?*"

She glanced at Max, but he wouldn't meet her eyes. Deacon seemed to be glaring at Laurence. She needed to sort this all out, but not during her mother's Christmas dinner.

The conversation ranged wide, from Laurence's insider scoop on the shoot for the most recent movie he'd worked on, to Carole's description of a story quilt she'd seen in a museum in New York and the four generations of women it described.

Finally, Carole put two trays of cookies down, one at

either end of the table. Henry turned to Deacon. "I've never met anyone who played pro ball. Of course, we all talked about it when we were kids—Geoff was sure he was going to the NFL. When did you know you wanted to go pro? I mean, not when did you know, but when did you start to think you might really be able to do it?"

"I don't remember a time when I *wasn't* aiming for the NBA. Just like anybody, I guess, you find something you're good at and do more of it."

He'd left out practically every detail that mattered. Because of a natural privacy or something else? Julia couldn't tell.

"Unless you grow up with a guidance counselor," Allison said. "Then you take test after quiz after interest inventory until you've determined exactly which career will suit you best."

"So all of you except Julia are best suited to practicing law?" Laurence asked. He leaned back in his chair so he could angle his body toward her. "Were you and your dad surprised your career planning headed along such a different path?"

Carole answered. "Julia was ten when my husband died. At the funeral she announced she was going to follow in her daddy's footsteps. She's never looked back."

"And she's been bending students to her will ever since," Allison said. "Julia is one of the few people I've met who thinks there's a way to win at life planning."

Julia was willing to let the insult go, but Deacon leaped to her defense.

"An awful lot of the kids who attend Milton don't grow up in circumstances like this," he said. "They need someone like Julia pushing them, exposing them to possibilities for themselves. Most of the guys I hung out with didn't have anyone at home who talked to them about college, let alone gave them an interest inventory."

"Yet you didn't go to college," Allison said. "Julia, remember how devastated you were you couldn't change his mind?"

"Allison, you're being totally inappropriate," Julia snapped. "Enough."

Carole stood. "Why don't we leave the dishes and go into the other room for a game? Who wants to play Scattergories?"

Deacon pushed his chair back from the table. Julia wanted to get a second to speak to him privately, but before she could, Laurence said to his son, "See, Max? That's why I turned the boosters down. Sports are entirely too important to some people. You have to focus on your education."

Deacon pulled his head back almost as if he'd been slapped. When he spoke, he made an effort to sound casual, but the anger behind his words was clear. "It wasn't the boosters pushing me into the NBA so much as the fact that my eight-year-old brother was getting shuffled around the foster care system and I needed an income to get him out." He locked eyes with Laurence. "That and the fact that I was good enough to get drafted out of high school, unlike every other kid in the country."

He excused himself to go upstairs to the bathroom, and Julia let him go. Max grabbed his dad's arm and whispered something to him, and even though she couldn't hear the words, she could tell the boy was mad. She was mad, too. She was the one who'd invited

Deacon and Wes here, and while she hadn't expected the tension that had sprung up, she still felt responsible.

"I'm just going to stack some plates," she said to her mom. "Allison will help me."

"Mom said we could leave them."

"I said you're helping me."

Allison snatched a platter off the table and went through the door to the kitchen. Julia put her plate on top of Laurence's and followed her sister.

Allison had her back against the sink, facing the door, obviously expecting a fight.

"What is the matter with you? Why would you bring up something so private about Deacon at the table that way?"

"I didn't know it was private."

"Of course it was private. He was my student. Obviously I shouldn't have talked about him at home, but as you mentioned, I was upset. I thought my family would keep my professional confidences."

Allison sniffed.

"I just can't imagine why you felt it was okay to mention it," Julia reiterated.

"Maybe I wanted him to know you don't like to lose and it's always bothered you that you couldn't get him to college. Maybe I'm worried you have unfinished business with him and that's why you called him up out of the blue to coach your team."

Julia looked over her shoulder but the door, thankfully, was closed. "I don't know what I've done wrong today, Allison, but you're being spiteful."

"Maybe next year don't bring a pity date to Christmas dinner for me."

Julia stepped forward and practically hissed at her sister. "I didn't bring you any kind of date. Forgive me if I thought you might like to meet a stunning, intelligent, single Hollywood producer. I mean, honestly, Allison. Most women would have thanked me."

"Then I guess most women like you to meddle in their lives," Allison said. "I don't."

DEACON KNEW HE shouldn't snoop around the Bradleys' house, but he had always been interested in how families lived. Probably if he went into therapy, the doctor would tell him it had something to do with the unsettled nature of his own childhood or some such crap, but Deacon liked the puzzle of putting people together with their stuff. If you knew what kind of stuff they had and how they kept it arranged and what they didn't have, then you could figure things out about them.

Victor, for example, had a TV in every room in his house. He couldn't stand being disconnected. Algae never marred his tank full of tropical fish, no incidents of cannibalism or incompatibility among species ever occurred, because he thrived on details and always studied up before he bought either one.

Deacon wanted to know about Julia. Wanted it enough that he turned left, away from the stairs, and started sticking his head into each of the five rooms upstairs. The first one was obviously Carole's bedroom and he ducked back out fast. The next one was more than likely a guest room, he decided. No one would choose the bland hunting-print wallpaper and striped comforter for an actual inhabitant. The next door was closed, and when he turned the handle he found a set of attic steps. Just past that, he hit pay dirt. A toy license plate was nailed crookedly to the door. He touched the letters that spelled out Julia's name. Under it, someone had written in what looked like red Sharpie, *No*

HENRY!!! Henry was underlined three times. Lucky for him he wasn't named Henry. He pushed open the door all the way and stepped inside.

He'd been expecting pink, but when he saw the bright, apple-green walls, he smiled. This was more Julia. Right up in your business with a happy smile. Oversleeping had no place in this room.

A twin bed was pushed against the wall between the windows and covered with a patchwork quilt faded from washing. A small, white wooden desk stood in front of a third window, looking out onto what he guessed was the backyard. He crossed the rug and lifted the eyelet curtain over the window. The curtain had fuzzy, apple-green pom-pom trim. He rubbed one of the pom-poms between his fingers, then pulled out the desk chair and sat down at the desk. A pair of heavy stone bookends shaped like rearing horses bracketed a small collection of paperbacks. He drew out one and opened it randomly. Poems—he could tell by the short lines. Putting his finger under the first word, he mouthed the letter it began with. *M.*

"Deacon?"

He jumped up, pushing the chair in again with one hand behind his back. "Sorry. I was taking a break."

"That's okay. I guess you found my room."

"I like the sign."

She half turned toward the door, and the play of shadow in the hollow of her throat, the slim muscles of her neck and shoulders, mesmerized him. She was gorgeous. She fit here in this house, where everything had been chosen with loving care and an eye for both beauty and function. Here in this room, surrounded by books and cheer, Julia made sense. Of course someone who grew up here would want to reach out to kids who didn't have these advantages. She'd want to share because she had so much to offer.

She lifted the book he'd had open. "I love these poems. I still remember some of them by heart. Do you know the Orphan Annie one? 'The goblins will git you?' Allison used to read that in such a dead-scary voice."

"She was just as charming as a kid as she is now."

"That's why I came looking for you, actually," Julia said. "Sorry about her. My mom thinks she's unhappy at work, and when Allison is unhappy, she likes to share."

"No big deal."

"Thanks," Julia said simply.

A framed picture of Julia in a baseball uniform, standing next to a tall man who resembled her brother Henry a lot, sat on the desk. "This your dad?"

"Yep." She picked up the picture and ran her finger over the frame. "I sang the national anthem for the minor league game."

"No kidding? You can sing?"

She nodded, tucking her chin in as if self-conscious about it. "I wanted to be a singer back then. I did a couple showcases with a kids' choir and sang at that ball game. I was getting really good."

"Do you still sing?"

"No," she said quickly, but then changed her answer. "In the shower. Sometimes at karaoke. One time at my cousin's wedding."

"What happened that you didn't pursue singing?"

"My dad died. Exactly a week after the game this photo was taken at. Like my mom said, I was at his calling hours, and all these people came through and they all had stories about how he helped them. So many stories. I promised him right then that I'd finish his job for him."

"You made that promise when you were ten?" he asked. "And you're still sticking to it?"

"How old were you when you said you'd care for Wes? It happens."

"But I've had to care for Wes. You don't have to keep that vow. It just makes you happy?"

"Mostly happy. Working under Ty gets worse every year. The paperwork is ridiculous. I have a lot more ideas than I have time. There are parts of the job I don't love, but that happens to everyone, right?" She took a few steps back, toward the tall white bookcases flanking the closet door. "My mom should really sort through these and donate some, but she says she's saving them for the grandkids." She pulled a tall, green book off the shelf. "*Make Way for Ducklings.* Henry and I used to make my dad read the ducklings names as fast as he could. Jack, Kack, Lack, Mack, Nack, Ouack, Pack, Quack and then we'd die laughing that anyone would name their kid Ouack." She flipped the pages, smiling to herself. "Did you have this book when you were a kid?"

"No," he said, and didn't manage to keep the frustration out of his voice.

"Oh." She shoved the book back on the shelf. "Sorry."

Now he'd embarrassed both of them. Why hadn't he just said yes and let it go? Was he worried she'd hand the book to him and force him to read out loud? The thought made him clench his hands into fists as he remembered the agony of being called on that way by teachers back in early elementary school.

"Not a problem," he said. "You and I just grew up different."

And they had. She'd grown up in this big house, and even though she'd worked in Milton for the past ten years, she'd never be from there. She'd never be from a trailer park, or a broken home, or have to watch a brother get put in foster care. She'd always be someone who took it for granted that adults could read a freaking children's book about ducks without breaking into a sweat.

He'd never be like her and maintaining his lie around her was depressing.

"I should take off," he said. "It was nice of your mom to have us."

She closed her eyes briefly, and when she opened them, she said, "I invited you, Deacon. I wanted you to be here. You and Wes," she added. "It's been such a good day. Please don't let my thoughtless remark send you home."

"That's not it," he said. "I'm just ready to go."

THE TEAM HAD a week off after Christmas. Oliver flew in and he and Wes spent hours playing some video game on the Xbox. He liked Oliver more now and could see what Wes enjoyed about him. The guy was nuts, no doubt. But he was smart and didn't give you any bullshit. What you saw was what you got with Oliver. It was refreshing.

Still, the constant stream of commentary on the video game that passed between Oliver and Wes made Deacon nuts. Plus, he hadn't seen Julia in a few days and he missed her.

He couldn't be with her. That much was clear. Just the fact that her family gave one another books for

Christmas. What if he married her and then he had to figure out some way to make one of them read his book title for him every year.

What Victor had told him way back before the whole thing with Julia started was true. Parts of him were off-limits. You couldn't be with someone and lie to her all day every day.

It would be a joke.

He was a joke.

But he wasn't quite as big a joke as Laurence, who'd ruined his kid's chances to play ball and didn't even seem aware he'd done it. How sad that Max's dad thought he was on the boys' team.

Deacon phoned Julia and asked her if they could meet to talk about Max. He told her he'd walk to her house. On his way out, he stopped in the living room and said, "I'm heading off. You guys can take the car if you need anything."

Wes's and Oliver's heads snapped toward him, and they both dropped their controllers and bolted for the door. He held out the keys and Wes snatched them.

"I gather you need something?"

"Soda!"

"Maraschino cherries!"

They shouted in unison, and then Wes shook his head at his roommate. "Maraschino cherries, man?"

"I was sure you wouldn't have them. I don't have a complete inventory of your pantry."

Wes opened the door and the two of them jostled each other as they passed through.

"We're two dudes living together, Oliver. We don't have a pantry."

"Where do you keep your food, then?" Oliver wanted to know.

"Don't speed," Deacon called to Wes. "And if Oliver drives, make sure he does a test run in a parking lot."

"I won't drive," he said. "I never got my license."

Wes sighed as they rounded the corner of the garage.

Deacon locked the door to the house and set out for Julia's.

SHE WAS SURPRISED to hear from Deacon. She'd been trying to figure out what had happened at Christmas, but with no success.

Maybe he'd explain now. Maybe she'd finally get a look at whatever he was protecting so fiercely.

She had a tray of cheese and crackers on the table. She'd been planning to have it later for dinner, but when he'd called, she'd pulled it out in case he was hungry.

"What's up?" she asked.

"I realize I'm just the basketball coach and you're the professional, but someone needs to talk to Max's dad and I wanted to give you a heads-up that I'm going to if you don't."

"Laurence? What about?"

"Do you know why Max got cut?"

Julia felt a prickle of tension up the back of her neck. Deacon seemed so cold and this wasn't the conversation she'd expected.

"Not exactly. I guessed. Knowing Max and Coach Simon," she said, "it's not much of a leap. You're not going to suggest that Max cut his hair."

"You think he's gay, don't you?"

"I never asked him," she said, "but yes."

"Well, I don't know if he is or not, but he got cut because Laurence humiliated Ty and Coach Simon. The worst part is, Max didn't even tell his dad. I think

Max knows exactly why he got cut. And I know Donny Simon well enough to know he'd want Max to know. Laurence is so caught up in himself he hasn't even noticed that Max is practicing with the girls' team. He must have made zero effort to go to the games he assumes Max is playing in."

"How do you know all this?"

"Cory Miller told me at the boosters party." Deacon sat on the end of the couch. "I figured it was none of my business, but now I've met Max's dad, and he needs to hear about it."

"But Max is fine with things the way they are."

"No," Deacon said. "He is not. He should be on the boys' team and you know it."

"He'd be eaten alive on that team, or worse yet, turned into one of them."

"No." Deacon pointed at her. "See? That's what you do. You decide what's right for someone, what they need and where they belong."

Julia was hurt. "But isn't that *exactly* what you're doing? *Deciding* Max isn't all right and *deciding* what his dad needs? And besides, that's not true. Max was new here and he didn't understand how the boys' team acted. He wouldn't have wanted to be part of them had he known."

"He wants to play basketball."

"Not Tigers basketball."

"Yes, Julia. He wants to play Tigers basketball. Sometimes, especially if you're a fourteen-year-old boy, basketball is just basketball. It's not empowerment or self-esteem or any of that other stuff you add on."

"So I should have let Coach Simon mold him into a Tiger?"

"Max wants to play. You should listen to him and not to yourself this time. Sometimes you're so good at your job you do know better than a lot of people what they want. But sometimes you push and push and you're wrong. People make choices you consider wrong, but they're actually right for them."

Clearly, he wasn't talking about Max anymore. Was he talking about himself? Was he still remembering ten years ago when he'd turned down her advice?

"Fine," she said. "Speak to Laurence. You and he can figure everything out together and leave me out of it."

"Are you sure you don't want to be involved? You appeared interested in getting closer to him at Christmas. He seems like a guy who'd be your type."

She was so mad she could have hit him. "My type? Interested? Is that the reason for the silent treatment? You're jealous of Laurence?"

"Well, you invited him home for Christmas, didn't you? Right in front of me," he said. Then he appeared to realize what he was implying. "And Wes. Right in front of both of us. Weren't we supposed to conclude you were interested? You sat next to the guy at dinner. You were all in sync with each other over book reviews."

"Stop it, Deacon." She held up a hand. "If I invited him 'for' anyone, it was Allison. I thought she might like to meet him, but she screamed at me for managing her life. Seems to be a theme."

He looked unsure whether to believe her.

"You can call my sister. She's not talking to me, but she'd probably pick up for you."

"No," he said. "I was out of line. I shouldn't expect you—"

"You should expect me to respect you enough not to invite an alternative date along to something I've already invited you to attend."

"I'm sorry, Julia. You're right." He stood up. "I'm going to go."

"Deacon, wait. Are you staying here after the season?"

He looked trapped.

"It's okay. I know you're not." She went to him and put her arms around his waist. "Can't we just enjoy each other while you're here? The team is coming together. Wes is doing good. Why not let things be good between us?"

He rested his chin on her hair. If he could keep his lies in place for just a few more weeks, this relationship would be okay.

CHAPTER THIRTEEN

THE SECOND TIME they played Leeds, the game turned ugly early and stayed that way through most of the first half. They needed a win. The Leeds players knew it and were not inclined to hand one over.

Oliver had set up his video equipment to tape the game and she winced every time the team missed another play. She wouldn't want to watch Oliver's tape. Tali got called for her third foul when she tripped and smashed into the Leeds shooting guard at the half-court line. That was typical of the way this whole game had gone. Bad breaks, bad luck, some bad shots and they were in a six-point hole they couldn't get out of.

Tempers were running hot on the court as well as the benches on both sides of the scoring table. Wes had run his hands through his hair so many times thick tufts stood up across the top of his head. Deacon's face was drawn. Max looked disgusted. Naya's mother had already gotten a warning from the ref for yelling at him.

Miri deliberately elbowed the stomach of a tall forward on the Leeds team. She grabbed her stomach with one hand and lashed out at Miri with the other. The ref blew his whistle, but Cora had to step between Miri and the other player to stop a brawl.

Julia felt sick when she thought that their season might slip away right here. Not only would they lose the game and their chance at States, but they'd lose it playing dirty and cheap instead of straight-up aggressive.

At the half, they filed into the locker room, where they took seats on the benches, none of their usual spirit or life in view. Max slumped against the door. The clipboard he usually scribbled notes on to give to individual girls about the players they were matched up with stayed tucked under his arm.

Deacon read them the riot act. They needed to step up and assume responsibility for their season. If they let Leeds win this game from them, they weren't the team he thought they were. He wanted to see them running hard, passing smarter, pulling down those rebounds as though they owned them and making a damn shot once in a while.

Wes didn't participate in the lecture. She scanned the room, and finally spotted him in the back corner near the showers. When Deacon called out Miri for the free throws she'd botched in the first quarter, Wes shook his head. There seemed to be dissension in the coaching ranks. When she looked for Wes again a few minutes later, he was gone.

They were subdued when they filed back outside. The ref stood at half-court, waiting to start the game, but apparently some issue with the scoreboard had cropped up.

The team took seats on the bench while the scorer and the Leeds coach looked at the clock. She had no idea what was wrong.

Clearly, neither did they.

The delay dragged on for more than ten minutes. The girls, already in a bad mood, turned sullen. The Leeds players had started to trash-talk sotto voce from their bench. She wondered if the Tigers should move back into the locker room.

She wasn't paying attention when Wes called Trey and Shawn over, but she did register that the three of them conferred with Oliver near the camera setup.

Just then the ref came by to say they could try to find a second clock in the storeroom. The Leeds coach knew they had one there, but he wasn't sure if it was in working order.

Music blared in the gym. She turned, along with everyone else, to look at the court. There, Wes, Trey and Shawn were lined up on the half-court line, doing the YMCA.

The gym was quiet for a few seconds, but then the fans started to sing along. Miri went to dance with them and then the rest of the team joined in.

"What is he doing?" she asked Deacon.

"Being Wes."

When the song ended, she expected the team to go back to waiting. Instead, the girls knelt along the sidelines while Trey and Shawn fiddled with the iPod. They gave Wes a thumbs-up and he set the speakers close to the Leeds bench. Like a dare.

Like he'd planned this. Being Wes. Where had he been during the end of the half-time lecture? How hard would it be to disable a scorekeeping clock? The music began again, and it was the Macarena. The Leeds players appeared confused and then Wes said, "It's a dance-off. Show us your stuff."

Deacon looked tense. "He's going to start a riot."

She wasn't so sure. "I think he can pull this off. Trust him."

No one on the Leeds side moved until Wes pivoted back to the Tigers. "I think we won this dance-off by forfeit," he called. "Nobody in Leeds High School knows the Macarena."

The girl who'd punched Miri stood up. "Oh, yeah?"

Turned out the entire team knew the Macarena. They knew it very well. Although they started off boldly, by the time they finished they were breathless with laughter.

They resumed their places on the sidelines and the boys queued up "Thriller." The Leeds coach had to dodge a horde of Tiger zombies on his way back to the table with the replacement clock.

She wasn't sorry when it didn't work, either. By then the teams were mixed together, doing a jig step to "Dueling Banjos."

Eventually someone ran into the locker room and got the bag of pink-and-white-striped balls Deacon had bought for them that they used for their dance.

"This is good," Deacon said. "Even if they lose, they'll have something to remember, right?"

She supposed he was right, but she wasn't anywhere near giving up on the season. Every time she thought about Ty giving that stupid thank-you speech, she felt so frustrated.

The girls did their routine, with Wes, Trey, Shawn, Max, even Oliver joining in. When they were finished, the fans in the stands on both sides roared with approval.

Just then the clock turned on, and the game picked up again. The Milton Tigers, fresh from their dance triumph, were unstoppable.

OLIVER UPLOADED THE video of the dance-off onto YouTube. He put the Tigers dance up separately. By the time their next game started, the videos had gone right through Milton. The Tigers were a sensation and ticket sales leaped ahead by a factor of ten. Tali's mom and dad finally showed up. Several of the families who were strong supporters of the boys' boosters started coming to games, even caravanning to the away game the same way they did for the boys.

After two more wins and several successful trips through the stands with the coffee-can bank, the Tigers were within sight of a trip to States and Julia winning the bet.

Until they lost to Carlisle Academy, the worst team in the league.

Tali couldn't hit a shot. Naya had a sore wrist and her shooting percentage was off. The center for Carlisle made some lucky rebounds. The loss wasn't a landslide but a slow erosion the Tigers couldn't seem to stop.

Julia was devastated and she turned to Deacon. She didn't even think about it. He was the one she needed. After the last car pulled out of the parking lot, taking the last player home, she walked right up to him and buried her head in his chest. He wrapped his arms around her and held her, not even asking why.

"We finally got boosters, you know? And now we lost to those stupid stinky Carlisle Academy girls."

"The Flippers."

"The Flippers. Who names a team the Flippers? Who loses to the Flippers?"

"Us, I guess."

"We've completely lost the season now. Our record stinks and we won't have anyone coming back to the next game, I know it."

"Hey," Deacon said. "You really don't understand the boosters, do you?"

"What's to understand?"

"Well, for starters, they love to win. But the real reason they come out for the Tigers is that it gives them somewhere to belong. If you're a Tiger, you're a Tiger for life. It feels good."

"But those other Tigers win."

"We're giving them something better than wins, Julia. We're giving them hope. You'll see. They'll be at the next game. I promise."

He was right. The fans came out, but Naya was home sick with bronchitis and they lost again. The season was over.

OLIVER WAS LEAVING that morning. Deacon had promised Wes he could borrow the car to drive him to the airport, and the two of them had been up and outside already, wiping down the exterior and washing the windows. Wes said the ladies liked a shiny finish, and even though Oliver looked skeptical, he'd started buffing with a rag.

Deacon was clearing up the dishes from breakfast when Oliver came in the back door. He shouted to Wes, "I'll be right there. I need to use the restroom."

Deacon figured he'd pass right by, but Oliver stopped behind him.

"Deacon?"

"Hey."

"Wes will kill me if he knows I gave this to you, but he won't tell you himself and you need to see it."

Oliver held out a small plastic case. Deacon's first thought was drugs. Wes couldn't be getting high without his knowing, could he?

"What is it?"

"It's video from his practices at school." Oliver moved closer and Deacon took the case, which he realized was a memory stick for a computer. "As you know, I held the video-support job for the team. One of my duties was to tape practice."

"Why wouldn't Wes want me to see his practices?"

Oliver hitched his backpack higher on his shoulder. "You have a power differential and he believes this will increase the imbalance."

Sometimes Deacon wished Oliver would just go ahead and speak Elvish if he was going to be incomprehensible in English anyway.

Wes beeped the car horn and then ran up the back steps to the storm door. "You coming, dude?"

Oliver shook Deacon's hand. "Thank you very much for the visit. I had a good time."

Deacon nodded. "It was good to get to know you."

He heard them outside. Wes was promising Oliver he'd send him updates from the game. He ran his thumb over the plastic case...the memory stick. He didn't turn it on right away. Whatever that load of crazy was that Oliver spouted, he'd been clear that Wes wouldn't want Deacon to see this tape. Deacon felt guilty, but he turned on his computer and loaded the video. He'd been worried about Wes for weeks now. Maybe this tape could clear up his questions.

Oliver had edited a clip reel together. It was like the highlight reel he and Wes had made to show to college recruiters, but it highlighted the exact opposite. In fact, it was a horror show. Coach Mulbrake seemed to have it in for Wes from the first practice. He called him Prep and constantly berated him for laziness and lack of dedication. At one point, Wes was running a passing drill and Mulbrake threw a ball at the back of his head so hard it knocked Wes down.

Deacon turned off the video after the first minute

because he felt physically ill, but then he thought about Wes, living through this and so much more, and he turned it back on. He'd stand witness for his brother. The abuse continued relentlessly for the entire five-minute video.

When it was over, he called Julia. "Do you have a second to look at something with me?"

"Sure. Bring it to practice?" she asked.

"I meant now. Can you come over? It's about Wes."

"Oh." Her voice got tense. "Is everything okay?"

"Can you just come here?"

She must have flown, because she seemed to be there in seconds. "Deacon?" she called from the foot of the stairs.

"I'm in my room. Come up."

He only showed her enough for her to understand what Wes had been dealing with.

"Why wouldn't he tell me that was going on?"

There were tears in her eyes. "Oh, Deacon. I don't know. Where is he?"

He touched her cheek where a tear slid out. No one had ever cried over his brother with him before. Not ever. "He took Oliver to the airport."

"What will you do?"

"Talk to Vic. Get my lawyer involved. Withdraw Wes from that freaking school tomorrow."

He touched the memory stick with one finger. "Apologize."

"For what?"

"I don't know. But kids don't keep stuff like that treatment a secret for no reason. I let Wes down some-how."

Julia moved behind Deacon and put her hands on his

neck. She rubbed, her thumbs pushing deep to circle the knots of tension. He relaxed into her touch.

"Thanks for getting here so fast. I hated watching that alone."

"Deacon, I'm always here for you and Wes. Anytime."

He slid his arm around her waist and pulled her down to sit on his lap. "I never talked about Wes with anyone. He was always my responsibility alone."

"Sometimes I wish I'd been in high school with you. I mean, it wouldn't have happened even if I had somehow gotten four years younger, because my family was in Jericho, but what if when we met we were both students. We could have been together all this time."

Deacon looked over her shoulder. He didn't want her to see his eyes when he said, "We'd have been great together."

He wanted it to be true, but it wasn't. If they'd been kids together in high school, she wouldn't have looked twice at him. Too tall, too serious, too far behind to ever catch up. He doubted their paths would even have crossed.

She opened her mouth and he kissed her. He didn't want to talk. He slid his hands up under her T-shirt and cupped her breasts, while their tongues dipped and explored. Her hands tugged at his hair until he tilted his head back and she kissed and licked the base of his throat. He loved the way she felt. All warm curves and eager, sexy mouth.

She turned her body to straddle him on the chair and he was quickly straining at the fly of his jeans, but Wes would be home any minute, so they had to content themselves with kissing, rubbing and the kind of frustrated, desperate grinding he hadn't done since high school.

He heard the rumble of the Porsche coming down the street in time to get his clothes sorted out and his hair finger combed.

"I should go," Julia said.

"Stay." Deacon held her hand. "Please?"

Wes raced in the front door and pounded up the stairs, probably taking them two at a time. Wes poked his head around the doorway.

"Hey, Julia, what's up?"

He tossed his hair back off his face, then realized they were both staring at him.

"What? Is my fly open?"

Deacon shook his head. "Oliver made me a tape of your practices from school. Wes, why would you keep this from me?"

Wes looked ready to bolt, but he stood still as Julia leaned over and stroked his arm.

"Why did Oliver do that?"

"He's worried about you."

"I'm fine."

"Wes!" Deacon said. "We saw what happened to you."

"So?"

"So," Julia said gently, "Deacon is worried. You've been acting like school is a joke ever since you got here, and then we find out your coach is treating you very badly."

"Why did you let me think you were screwing around?"

"Because." Wes sat down on the bed. Julia sat next to him. "Because it's easier if you think I'm screwing up than if you find out I suck at basketball. I'm supposed to play ball at school. That's what you want and I just— I want to give that to you." Wes drew in a deep breath. "But I couldn't. I couldn't make him stop yelling at me and I thought…I thought he was going to take back my scholarship."

"So you messed up on purpose?" Julia asked. "Why?"

"So I'd get kicked out. So it would be over."

"But what did you think would happen then? If you got kicked out."

Wes lifted his shoulders and let them fall. "I didn't really think. I just wanted to get through the next day."

Deacon understood what Wes meant. When he was in school, every single day was so freaking hard. He never knew how to keep up and he never knew how to get out. He had to show up every day and hope for the best.

"What I saw on that tape wasn't right, Wes. You have to realize I would have wanted to know. My job is to take care of you."

"But you've been doing that since you were a kid. I'm dead weight just like Coach Mulbrake said. I don't want you to take care of me the rest of my life."

Deacon stood up and crossed to stand in front of Wes.

"I have no intention of taking care of you your whole life," Deacon said. "But I will protect you. I will stand with you. I will care, Wes, if things have gone wrong."

Wes wrapped his arms around his middle. Deacon reached for him and pulled him into a hug. Julia's arms came around them from behind.

"Vic has a fantastic lawyer," Deacon said. "Mulbrake is going down, and if I know Vic, they'll even give you your year of eligibility back when Vic's finished with this thing."

IT WAS A RELIEF, of course. Now that Deacon knew everything, Wes could stop worrying. Standing with D and Julia, he felt sheltered. Safe. Vic would clean up the mess, and between Deacon and him, he'd wind up with a clean slate. He could apply to another school, find another basketball program and move on.

He should feel terrific with the weight off his mind.

He didn't. He felt low and small. Once again he'd had to call on Deacon for help.

JULIA WAS IN her office when the league commissioner called her. She wasn't really paying attention until she realized he was talking about Leeds.

"Can you repeat that?"

"I said the league found out they rostered players from the next school district. They had a fake mailbox and everything. Their entire record is vacated."

"What does that mean?"

"Your loss against them is now a win." She thought quickly about the standings, trying to calculate what this all meant.

"That means we have a shot!"

She went room by room through the school and told each of her players individually. She wanted to be sure they came to practice prepared to work.

"We still have to win one more game," Tali said.

"Yeah, but this time it's a game you *can* win. You beat Westview last time you played."

"By eight points."

"You're better now. No worries."

JULIA SPENT THE night before the final game watching clips from every famous sports movie she could find. She Googled famous coaches and read transcripts of their best speeches. She thought there must be something in them she could adapt and bring to the girls tomorrow to inspire them to do their best, be their best, and end this improbable season in triumph.

She didn't find the words she wanted, but in the end it didn't matter.

The girls dressed quickly, eager to get out of the "dressing room," as Tali had started calling the locker room, and into their real team room. When they walked through the doors of the weight room, Deacon, Wes and Max were waiting for them. Max had a stack of new warm-ups, and as each player passed him, he handed her the customized pants and jacket, number and name proudly printed on the back.

"Here's yours, Coach," he said. She took the warm-up and slipped her arms through the jacket sleeves. The warm-up suit was Tiger colors, black and yellow, but just above the large Tiger logo on the back was printed "My Tigers."

The girls put on their warm-ups and then settled down. Julia looked around the room and met their eyes, then she looked at Deacon. They were ready. They'd made it this far together and nothing could stop them now.

Ty didn't knock when he came in. He just opened the door and beckoned to Max. "Max Wright, I need to see you."

Max hesitated, but Ty beckoned again. "This is serious, Wright. Is your father here?"

"Mr. Chambers," Julia said. "Is there an emergency?"

"As a matter of fact, yes. Mr. Wright is ineligible to serve as student manager because he doesn't have a current parental consent form on file." Ty put one hand on Max's shoulder. "You've been in violation of league rules every time he rode the bus this year."

"What!"

The weight room exploded with shocked voices. Max twisted, trying to move away from the principal, but Ty held on to his shoulder.

"I'm sorry. Didn't you know student managers are subject to the same rules as players?" Ty asked. "It's all laid out in the rule book. 'No nonrostered student shall ride the school district–supplied vehicle without proper parental consent.'"

Max tried to pull away again and when Ty's hand tightened, the boy flinched. Deacon was across the room in three steps.

"Let him go, Chambers," he said. "You made your point."

Ty looked as if he was going to refuse, but Deacon moved up closer to him and he swallowed, but gave Max a little shove, causing him to stumble as he moved away. Then Ty smiled. "It's ironic. I wouldn't have had to call the league about your illegal student-manager if the Leeds team hadn't been cheating. This league is just full of folks who think they're above the rules."

"You knew about this?"

"I knew about it from the time Wright stepped foot on the bus the first time."

Deacon went for him. Despite his extra bulk, Ty could still move fast. That, coupled with Wes stepping between his brother and the principal, allowed him to escape from the locker room unscathed. Julia would have hit him herself if she hadn't been so shocked.

Max's face was pale and he stood frozen in the center of the room. He didn't look at any of them as he said quietly, "I can't believe I lost the season for you. This is a nightmare."

Julia was still trying to decide what to say, when Tali kicked the side of the trainer's table. "Shut up, Max." She put an arm across his shoulders. "Just shut up." She patted him. "Mr. Chambers has been taking stuff from us all year, or trying to. We have one game left. This team is ours, not his. Who cares about the stupid rules?"

Julia turned to Deacon, wanting to share the moment when those two kids joined forces, knowing that even though she'd lost her bet, they'd just had a big win. He was gone. She pivoted, scanning the room, but he wasn't there anymore. Wes went out to check the parking lot and reported back that the Porsche was no longer there.

Finally, they couldn't delay anymore and they filed out to start down the short hall to the gym. Julia stopped short when she realized most of the players from the boys' team were lined up along either wall.

Seth stepped forward. "Mr. Chambers told us about Max." He made eye contact with the other boy. "That sucks, dude."

Max shrugged, a purposeful, overacted nonchalance in every inch of the movement.

"Anyway, good luck."

The girls went through the doors into the gym, the cheering from the Milton Tigers beating time for them as they went.

She instinctively looked for Deacon. He'd been there all season sharing the large and small triumphs with her and he'd have known exactly how much that cheer from their former in-school rivals meant to the girls and to her. For the first time since she'd called and asked him for a favor, Deacon wasn't there when she needed him.

Julia and Wes did their best and the team played hard, but a spark was missing and the final score showed the Tigers down by two. The season was over. The girls were subdued as they changed for the final time. Several of them asked her if she'd heard from Deacon. She had to reassure Max three times that Deacon didn't blame him. She was confused. Why would he leave them?

The door to the locker room opened and Deacon stuck his head in. "The gym is almost empty. Can you bring the team in there for a meeting in five?"

He ducked back out again before she had time to do more than nod.

CHAPTER FOURTEEN

THE GYM AT Milton was one of the few places in the world Deacon had never felt stupid. Until tonight. When he'd left earlier, all he could think about was getting away from the team, from Wes, from Julia, from everyone he'd let down. He hadn't even listened to the game on the radio. He'd just driven, aimlessly, mindlessly, looking for escape, but of course there was none.

He was finally coming clean and it was right that he do it in the gym. The gym was the place that had let him conceal the truth for so long. If he hadn't been necessary for the team, they wouldn't have passed him along, fixed his schedule, let him skip the SATs, and still sign that fat contract and look like a hero.

He'd also been in charge in the gym and it was right that he face this there.

The kids sat in the bleachers. Wes and Julia were with them, in the front row. He glanced at his brother but couldn't look at him. He wished like hell Julia wasn't there. If only he could have kept this from her, maybe they'd have had a chance. But he'd known all along they had no chance.

Relationships can't be built on lies and he couldn't have a relationship with her knowing he could never keep up with her in the one area she cared about most.

He locked the doors to be sure the parents waiting

outside to take their players home didn't come in until he was finished.

"Um." He cleared his throat. He had expected this to be hard, but he hadn't expected to be so... Screw it. He just hoped he didn't cry. He began, "When I got here and Coach Bradley told me about her dream to bring you guys to States, I thought she was nuts. That first day of practice, only one kid in the gym was any good and, although I didn't know it at the time, that kid wasn't technically eligible for the team—even if he is one of the best ballplayers ever to take the court at Milton."

He made eye contact with Max. It mattered to him that the kids heard what he had to say. He wasn't going to let them feel like losers. They weren't losers and they needed to know it.

Max's lips twitched. It was almost a smile, even if it was gone quick. Good enough.

"Then the season started and we... You...put yourselves together and you became a team. We caught some breaks, but lots of teams catch breaks and can't capitalize on them. I want you all to look around and know that the kids sitting next to you are your team. You took one another further than you should have been able to go and it worked because you are a team."

A couple of them turned their heads and he saw a few smiles exchanged. Tali gave a fist pump. He accidentally looked at Julia and she was glowing. Even after everything, she still believed in him. She thought he was going to inspire them. He almost quit when he saw that. She was proud of them. Proud of him. He wanted to walk out of the gym now and leave this the way it stood. No one had to know. Except he'd always know and he needed to come clean.

"You know what you brought into this gym at the beginning of the season and you know what you left out there on the floor at the end of the Westview game. Cora took every rebound that came her way and more than a few that didn't. Miri put points on the board in practically every game. Iris boxed out the defense, protected her perimeter and shot consistently every time she got the ball. Naya, you showed up and gave us a chance. You're a gifted girl and I'm proud to have had the chance to coach you. And Tali. You went from an okay player with a lot of attitude to our dependable star. Not once did you let this team down, because you delivered every time we asked for a shot or a fast break or one of your sweet, smart passes. Every one of you brought something."

He met Wes's eyes. "My brother never coached before in his life, but without him, we'd have been sunk after our third game. He brought us a dance and you guys gave the team a heart. No one will forget this team."

He tipped back his head, staring at the fluorescent lights and wishing with everything he had that he hadn't screwed up again. If he could only go back. But he knew… He'd known since he was a kid that life didn't hand out do-overs. He had to get through the next five minutes and then he could leave this gym and figure out what he was going to do with the rest of his life. He cleared his throat again and finally looked Julia in the eye.

"Coach Bradley knew this team was great before any of us. None of us would even have had a team this year if not for her. We'd have missed out on…everything." She swiped her fingers across her cheeks and smiled at him. "Coach Bradley never let us down. Not once."

She jumped up then and crossed the floor to him. She faced the girls and started talking before he could stop her. "No one let us down. Mistakes happen. That's something we've learned as a team and this paperwork snafu is nobody's fault. The thing we can take away from this year is knowing we all faced our fears, met our challenges and did our very best."

Some of the girls clapped and started to get up. He held up his hands and motioned them to sit back down, but they were too charged up, crying and hugging one another. He needed them to listen because he wouldn't be able to work up the nerve to do this again.

He reached for his whistle and put it to his lips. He realized Wes hadn't moved. His brother was watching him. He'd spent a lifetime trying to take care of Wes and he knew how his brother had seen him. Deacon decided to tear down any remaining hero worship right now. He blew his whistle.

The girls stopped and looked at him. He scanned their faces, saw nothing but curiosity and warmth.

"I let you down. I'm sorry. I—"

"Deacon, no," Julia said. "It was just a mistake. That rule is buried in the rule book. No one could have expected you to memorize every last thing. I've been coaching for five years and I forgot about it."

He continued as if she hadn't spoken.

"I let you down because I lied. I've been lying my whole life. I didn't know about the student-manager rule because I never read the rule book." He sucked in a deep breath. Wes stood, but didn't come closer. "I didn't read the rule book because I can't read."

"No way," Tali whispered. Deacon felt as if he'd

stopped breathing. He was racing through this because if he paused to think or feel or anything, he'd never go on.

"I let you down because I'm embarrassed that I can't read, so I never told anyone. I let Coach Bradley and my brother think I'd read the rule book, and that was wrong. I'm sorry I let you all down. You..." And here he did look up, to see their faces, to make sure they heard this. "You all did everything right. You showed up and put in your honest best efforts, and I was too ashamed to admit I couldn't do my job. I'm sorry."

He couldn't watch. Couldn't stand there and see their expressions change from warm, welcoming and embracing to horrified, disgusted and ashamed. He turned on his heel and walked out of the gym. He didn't know if Wes was following him. He hoped not. He wanted to be alone because he didn't know how he'd ever look at his brother, the kids or Julia. God, *Julia.* How could he face her?

SHE YEARNED WITH every ounce of her body and heart to rush out the gym and find Deacon, but the kids crowded around her with questions and tears. She couldn't leave the team until they'd talked this out. He would have expected her to be there for the team and she didn't want to let him down. She'd do this for him and then she'd find him.

Wes's face was drawn. None of his usual joy showed as he put an arm around Max and met Julia's eyes. He hadn't known—that much was obvious.

Oh, Deacon. He hadn't trusted any of them. Why hadn't he seen that none of them would have loved him less?

She loved him. She hadn't quite let herself acknowledge that before his speech, but watching him stand in front of the kids and admit the secret he'd kept all these years, she'd known she loved him. He was the bravest, strongest, most loyal guy in the world, and if she could just settle these kids down, she'd make sure he knew how she felt.

"Ms. Bradley, we have to find Coach. Why'd he leave like that?" Tali's voice rose above the others.

Julia reached for Miri's hand and put her arm across Cora's shoulders. "He's hurting, guys. He thinks he let us down."

"Did you know he can't read?"

She shook her head. She'd missed that. She'd missed so many things. How could he forgive her for making it so hard for him to be with her?

Eventually she convinced them that she would go after Deacon and bring him back. Not that evening, but as soon as she could. She'd reconvene the meeting. She'd bring their Tigers back together. If he'd let them.

"HE'S RIGHT," WES said. He could feel how tight his mouth was. Julia had thought in the gym that he was hurting the way she was, but he was angry. "He let us all down," he told her. "All he needed to do was give me the damn rule book and I'd have read the stupid thing to him."

"Wes," Julia said carefully. "He couldn't do that. It was too painful for him."

"Too painful for him to ask me for a simple favor?" Wes said. He was so mad he could barely speak. "My entire life I've owed him. He saved me, Julia. He bought and paid for this life I have—everything I ever wanted, he got for me, and he never once asked me for anything. I'm a screwup and I've constantly let him down, and all this time, if he'd only—" He was shaking. "He needed me and he never asked." He couldn't stop yelling and he needed to stop. Julia didn't need to hear all this. No one did.

The main thing he'd learned today was that his brother didn't trust him. Didn't matter how much time they spent together, Deacon would always be the hero and there could never be a way they could just be... brothers.

DEACON WAS AT the small park. She and Wes should have thought of searching there first because it made sense that he'd be on a basketball court, and especially on this one that he'd built and where the kids on the street had already had such good times.

He did that kind of thing. Made it possible for other people to succeed. It was what she was supposed to do. She couldn't believe she'd missed his reading issues when he'd been her student. She could make a million excuses about her lack of experience, his skill at faking, the complicity of so many of his teachers and other adults. But the fact remained. He'd been her student and she'd missed it.

Was what he'd said to her true? Did she fixate on the course she thought was right for people and refuse to back down? If she hadn't been so busy trying to get him to accept a scholarship, would she have picked up on his difficulties? She didn't know.

What mattered now was what she was going to do about it. Had he ever been tested for a learning disability? Did he need or want a tutor? How did he get along in so many basic ways? She had a million questions and not nearly enough answers.

"I want to talk to him first, okay?" Wes said.

She nodded. He deserved the chance to confront Deacon. She prayed it would go well.

Deacon was sitting on the bench under the basket. The winter had been dry so far, so the court was cold but free of snow. Wes grabbed a ball out of the backseat and advanced on his brother. She stayed a few yards behind him and stopped a short distance away.

"I want you to play me."

"No."

"Yes, Deacon. Get up and play me."

Deacon got to his feet, but he didn't make a move toward the ball Wes was holding out to him.

"Why?"

Wes bounced the ball to him and Deacon caught it, those ingrained instincts for the ball taking over.

"Because you lied to me. You owe me one honest game."

Deacon sounded tired when he said, "I'm sorry I lied."

"Prove it. Play me."

Julia moved to the bench as soon as they began playing. The half-court was intimate. Not nearly big enough to contain the anger Wes brought to the game. Deacon started out playing him soft. He put just enough effort in to keep the score close, but Wes was the one who was actually competing.

When the score was 12–10, Wes's patience finally snapped and he slammed an elbow into Deacon's face as he brought down a rebound. Deacon staggered back, his hand pressed to the bone above his right eye.

"Goddamn it, Wes. Watch out."

"Play me," Wes repeated and he checked the ball at his brother hard.

Deacon did play him. The game turned brutal and

Julia wondered if she should step in. She didn't want to see either of them hurt. That first elbow Wes threw didn't draw blood, but he brought a shoulder up into his brother's mouth and that did. Deacon recoiled and took a second to wipe his mouth with his shirt, leaving a bright red streak behind.

Then Deacon took the ball, shot a huge jumper from the three-point line and he had the lead for the first time. Wes came roaring back, fighting through his brother's defense and powering past him for a layup.

Wes had his back to Deacon, so he missed the quick series of reactions Julia saw. Surprise. Shock. Respect. Determination. Deacon wiped his face again, using the hem of his shirt and streaking more blood across the fabric. Then he went back to the game.

The score stayed tied as it climbed closer to thirty. Deacon was tiring. His shoulder was giving him trouble, and that told her how wiped out he must be because for the first time since she'd met him, he showed signs of the old injury. Watching him play his brother was a revelation to her. He would have kept on protecting him, doing for him, for as long as his brother needed him. But now that Wes was asking for his independence, demanding status as an equal, Deacon was up for the challenge of showing him that he saw him as a man. Wes was going to win this game. She knew it, and Deacon knew it even if Wes didn't yet. And when it ended, after Deacon left it all on the court, his brother would have no more doubts about himself as a ballplayer. Or a Fallon.

Deacon had humbled himself in the gym for the team. He was humbling himself here on the court for his brother. He was strong enough to bend when that was the right thing to do.

Wes beat him on a power drive straight up the middle. He went up and over, his few extra inches of height giving him the slight advantage he needed to sink the shot.

Deacon put his hands on his knees and hung his head, sucking in deep breaths. Wes threw the ball and it bounced hard an inch from his brother's foot.

"Why would you lie to me?"

"To protect you. You lost everything. You needed someone to count on."

"I need," Wes said, walking up to Deacon, "for my brother to let me be his brother, not his kid. That's what I need. I need you to ask me for some freaking help if *you* need it."

When the Fallons hugged, the embrace was fierce and wild and showed her that Deacon understood. He had Wes now. Not to worry over, although he'd probably continue to worry, but to be his family.

A few minutes later, Wes walked past her on his way home. "You're up," he whispered. "Good luck."

Deacon had his hands on his hips, waiting for her to approach.

"So now you know," he said. "Now you know why I didn't go to college."

It hit her that she did know, but not because she'd found out he couldn't read. Because she understood Deacon. He could no more have gone to college and ignored the money being offered him, money he saw as a secure future for Wes, than he could have flown to the moon. He wasn't built that way.

She wanted to tell him how much she admired him and how much respect she had for the boy he'd been. But he spoke first.

"Now you know why nothing can happen between us."

"What?"

"I can't read, Julia. You…your whole life is about education. You can't be with a guy like me. It would never work."

"It's been working pretty well all season."

"I've been lying to you."

"That's behind us. You're not lying about anything else, right?"

"No."

"So why can't we be together?"

"Julia, you did everything in your power to get me to go to college. You can't tell me that suddenly you're all right with my high school diploma and this additional twist where I can't even read a menu. What if we had a kid and we went to a parent-teacher conference? Would you lie for me—pretend you want to read the report card out loud just so I can listen? What if the kid wants me to read a bedtime story? Who's going to cover for me there? My life is a lie. You don't want to be part of that."

"Deacon, I don't know what's going to happen tomorrow to me or to you. One of us could get sick. One of us could get hurt. What I know is that I love you. You're strong. You're brave. You're loyal and you love your family in a way that's so uncommon I wouldn't believe it was true if I hadn't met you. Why wouldn't I want to be with you?"

Deacon hesitated. He wanted to believe but he couldn't. She took his face in her hands.

"I'd love you even if you grew that mustache back."

She kissed him and he closed his eyes and held her. There would be more issues between them, just as there were for any couple. What mattered now was being with him. Knowing he wanted to be with her.

"We can work this out, Deacon. I mean, in a way it's perfect that you and I got together."

He leaned back tentatively, his arms still around her, but making space so he could look at her. "What do you mean?"

"I mean, I can help you. There are so many programs, and if you haven't been tested, I have contacts who can do that first. I don't know what you've tried—"

"Are you talking about finding out why I can't read? Teaching me?"

"Well, yeah."

He dropped his arms. "No. I'm the way I am. This is me. You either take me the way I am—flaws and all—or don't."

Deacon had this way of standing, arms slightly apart from his body, shoulders angled forward, that was both vulnerable and defensive at once. She wanted to make things right between them, but she wanted to give him hope, too. He felt being illiterate made him unlovable. She wanted to take that painful feeling away from him. She hesitated too long, looking for the right thing to say. He interpreted her silence as affirmation that he wasn't what she wanted.

"Forget it," Deacon said. He had bared his freaking soul for her. Showed her his biggest flaw, and she was attempting to fix him! He'd told her to love him as he was, and she couldn't do it. She wasn't the kind of person who could rest when a puzzle had to be solved, and that was how she saw him—as a puzzle. He wouldn't be her man, he'd be her project.

He walked away.

"Deacon!" she called after him.

"Stop it, Julia. Just stop. I love you. I really do. But we can't be together. I'm never going to be the guy you want me to be and you're not going to stop trying to fix me. Let me go. Please."

She did. She was crying, big fat tears rolling out of her eyes and down her face, tracing across her chin and down her neck. She didn't lift a hand to wipe them away.

"I'm sorry, Deacon. This was not the time for what I said, but I won't apologize for saying it. I can help you, but you won't let me. You're afraid to let me try. Ever since I met you, you've had these boundaries. As long as I stay on my side of them and don't ask you to share your whole self, then we can be together. It doesn't work that way. If we're together, then we're really together and you will stop drawing fences around the things I'm not allowed to discuss."

He walked away, because if he looked at her for one more second, he'd stay.

When he got back to the house and told Wes he'd broken off with Julia, his brother took a swing at him. Deacon let the punch land and he savored the pain. He wanted whatever Wes could dish out and more. He wanted to be punished. He wanted to hurt physically so he could forget how he felt in his soul.

But Wes stopped. "You have to say goodbye to the kids. You owe them."

"I said what they needed to hear."

Wes clenched his fist again, but then looked at the ceiling and took a deep breath. "You're an idiot, D. But I'll give you some time."

They hadn't brought much with them to Milton. Packing the car didn't take long.

All in all he was leaving Milton with more than he'd expected when he'd come. He and Wes were solid now, even if his brother was pissed about Julia. They'd accomplished a lot with their team, even if the girls did lose. Tonight, playing Wes on the neighborhood half-court, he'd realized that he wanted to build spaces just like that in other neighborhoods. Spaces where families and communities could come together. He even had some amazing memories from his time with Julia. He was glad he did, because he knew he'd never meet anyone like her again.

CHAPTER FIFTEEN

HENRY BROUGHT HER a pie. They sat in her living room and ate silently. Finally, he asked her what happened.

"I told him I loved him." She put down her fork on the edge of her plate. "He told me he loved me. And then I screwed it all up."

A few silent tears slid down her face. She wanted to be done crying, but apparently she wasn't quite.

"That's not the whole story, Julia. What happened?"

"Well, he was hurt. If you could have seen how he looked when he was telling the kids he couldn't read. He's amazing, Henry. Talented and smart. I told you how he rearranged my office. The way he loves Wes... I imagined what a good dad he'd be if we had kids. And he felt terrible about not being able to read—he's thought about having kids and he imagined all these scenarios where his illiteracy would cause problems."

"So after he said he loved you, you suggested academic testing and perhaps a nice course of tutoring?"

"I didn't just suggest like I knew what he needed. I said I didn't know what he'd already tried. I said he needed to be comfortable with the idea. I tried to give him some space."

"You were problem-solving your boyfriend."

"No. I love him. If he never learned to read, I'd be fine with that." Julie tapped the table to emphasize her point. "He's the one who is not fine with it." She stood up and crossed to the bookcase. She pulled out *Make Way for Ducklings* and remembered the night he'd looked at this book. "Reading's not the issue, Henry. He can't ask for help. I guess it's understandable because he was on his own so young, trying to keep his brother and him together. He probably learned that the only person he can rely on is himself."

Henry nodded. "I get it."

"I can't be with someone who can't let himself need me."

She started to cry again, and when her brother hugged her, she put her face against his shoulder and let all her hurt come out. She couldn't ever get over Deacon Fallon. But somehow, she had to find a way to live her life without him.

The boys' season came down to the last game. If they won, they'd go to States. If they lost, they'd be sitting home the same as the girls. Deacon kept track of the prognostication as best he could by pumping Wes for information.

He asked Victor to come over in the afternoon before the game. Vic asked Deacon if he wanted to shoot around, but Deacon hadn't picked up a ball since he'd been back. He wasn't sleeping, either.

They went into the living room and Deacon described his idea for the community centers he wanted to start building. He'd expanded the plans past just the simple half-court basketball courts. He wanted to impact kids' lives and he wanted to be sure there were support and resources in the neighborhood to make changes.

"You should have seen the kids' faces when they saw the new court, Vic. If we could take that feeling and multiply it in other parts of their lives, we could make magic for kids and their families."

"So these community centers you're envisioning… they'd have athletics and academics?"

"And art or music or something."

"Obviously," Vic said. "And you'll be the public face. You'll go out and get donors to support the foundation and you'll work with the teams at one of the centers."

Deacon nodded. "I have a lot to learn about fundraising, but I'm ready, Vic. I've been sitting around in the shadows too long."

"Okay," Victor said. He got up and walked across the room then back. "You pay me to be honest so I'll be honest. You won't like it, though."

Deacon felt his muscles tighten. Vic's honesty had saved him all those years ago. He'd trust it again. "All right."

"You have to address your reading issues or this won't work. You can't ask people for money to fund centers like this if you haven't dealt with your own problems first."

"What is it with everyone? I'm twenty-eight years old and I've been doing just fine for myself without knowing how to read." He pointed around the room. "This place? Bought and paid for by a guy who can't read. Your salary? Ditto. Rehab facilities in two states. I didn't have to read to get those built."

Victor tilted his head back and sighed. "I told you you wouldn't like it. But you pay me to be honest and that's what I'm doing. Look at it this way. What if you wanted to open a Chevy dealership, but your personal car was a Honda and you weren't going to give it up?

I'd tell you the same thing. You can't sell a solution if you're not willing to use it yourself."

"What solution, Vic? I'm not selling reading lessons."

"You're selling the idea that people can solve their problems. You have a problem, and it's one some people in the communities you want to help are going to have. Your donors are going to want to see you address it."

Deacon's stomach twisted with the same nervous tension he felt whenever he tried to read something. Victor was right and he knew it. But he wasn't sure he could follow through. What if he tried... He remembered the optimism on Julia's face when she'd listed the possible ways to diagnose and fix his issue. He'd felt the opposite. Dread. Fear.

"With the rehab centers, you do one small part and you let the team do the rest. With this...won't you want to be fully involved? Won't it kill you to let other people run the show when you know damn well you're more than capable?"

What if he wasn't capable?

What if he did the testing and the answer came back that he was just too dumb to read? How would that solve anything? He couldn't be with Julia then. He couldn't run a foundation then. Testing would only validate the fact that he didn't belong in the same league with Wes, or Victor, or most especially Julia.

If he didn't try the testing, he wouldn't have to know.

He told Victor he'd think about it, but he didn't mean it. It was the first lie he'd ever told his friend.

When the boys' game started, Deacon, Victor and Wes huddled in front of Wes's laptop. A local station out of Jericho was broadcasting the game live on their website.

The three of them watched the game with silent intensity. At the half, Milton was up by four. Deacon kept a close eye on the screen whenever the crowd was visible. He couldn't stop scanning the rows, looking for some hint of Julia's brown hair or bright smile. He didn't see her.

One of the Tigers sank a three-pointer. Deacon cheered.

Wes and Victor stared at him. "Traitor."

He stared at the screen.

Wes shook his head. "You want them to win so you can go back, don't you?" He poked Victor. "That's it. If the Tigers win, Julia has to run that party and Deacon wants to swoop in and save her. Did you already call a party planner?"

He'd called a caterer, not a party planner, so he shook his head and told Wes to shut up.

With three minutes left, Milton was ahead by ten. He leaned closer to the screen, willing the Tigers to hold on. He wouldn't leave Julia to run the party on her own. He'd pay for everything and spare her having to deal with Ty or the Tigers. He knew going back wouldn't change anything long term between them, but he wanted to give her one more gift.

The Tigers had the season in the bag and then... they lost it. Their big forward tripped getting back on defense and the other team put in an easy layup. The point guard made a terrible pass on the next play and the ball got taken down the court for another layup. The lead that had been inching toward comfortable had been cut in half.

The two lucky breaks woke up the other team and

by the time the buzzer sounded, Milton had lost the game and the season.

"Freaking Tigers." He smacked his hand on the table and slammed his chair back. "What were they thinking?"

Wes met his eye. "Sorry, D."

Victor nodded.

"You know you could just go and see her," Wes ventured.

"No."

"You're being ridiculous. If they'd won and the bash was on, you were totally going. But now that they lost and you don't have a built-in cover story, you're not going?"

"No."

"You're leaving your fate up to a bunch of high school boys?"

He told Wes to shut up, and walked out before he killed him.

That night he dreamed about Julia. Which was nothing new, because he dreamed about her almost every night. But this time, he dreamed that when she offered to help him, he said yes. In the dream he felt good. Really good.

TY WAS IN a foul mood after the loss. She stayed out of his way, but he made a point of stopping in her office.

"So the bet is off and the girls' team is gone next year. Just wanted you to know."

She didn't get up from behind her desk, because that way he couldn't see her hands clenched in her lap. If she kept her mouth shut, he'd leave and she could continue as she always had, doing her best by the kids who came through her office.

She repeated a silent mantra in her head. *Please leave, please leave, please leave.*

He either got tired of waiting for her to react or her thought waves finally succeeded in pushing him out the door, because the door eventually closed behind him and she was alone in her office. She didn't cry. She was getting better. Maybe. Except she still ached so deeply in her heart. She wanted another chance with Deacon, but she couldn't see how they would work. He didn't trust her and she couldn't watch him live his life with pain.

WES FOUND HIM in the kitchen. He was holding a small gold postcard. "Check this out."

Wes read the card aloud: "'To Coach Wes and Coach Fallon. Please come to the first-ever Milton Sports Lovers and Athletes Appreciation Extravaganza.' Then in parentheses it says 'Please come.'"

"We're going, right?" Wes asked. "The envelope was hand printed in glitter pen. Somebody took some time with this thing."

"Fine."

He was going to see Julia again. The lie that had been between them was gone, but what was left in its place? He and Wes were adapting. Now that he'd stopped hiding his problems with reading, Wes naturally picked up the slack. The first few times his brother read something to him, it made his skin crawl with shame. He'd felt the same as he had in school when everyone around him was reading and he couldn't make it work. But he'd forced himself to let it happen—more for Wes than for himself. Wes... Wes surprised him. He treated reading out loud like a natural addition to his normal activities. He did it and moved on. Oddly, now that he wasn't working so hard to cover up his vulnerability, Deacon felt a curiosity about reading that was new. He'd tried over the years to force his brain to spit out words, but he'd never tried to get professional help. He'd assumed it was hopeless. Everyone else learned to read in school, but he didn't. Why would a different professional work better?

But Victor seemed to think there was hope. Wes thought it. Julia…well…obviously she did.

Victor hadn't mentioned the community centers again, but when Deacon wasn't missing Julia, he was thinking about his idea. He knew with absolute certainty that he could make a difference for kids and families if he got the chance. The only obstacle in his way was his fear.

The same obstacle stood between him and Julia. What if he saw her and said, "I'm ready to learn." It would change everything between them. But would it be better? Lying hadn't worked. Staying stuck wasn't any better. Could he work on his problem…and still be the man he wanted to be for her?

SHE'D TRIED PUMPING each of the girls on the team for information. She'd even sunk so low as to corner Shawn and ask him what was happening, but he'd zipped his lips.

She didn't know who was putting this extravaganza together or how. Finally she realized she had to just sit back and enjoy the ride.

She wondered if Deacon and Wes were coming, but she wouldn't call them. She couldn't be the one to reach out—it would smack of trying to help. No. If Deacon wanted to talk, he could call her.

The night of the extravaganza, she pulled into the

parking lot at the high school and was surprised to find it as full as it would be for a Friday-night basketball game.

She checked in at the registration table staffed by Miri, Cora and three of the boys' basketball players. Trey and Shawn appeared and led her to her seat of honor, which was a folding chair decorated with black-and-gold crepe paper.

Ty and Coach Simon were already in their chairs. They didn't acknowledge her and she pretended not to see them. Two more chairs stood empty next to hers.

The Fallons arrived just as the lights in the gym were going down. She caught her breath. She'd missed Deacon so much, just seeing his familiar outline striding through the doors of the gym took her back to the time when they'd been a team, working together, learning to…well, she'd been learning to love him.

Deacon sat in the chair next to hers.

"Hi," he said softly.

"Hi."

"So you ended up running a sports party after all," he said.

"Nope. I have no idea who put this together."

But then Tali's voice came through the loudspeaker. "Last year our school lost all our sports programs. Different groups tried to do what was right for them and put their own sports back in business. One thing the girls' and boys' basketball teams learned is if we work together, we can get further on less."

Next up was Max. "So that's what we want to do next year. We want everyone in this room to think about what high school sports means to any kid and then give a donation—time, money, even a pledge to drive a carpool or bake a snack."

Then Seth, from the boy's basketball team, spoke. "The student athletes at Milton high school are committed to working together to get something good for all of us. We're asking you all to join in."

Finally Max came back to the microphone. "We've secured matching funds from a generous sponsor." She looked at Deacon, but he shrugged. Then she noticed that Max's dad was standing across the gym, watching his son intently. It looked as if Laurence had changed his mind about the place of sports in his son's life. "So if we pull together, we'll have more than enough money to share around. We're all Tigers together."

When the kids finished speaking, a whole group of them filed out into the middle of the gym. The girls' and boys' basketball teams were there, but a lot of other kids were, as well. All of a sudden the music for their dance started to play. Every kid on the gym floor picked up a basketball and they all began to dance.

She was in awe. She'd known all along what the solution was. Fund the girls' team and take the boys' team down a peg. She was one of the people Tali was talking about who'd pulled separately for her own small interest. The kids new better. They understood that even with their differences, they were stronger as a team.

Wes stood up at his place and joined in. She was watching the dancers when she realized Deacon was holding out his hand to her. He'd never once participated in the dance all season.

"You want to do this thing?" he asked.

She took his hand and the two of them danced together. By the time the dance was over, she was breathless and smiling so hard her face hurt. She'd missed him so much.

The lights came back on and she stepped closer to him.

"Can we talk?"

He nodded. They were surrounded by the players, the other kids, everyone celebrating together. She reached for his hand and when their fingers touched, he gripped her as if he'd been as hungry for her as she'd been for him. She let herself hope.

He pushed open the weight-room door and she flicked the wall switch to turn on the overhead lights. She held on to his hand, rubbing her thumb across his skin, letting the memories of his strength and surety and sweetness roll back into her soul. She didn't want to lose him again. She couldn't.

"The kids are smarter than me."

He looked confused and she went on. "They're kinder and wiser and they put me to shame. You were right about me. I see the answers so clearly sometimes, and I don't stop pushing. The way I tackled this season was wrong, and what we just watched proved it."

He broke in. "You made that happen, Julia. You might have made some mistakes, but what we just watched came from you. Your girls know they matter. Without you, they wouldn't have cared enough to make this night happen. Without you, Max would be home alone. Without you—"

She interrupted him. "I missed you, Deacon. There's nobody else in the world for me. There's just you. You, exactly how you are. We belong together. I've been wrong about so many things this year, but I'm not wrong about us. I'm not." She met his eyes. "Am I?"

"You're not," he said. "I've got plans, Julia. Big plans. For you and me and a whole bunch of kids I want to help. Whole towns full of kids. But I need you.

I promise I won't shut you out if you promise you'll stick by me no matter what."

"No matter what," she agreed.

When they kissed, Julia thought there might have been fireworks, because she thought she heard them going off. But then she realized it was just her and Deacon. Fireworks hadn't been in the budget. She and Deacon had to make their own. *Go Tigers.*

* * * * *

HEART & HOME

COMING NEXT MONTH
AVAILABLE JUNE 12, 2012

#1782 UNRAVELING THE PAST
The Truth about the Sullivans
Beth Andrews

#1783 UNEXPECTED FAMILY
Molly O'Keefe

#1784 BRING HIM HOME
Karina Bliss

#1785 THE ONLY MAN FOR HER
Delta Secrets
Kristi Gold

#1786 NAVY RULES
Whidbey Island
Geri Krotow

#1787 A LIFE REBUILT
The MacAllisters
Jean Brashear

REQUEST YOUR FREE BOOKS!
2 FREE NOVELS PLUS 2 FREE GIFTS!

Harlequin®

Super Romance®

Exciting, emotional, unexpected!

SPECIAL EDITION

Life, Love and Family

USA TODAY bestselling author

Marie Ferrarella

enchants readers in

ONCE UPON A MATCHMAKER

Micah Muldare's aunt is worried that her nephew is going to wind up alone in his old age...but this matchmaking mama has just the thing! When Micah finds himself accused of theft, defense lawyer Tracy Ryan agrees to help him as a favor to his aunt, but soon finds herself drawn to more than just his case. Will Micah open up his heart and realize Tracy is his match?

Available June 2012

Saddle up with Harlequin® series books this summer and find a cowboy for every mood!

Available wherever books are sold.

www.Harlequin.com

A grim discovery is about to change everything for Detective Layne Sullivan—including how she interacts with her boss!

Read on for an exciting excerpt of the upcoming book UNRAVELING THE PAST by Beth Andrews....

SOMETHING WAS UP—otherwise why would Chief Ross Taylor summon her back out? As Detective Layne Sullivan walked over, she grudgingly admitted he was doing well. But that didn't change the fact that the Chief position should have been hers.

Taylor turned as she approached. "Detective Sullivan, we have a situation."

"What's the problem?"

He aimed his flashlight at the ground. The beam illuminated a dirt-encrusted skull.

"Definitely a problem." And not something she'd expected. Not here. "How'd you see it?"

"Jess stumbled upon it looking for her phone."

Layne looked to where his niece huddled on a log. "I'll contact the forensics lab."

"Already have a team on the way. I've also called in units to search for the rest of the remains."

So he'd started the ball rolling. Then, she'd assume command while he took Jess home. "I have this under control."

Though it was late, he was clean shaven and neat, his flat stomach a testament to his refusal to indulge in doughnuts. His dark blond hair was clipped at the sides, the top long enough to curl.

The female part of Layne admitted he was attractive.

The cop in her resented the hell out of him for it.

"You get a lot of missing-persons cases here?" he asked.

"People don't go missing from Mystic Point." Although plenty of them left. "But we have our share of crime."

"I'll take the lead on this one."

Bad enough he'd come to *her* town and taken the position she was meant to have, now he wanted to mess with *how* she did her job? "Why? I'm the only detective on third shift and your second in command."

"Careful, Detective, or you might overstep."

But she'd never played it safe.

"I don't think it's overstepping to clear the air. You have something against me?"

"I assign cases based on experience and expertise. You don't have to like how I do that, but if you need to question every decision, perhaps you'd be happier somewhere else."

"Are you threatening my job?"

He moved so close she could feel the warmth from his body. "I'm not threatening anything." His breath caressed her cheek. "I'm giving you the choice of what happens next."

What will Layne choose? Find out in
UNRAVELING THE PAST by Beth Andrews,
available June 2012 from Harlequin® Superromance®.

And be sure to look for the other two books
in Beth's THE TRUTH ABOUT THE SULLIVANS series
available in August and October 2012.

HSREXP0612